Michigan Motors was a firm of which Miss Corsa, John Thatcher's super-efficient secretary, would approve.

They shot their objectionable executives. And Ray Jensen was objectionable—as his wife and his associates were happy to testify. For Thatcher, it was a matter of sentiment as well as banking business to unmask Jensen's ingenious murderer. . . .

"As usual, Miss Lathen is noteworthy for her quiet dry humor and her skill in making big-business intricacy clear and plausible."
—*The New York Times Book Review*

"She is peerless in style, wit, inventively credible plotting, and character bits."
—*Los Angeles Times*

Books by Emma Lathen

Accounting for Murder*
Ashes to Ashes*
Banking on Death*
Come to Dust
Death Shall Overcome*
The Longer the Thread*
Murder Against the Grain*
Murder Makes the Wheels Go 'Round*
Murder to Go*
Pick Up Sticks*
A Place for Murder*
A Stitch in Time*
Sweet and Low*

*Published by POCKET BOOKS

 *Are there paperbound books you want
but cannot find in your retail stores?*

You can get any title in print in **POCKET BOOK** editions. Simply
send retail price, local sales tax, if any, plus 35¢ per book to
cover mailing and handling costs, to:

MAIL SERVICE DEPARTMENT
POCKET BOOKS • A Division of Simon & Schuster, Inc.
1 West 39th Street • New York, New York 10018

Please send check or money order. We cannot be responsible
for cash.   *Catalogue sent free on request.*

Titles in this series are also available at discounts in quantity
lots for industrial or sales-promotional use. For details write our
Special Projects Agency: The Benjamin Company, Inc., 485
Madison Avenue, New York, New York 10022.

Murder
Makes the
Wheels Go 'Round

EMMA LATHEN

PUBLISHED BY POCKET BOOKS NEW YORK

MURDER MAKES THE WHEELS GO 'ROUND

Macmillan edition published 1966

POCKET BOOK edition published July, 1976

3rd printing .... November, 1976

This POCKET BOOK edition includes every word contained in
the original, higher-priced edition. It is printed from brand-
new plates made from completely reset, clear, easy-to-read type.
POCKET BOOK editions are published by
POCKET BOOKS,
a division of Simon & Schuster, Inc.,
A GULF+WESTERN COMPANY
630 Fifth Avenue,
New York, N.Y. 10020.
Trademarks registered in the United States
and other countries.

ISBN: 0-671-80545-2.
Library of Congress Catalog Card Number: 66-13562.
This POCKET BOOK edition is published by arrangement with
The Macmillan Publishing Company, Inc. Copyright, ©,
1966, by Emma Lathen. All rights reserved. This book, or
portions thereof, may not be reproduced by any means with-
out permission of the original publisher: The Macmillan
Publishing Company, Inc., 866 Third Avenue,
New York, N.Y. 10022.
Cover art by Roger Kastel.

Printed in the U.S.A.

CONTENTS

1 Down Payment 7

2 Universal Joint 14

3 F.O.B. Detroit 19

4 Merging Traffic 29

5 Body Work 39

6 Automatic Transmission 47

7 Under the Hood 55

8 No Passing 65

9 Hairpin Turns 74

10 Unimproved Surface 82

11 Abutters Only 91

12 Rotary Ahead 100

13 Men Working 109

14 License Suspended 119

15 Financing Arranged 127

16 Overtime 135

17 Stop, Look, and Listen 142

18 Flat Tire 151

19 High Octane Rating 159

20 Fringe Benefits 166

21 The Open Road 172

22 Pedestrians Only 181

The Principal Characters

"Michigan Motors' Monarchs of the Road"

Plantagenet: The Crown Jewel of Motoring
  Sceptre: Symbol of Achievement
  Royale: The Executive Car Without Peer

Lancaster: Beauty Bred to Service
  Majestic: The First Family Car
  Viscount: Elegance in Driving
  Victory: Flagship of Convertibles
  Chancellor: The Thoroughbred Station Wagon

Buccaneer: The Sea Dogs of the Michigan Motors Fleet
  Drake: The Lively Fun-Loving Compact
  Howard: Compact Economy with Big Car Comfort
  Raleigh: The Cavalier Convertible

Hotspur: The Golden Sports Car

1 • Down Payment

SPRING ARRIVES on Wall Street without crocuses and robins, let alone newborn lambs. There is no season to mergers between large cigarette firms and small carpet companies, to optimistic bond issues proposed by Massachusetts public authorities, to tricky auditing methods in small electronic firms. As the earth rotates on its axis, only legal holidays disrupt the serious business of buying, selling, borrowing, and lending in the world's money market. If the April breezes whistling up Broad Street are raw and biting instead of mild and balmy, the one sign that winter is over is the Easter finery defiantly sported by the secretaries.

Forty floors above the Street (Exchange Place, to be literal, not Wall Street), in the vast conference room of the Sloan Guaranty Trust, John Putnam Thatcher, senior vice-president, was at his wintriest although it happened to be a particularly pleasant April day. Much as he disliked meetings, he was attending one.

It was true that Thatcher was, *ex officio,* a member of the Sloan Review Committee. But as a rule he liked to interpret this as synonymous with *in absentia,* and let subordinates shoulder the burden of regular Tuesday discussions with the underwriters. Nevertheless today he himself sat at the head of the table, waiting for the representatives of Waymark-Sims to appear. The reasons for this departure from normalcy were still not altogether clear to him, but John Thatcher, whose instincts along these lines were highly developed, had sensed dark forces at work since early in the week.

First, Walter Bowman, his chief of research, had waylaid him in the corridor to urge him to attend today's meeting.

"Why?" Thatcher asked, bracing himself for Bowman's usual hard sell.

7

Instead Bowman, huge, jovial, and forthright by nature, had muttered something about hot prospects, then suddenly recalled an appointment in his office.

The next day Bradford Withers, president of the Sloan Guaranty Trust and a man usually far removed, not to say insulated, from its day-to-day workings, forwarded an unintelligible memorandum to Thatcher's office. Careful reading suggested that it was meant to convey the president's belief that Waymark-Sims had something interesting to present to the Sloan, together with his desire for Thatcher to attend the Review Committee meeting.

Then ancient Bartlett Sims, encountered by chance at the Downtown Club, had favored Thatcher with a disjointed speech about the dangers of financial men becoming overconservative. Bartlett Sims still affected a pocket watch, complete with across-the-vest chain.

All of this would have been enough to make anybody wary. John Putnam Thatcher confidently expected the worst.

The door opened. Charlie Trinkam, one of the Sloan's senior trust officers, ushered in Hugh Waymark, exuding enthusiasm, and one of his associates, Arnold Berman. Berman, a round, untidy man with a shiny bald pate, looked doleful. After a quick round of handshaking Waymark shot his cuffs and spread his papers. The meeting began.

He had wanted to come in person, Waymark said, because the investment opportunity he was about to discuss promised to be the most profitable in Waymark-Sims history. Over at his shop everybody was really sold on it. He thought he could safely say the same for the Sloan people already in the know.

Charlie Trinkam, who never let personal extravagances interfere with professional orthodoxy, cast an inquiring glance at Walter Bowman. Bowman, Thatcher noted appreciatively, was avoiding his colleagues' eyes by rapt absorption in the papers on the table. Hugh Waymark continued.

"We're thinking in terms of an offering of one million five of the common," he said impressively. "If the market holds up, we should be able to get at least fifty-five for it. Of course we haven't worked out all the fine print."

To a degree, this was intelligible to his listeners. Waymark-Sims was planning to underwrite one million five hundred thousand shares of common stock issued by a corporation. The corporation would hand over the shares, get the money it wanted promptly, and go about its business of producing bigger and better widgets. Waymark-Sims would make a healthy profit by marketing the stock as advantageously as possible, in this case at fifty-five dollars a share.

But hundreds of million of dollars argued a very big widget maker, and a commitment so large that Waymark-Sims had to split the pie by forming a syndicate—including, it hoped, the Sloan Guaranty Trust.

"Fascinating," said Charlie Trinkam blandly. "Are you planning to tell us what you're talking about, Hugh?"

Thatcher waited with mild interest. Waymark's shrouded approach had already confirmed his worst fears. Only the spine-chilling particulars remained.

Waymark smiled, took a deep breath, and said, "Michigan Motors! That's what we're talking about, Charlie! And this is going to be big! Out in Detroit the Big Three is a thing of the past. It's going to be the Big Four pretty soon—with MM right up there! Here, look at these figures."

He shoved sales charts, diagrams, and a sheaf of reports across the table, still developing his theme. The Plantagenet was fast becoming America's leading prestige car. No compact was selling better than the Drake. Why, in the middle-priced market . . .

But even professional underwriters are not immune to atmosphere. First Hugh Waymark's voice lost its practiced conviction, then trailed away altogether. There was a long, pregnant silence.

"Now, let's see," said John Putnam Thatcher in a thoughtful tone that made Walter Bowman regard him with quick suspicion. "Exactly when was Michigan Motors convicted of rigging government bids and price fixing?"

Rightly assuming the question to be rhetorical, his companions did not reply.

"I seem to recall that it was last October, wasn't it?" Thatcher mused aloud. This was pure malice. Neither he nor anybody else in the room could have forgotten.

The biggest antitrust case in American history had been covered with the loving attention normally reserved for a spacecraft launching or a Hollywood matrimonial fracas. October had been a riot of fascinating headlines:

AUTO CONSPIRACY CHARGED BY GOVT
MULTIBILLION-DOLLAR PRICE FIXING IN CARS
RIGGED BIDS IN DEFENSE CONTRACTS
NINE AUTO EXECS GO ON TRIAL

And finally,

GOVT PRODUCES RECORDS OF MARCH 15 PLOTTING
CAR CONSPIRATORS GUILTY
NINE AUTO EXECS GET SIX MONTHS

"Yes, it was October," Charlie said, incurring a reproachful look from Hugh Waymark. "I was just coming back from Toronto when the government produced the photostats of that meeting in March. Remember, Walter?"

"I remember," said Walter Bowman, sharply for him.

In a game attempt to steer the conversation out of these undesirable channels, Hugh Waymark flicked some papers and said, "Of course I don't deny that the trial was important. But what's past is past! MM has a great future!"

Unfortunately this merely prodded Charlie Trinkam into further reminiscence.

"That's just it, Hugh. Is it past? Michigan Motors was the ringleader of the whole price-fixing plot, after all. Don't you remember?"

Waymark, who remembered perfectly well, opened his mouth to retort, but Trinkam continued. "And even worse, the tipoff to the Justice Department came from inside MM."

He was referring, Thatcher recalled, to the information that had first alerted the Department of Justice to the conspiracy, then enabled it to document every clandestine meeting in March, April, and May with photographs, witnesses, and receipted bills from several luxurious mountain resorts in secluded areas.

"That's a company with a past," Charlie was saying. "But I'm not so sure about the future. They broke the law, they got caught—just like the others. But MM has an inside informer willing to pull the rug from under them."

"Nicely put," said Thatcher.

Waymark hurried into rebuttal. In the next ten minutes Thatcher learned that Detroit, pained by this reminder of the dangers of federal intervention in business, had been carrying on bravely since jail doors closed behind nine of its top executives. Almost immediately advertising agencies from New York to Los Angeles had begun to work overtime erasing old corporate images and projecting new ones. It had been a winter of heavy snow and record-breaking management shake-ups.

"What did that entail at MM?" Charlie interrupted to ask. He had adopted a rollicking view of the meeting and any Sloan involvement with Michigan Motors Corporation.

Waymark glanced at his associate. Obediently Arnold Berman, who had been balefully studying his cigar, hitched himself forward. When he spoke, it was not with Hugh Waymark's vigor but with a philosophical skepticism.

"You know, of course, there's a new president. A capable, competent accountant named Frank Krebbel. He was controller. Didn't have anything to do with the price fixing—the board made sure of that. He's got a good head on his shoulders." Berman came to a halt, decided he had nothing further to add, and leaned back in his chair. His chief looked disappointed.

"Who was the ex-president? Oh, yes, Eberhart, Stuart Eberhart. Did they get him on the antitrust violations?" Charlie asked with every outward sign of genuine interest.

With a sad smile Berman replied, "They couldn't prove a thing, Charlie. But he had to resign—for reasons of health. You remember what the judge said about him."

Hugh Waymark was pained, but before he could speak, Thatcher intervened.

"Is this new president the extent of the management shake-up?" he asked.

In man-to-man tones Waymark spoke of sweeping internal reforms. He spoke of a staff once demoralized, now full of the *esprit de corps* that produces great cars. He spoke, as Thatcher pointed out finally, in very broad terms. Waymark took this in good part and explained that Arnie Berman, just returned from a fact-finding mission to Detroit, had the details at his fingertips.

Again Berman removed himself from his cigar. "Michigan Motors has three people in jail—just like the other firms. At MM they caught the head of Plantagenet and his assistant—"

"I remember," Trinkam said. "Wasn't he the big brain behind all the meetings?"

Berman nodded. "Ray Jensen. One of the real whiz kids of the industry. He set up that March fifteenth gathering of the whole bunch."

At a guess Thatcher would have said that Arnold Berman was not favorably impressed by whiz kids.

"Yes, yes," Waymark said impatiently. Berman could not, however, be hurried.

"Jensen went to jail, together with his assistant, a kid named Dunn. And the other MM man in the clink is Buck Holsinger. He ran MM's whole Buccaneer line, the compacts. They've been in jail since October. Then a couple of other division managers had to resign. Not enough evidence to indict, but plenty of suspicion. And a new president. I suppose you could call that a sweeping management turnover."

Thatcher listened to this careful recital and decided that it was a shade too careful.

"Does that mean that Jensen and Holsinger are out of the company for good, or only for the duration of their jail sentences?"

There was another long silence.

"That," said Arnold Berman, inspecting a lengthening ash with the ghost of a smile, "that hasn't been decided yet."

This elicited a bleat from Hugh Waymark. "They were fired! They're both out of the company for good."

"At the other companies," Berman corrected him gently, "the big boys who went to jail got the bounce. But MM hasn't announced any decision yet. Raising a lot of talk."

"I'll bet it is," said Charlie Trinkam with great good humor. "And things must be just dandy for the guys running Plantagenet and Buccaneer now. I have to hand it to you, Hugh. You've really got a beat, here. All of this— and an informer, too."

"Now, now," said Waymark, getting his second wind. "Just because a public announcement hasn't been made doesn't mean that there isn't a clear policy in the front office. I assure you that out at MM the difficulties associated with the trial are over. That includes . . . er . . . the informant."

Walter Bowman, who had been heroically holding himself in check, now broke in. "Hugh is absolutely right. The antitrust trial and conviction are history." Ignoring Charlie Trinkam's sardonic smile, he picked up steam.

"Let's forget about price fixing. Just look at these earnings estimates. Michigan Motors is a damned good buy."

At this point, despite his best intentions, John Putnam Thatcher yielded to temptation. He discovered a previous engagement.

2 • Universal Joint

THATCHER ESCAPED to his sixth floor office, pausing only to inform his secretary, Miss Corsa, that he wanted to be undisturbed for the remainder of the afternoon, particularly by Walter Bowman.

"Yes, Mr. Thatcher," she replied. Miss Corsa celebrated the arrival of springtime with a chaste bunch of violets on her desk instead of unseemly colors on her person. As usual, she looked trim and efficient in a navy blue dress. Thatcher decided to put her efficiency to work.

"Miss Corsa, are you prepared to do some stealing for me?"

Patiently Miss Corsa waited.

"I want you to get the Michigan Motors file from Research before Bowman and his men have a chance to doctor it."

"Oh, they wouldn't do that, Mr. Thatcher." Her tone was reproving.

"You never know," Thatcher said, proceeding into his office. He had complete confidence in Miss Corsa's ability to abstract the files from Research before the meeting upstairs ended, and a similar respect for Walter Bowman's capacity to submerge any material unfavorable to a company he was selling to the Investment Committee.

Both feelings were justified. Miss Corsa, supremely indifferent, produced a bulging folder within twenty minutes. And fifteen minutes more told John Thatcher that many of the enclosed clippings would be ruthlessly pruned from the inevitably optimistic research report on Michigan Motors. The contents were in rough chronological order; first, September articles describing rumors of a gigantic anti-trust case in the offing, then the bombshell with its screaming October headlines. Thatcher flicked through long accounts of the trial, through thumbnail profiles of the defendants—MM's Ray Jensen was the "lantern-jawed, hard-nosed boss of prestigious Plantagenet Division," Buck

Holsinger was the "jocular, glad-handing No. 1 man at Buccaneer," and Orin Dunn was "pale but composed"—and through the summing-up from the bench. Events were roughly as he had recalled. The Department of Justice had struck in October, charging price fixing and rigged bids. Contemptuously Detroit had countered with a *nolo* plea.

At this point the party started to get lively. The Solicitor General of the United States appeared in court in person; the *nolo* plea (which could have saved the automotive industry untold millions in treble damages) was rejected. Detroit muttered resentfully about vindictive public officials in high places, insiders said that the Justice Department must have a sure thing, and something else happened.

Overnight fifty million Americans suddenly realized what this legal palaver about artificially maintained prices really meant; they might have been suckered when they bought last year's car. Avidly an outraged public read about bids to the government, about price collusion, about bellboys who had borne refreshments to price fixers, and finally about what even the *Wall Street Journal* called "a prosecution blockbuster"—photostats of Ray Jensen's handwritten notes covering the March fifteenth meeting, including a detailed explanation of the famous code system used by the conspirators to exchange price information and to allocate government contracts.

The decision was a foregone conclusion. The next set of clippings, with photographs, showed convicted felons, including a scowling Ray Jensen and a Buck Holsinger whose jocularity looked impaired, being led behind prison bars. Then came a playful account of Christmas gifts from the union to the imprisoned: gift-wrapped sets of Monopoly. Thereafter the press coverage had abated until early April, when Walter Bowman's research assistant hit another covey of clippings.

EARLY RETIREMENT FOR MULDOON
BLAKESLY TO RELOCATE
MCKAY OFF PAYROLL, PREXY ANNOUNCES

They added up to a clean sweep of the executive-conspirators by virtuous corporations, with the conspicuous exception of Michigan Motors. The firms involved proclaimed (1) they had not known their employees were violating the Sherman Act, the Clayton Act, or even local parking ordinances, (2) they could not countenance such malefactions.

Thatcher smiled. He well recalled the judge's tart observations when the ex-president of Michigan Motors, Stuart Eberhart, Jr., had delivered himself of similar sentiments in the courtroom.

No, Charlie Trinkam was right. MM did not emerge happily from the great price-fixing conspiracy—if, indeed, it had emerged.

Turning over several woolly-headed pronouncements on Ethics in Business by assorted pastors, educators, and social commentators ("Though I cannot deny that perhaps he erred in rendering unto Caesar that which is Caesar's, I know that this fine man, devoted to his family, responsible to his community, and untiring in his support of the church, did not stint in his rendering unto God . . ."), Thatcher finally came upon a small item:

SPECULATION RIFE AT MM

Industry sources are buzzing with questions about the future of Ray Jensen and Buck Holzinger at MM. MM is keeping plans to itself . . .

It had a recent dateline.

Upstairs Charlie Trinkam and Walter Bowman were deep in profit and sales projections with Hugh Waymark. It was a tribute to their single-mindedness as financial men. Thatcher closed the folder. Until he knew who had tipped the Department of Justice to the conspiracy, and until he learned what Michigan Motors planned to do with its erring executives, he did not think that projections were a sound enough basis for a Sloan investment.

As it happened, this eminently sensible point of view was being presented some seven hundred miles away.

"We have to make some sort of announcement if we want to go ahead with a new issue, you know," said Frank Krebbel, new president of Michigan Motors. He said it dispassionately.

"It's a shame to rake the whole thing up again," replied Lionel McC. French, chairman of the board, with his usual ponderous air of regret. They were in conference in the president's office, which was as vast as the Sloan conference room and even more Danish.

In silence Krebbel looked down at his desk. His neutral appearance covered formidable energy. He had spent long months pulling Michigan Motors through a very bad time. Now, despite the dislocations and disruptions, he had the satisfaction of knowing that production was again flowing smoothly. Car buyers were enthusiastic about the new models, and the marketing men were predicting a record year. The only clouds that Frank Krebbel saw on MM's horizon were the forthcoming wage negotiations—and, of course, MM's board chairman, Lionel French. French was not making a rapid recovery from the shock of the antitrust conviction.

"We should make some sort of announcement," said Krebbel mildly.

French indicated dignified distaste.

Krebbel said, "Yes, I know it's a shame. But Ray and Buck are getting out of jail early next month. We've put this off long enough. It doesn't do us any good to have rumors flying around. Particularly if we want to raise capital."

French drummed his fingers on the corner of the irregularly shaped desk.

"Damned unfair," he said aloud. "All this trouble because some secretary went running to the Justice people!"

Krebbel suppressed a sigh. Patiently he said, "It wasn't a secretary, Lionel. We've checked the clerical staff. It was somebody with access to Ray's notes, somebody who knew about all the meetings. Somebody at executive level." He paused, then added, "If you're still worrying about the informer, I'm willing to start another investigation—at a much higher level. I've always thought it should be cleared up."

"For God's sake, no! Leave it alone."

"Well, then," said Frank Krebbel with unimpaired calm, "what about the announcement?"

Lionel French frowned and pursed his lips. Krebbel waited. Finally the chairman said, "Look, Frank, perhaps we should come to some arrangement with Ray Jensen when he gets out. He's . . . er . . . very well informed about the company. And he did go to jail without telling the government anything that they didn't already know."

This produced no reply. Much against his will, French

was forced to be direct. "Do you think Ray is likely to make trouble—if we fire him now?"

"He'll try," said Krebbel. He did not look concerned at the prospect.

French shook his head. "Then take Buck Holsinger," he continued. "You never can tell what he'll come up with. After all, he did develop the Drake."

Frank Krebbel duly considered Buck Holsinger. "As you say, it doesn't pay to underestimate Buck."

French stood up. "That's just it. I tell you, Frank, we're going to have to hold up the announcement," he said decisively. "The board will need more time to . . . think things over."

The president looked at him without sympathy. Lionel McC. French and the board of directors had been taking a little more time to think things over for six months now. But Krebbel knew when to push and when not to push. He assented to French's decision without protest.

At the door the chairman of the board hesitated, then voiced a new worry. "Frank, you know Ray Jensen can be quite difficult on occasion. You don't suppose . . . that is, do you think he might be tempted to go to the Department of Justice with . . . oh, say, information to implicate Stuart—or anybody?"

He got only cold comfort in return.

"Let him," said Frank Krebbel evenly.

3 • F.O.B. Detroit

BY THE SECOND WEEK in May, Michigan Motors had still made no public announcement of plans for its jailbird executives. Nobody had identified the Michigan Motors informer. But descending on Detroit, with varying degrees of enthusiasm, were five men determined to dispel these clouds of uncertainty.

The first to arrive was Ray Jensen, until last October, at least, head of MM's big Plantagenet Division. Jensen brushed off reporters after he left jail on Monday and proceeded directly to the Executive Building of Michigan Motors. Within twenty minutes he was in conference with the president. He did not emerge for over an hour. The grapevine, which spread this information, did not know what had been said. It did know that after leaving Krebbel, Ray Jensen had gone immediately to his old office, currently occupied by Ed Wahl, acting division manager of Plantagenet. Fortunately a secretary witnessed their encounter.

"I want to thank you personally, Ed," said Jensen.

"What for?" Wahl asked cautiously.

"Why, for minding the store while I was gone."

The grapevine reported that Jensen was smiling coldly and Ed Wahl was pale at the end of the interview. The more knowledgeable portions of the grapevine—secretaries who had been at Michigan Motors more than five years—whispered one further item: Ray Jensen had not yet bothered to go home to see his wife.

Next to make the trip from jail to Detroit was Orin Dunn, Ray Jensen's erstwhile assistant. More domestically oriented than his superior, he went from the train directly to his home in Bloomfield Hills. His wife, who had firmly taken the position that he was a persecuted innocent, cooed sympathetically and lacerated his sensitivities by her total inability to comprehend the problem.

"Look, can't you understand?" he was shouting within

19

minutes of arriving under his own very extensive roof. "What if they don't take me back? I'm too young to be a has-been!"

The third, Buck Holsinger, was met by his wife at the gates of the Federal Correctional Facility. One look at her husband's unshadowed countenance told Diane Holsinger that he was going to be difficult. Accordingly she was prettily attentive on the drive to Grosse Point Farms, holding her fire until they got home.

"Now, we should face facts, Buck," she said, gracefully stepping onto the gravel driveway. Diane Holsinger was forty-five, but even in the full light of the afternoon sun she looked ten years younger. "Getting back into the company won't be easy. You're going to have to fight for it."

Buck assumed his place at her side. "If we're going to face facts, honey, we might as well face the fact that I'm through." He shrugged slightly, surveyed his home, then added, "It's hard, but you have to roll with the punches. Say, I like that new fence."

His wife replied with emphasis. "Nothing has been announced up at the company. There's a lot of talk that they're going to take Ray back."

"So?" Buck Holsinger opened his front door and looked at his entrance hall with undisguised pleasure.

"You're not going to take that lying down!" Diane told him. "You and Orin will have to spike his guns. There's nothing Ray would like better than keeping you out in the cold."

"Not much I can do about it," he replied absently. "God, it's good to see the old place."

Diane Holsinger gripped her purse with white knuckles for a moment. "It's Frank Krebbel who counts right now. Ray's probably gone up to see him today. You have to do something about it, Buck."

From the entranceway to the living room he looked back at her. "It means a lot to you, doesn't it, Diane?"

She bit her lip, then forced herself to smile at him. "Yes, Buck, it does."

The last visitors came two days later, on Wednesday, from Wall Street, not the Federal Correctional Facility. They represented Waymark-Sims—which was not surprising since Hugh Waymark was an incorrigible optimist— and the Sloan Guaranty Trust—which was a tribute to human tenacity in general and to Walter Bowman's tenacity in particular.

Since the Review Committee meeting, Bowman had labored valiantly. For weeks an unremitting barrage of material had rained down from his Research Department about "1965-level sales for Viscounts," "dazzling cost-cutting in Majestic," and "improved MM-dealer relations." One notable afternoon Thatcher had returned to his office to discover Miss Corsa contemplating a two-foot model of the MM Lancaster.

"Mr. Bowman thought you would be interested. 'Beauty bred to service,' " she quoted.

"Well, send this half-breed back to Research, Miss Corsa, and tell Mr. Bowman that I am convinced there is no future in cars without running boards."

Undaunted, Walter Bowman not only persevered, he managed—Thatcher would never know how—to convince the unimpressionable Investment Committee that the Sloan Guaranty Trust would lose nothing by a tentative exploration of the Michigan Motors situation. Then, having packed his bags for Detroit in well-merited triumph, Bowman proceeded to break his left ankle alighting from a taxi at La Guardia.

"For a man who has been littering my desk with information about cars, I regard that as inexcusably clumsy," Thatcher said unsympathetically upon hearing of the mishap. "And with Bowman in traction, who goes off on this wild goose chase?"

"I'll send flowers," said Miss Corsa by way of remonstrance. "Do you want to talk with Mr. Gabler?"

But Everett Gabler was negotiating Swiss credits; Charlie Trinkam was reorganizing liaison between the Trust Department and the Collateral Loan Department (a move necessitated by the discovery that the innocents in Collateral Loan were lending money on securities that the Trust Department had long since apostrophized as worthless). Sinclair was in Washington, testifying. Blaisdell was in Iraq. Innes had the mumps.

"Mumps." Thatcher repeated sourly. "What about Nicolls?"

"Mr. Nicolls is Too Junior," said Miss Corsa.

"Nonense. It will do him good."

But he had to bow to her higher realism. Mr. Nicolls was Too Junior.

As a result, on Wednesday it was John Putnam Thatcher who strode into the richly appointed cavern that
served Michigan Motors as a lobby.

Arnold Berman, looking more melancholy than ever,
performed the introductions. There was Glen Madsen, tall,
rugged, and generally forbidding, MM's director of economic planning and research. Madsen was the senior member of the clutch of executives assembled to greet Berman
and Thatcher. He shook hands vigorously, introduced his
associates, and allowed one of them to describe the domestic arrangements made at the nearby Telegraph Motel.

Madsen was masterfully shepherding Thatcher and Berman forward, when their path was blocked.

Before the elevator stood a young woman clutching a
folder. Oblivious of bystanders, she scowled at the bespectacled young man facing her. While assorted secretaries
peered around the decorative foliage and visiting car
dealers swiveled their heads, the couple exchanged hos-
tilities.

"You're not seeing these reports until I've typed them
and sent them to Mr. Wahl," the young man said hotly.
"Or Mr. Jensen!"

"Glen, maybe we'd better walk upstairs," Thatcher
heard somebody whisper.

"Listen, Miss Price," her opponent retorted. "I know
you were Jensen's secretary, and now you're Wahl's, so
you're willing to fight all the way for Plantagenet. But I
know as well as you do that Jensen has been keeping out
of sight since he got back Monday. Either you give me
that report or we check with Mr. Wahl . . . or . . . there's
Mr. Madsen."

Madsen swore under his breath. "Now what's the trouble, Riley?" he demanded as a twittering subordinate
made a manful attempt to divert Thatcher and Berman
with a description of the Burpee Plantagenet Rose, newly
developed for tie-in advertising.

Naturally finding the conflict more interesting than roses,
Thatcher and Berman gave only perfunctory responses.
Miss Price and Glen Madsen had lowered their voices:
Mr. Riley had not.

"Miss Price doesn't seem to know that our court order
covers current records at Plantagenet," he said pugna-
ciously.

Involuntarily Berman repeated, "Court order?" His companion doggedly talked about American Beauties.

Glen Madsen wasted no time. "All right. Just give Mr. Riley any records he wants." He turned to rejoin the official party.

Miss Price, however, had her loyalties. "Don't you think I should get Mr. Jensen to O.K. them first, Mr. Madsen?"

"Give him the records," Madsen barked, gesturing his guests to the elevator.

As they passed Miss Price she thrust her folder forward. "All right," she spat. "Read it. But read it now! Mr. Wahl has to have it this afternoon."

Desperately the rose fancier stabbed the button. The elevator, however, took several moments to arrive, during which Thatcher and Berman unashamedly eavesdropped on Riley, dictating to himself as he jotted notes.

"Oh, the Tuesday Work Report. Let's see. Two cutters dismissed for brawling in the fender assembly men's room. Check with Casimir and Grievance Committee. Guard Stanislas Novotny's gun stolen . . . gun stolen! Why are people stealing guns at Plantagenet, Miss Price?"

"To shoot snoopers!" she replied venomously.

"Reported this to the police?" he asked sternly.

"Of course."

As they were wafted upward Arnold Berman cleared his throat. "What's this court order, Glen?"

"Riley's from the Department of Justice. He's ensuring that MM complies with the cease-and-desist order." When neither Thatcher nor Berman commented, Madsen dropped his belligerence and added, "It's a damned nuisance, you know. Only a formality. Around here price fixing is over —for good."

A general murmur of assent attended this company line. Thatcher was to hear it repeated almost immediately in MM's presidential suite. During the preliminaries Thatcher inspected the new president with interest. In contrast to Madsen, Frank Krebbel was middle-aged and colorless. But rimless glasses and a receding hairline did not impair his aura of competence. He referred to his predecessors, and to the current chairman of the board, in terms leaving no doubt that Frank Krebbel was master in his own house. Nor did a question about price fixing embarrass him.

"It was a big problem, but I can assure you we've solved it," he said with calm finality. "Now, before you talk to our financial men, you'll want to inspect one of our plants."

Neither John Thatcher nor Arnold Berman was discourteous enough to disagree, although each had toured Willow Run and one assembly line is, after all, much like another.

"Glen," Krebbel continued, "what about calling Ed Wahl? Mr. Thatcher and Mr. Berman could go through Plantagenet right after lunch."

Madsen nodded approval.

"We've got a Super Plantagenet we're building to specifications for the Sheik of Shahoda," Krebbel said. Then, noting Thatcher's look of polite inquiry, he smiled slightly and said, "Ed Wahl's the man who's directing Plantagenet. Sorry I can't join you for lunch."

As the brief encounter ended, John Thatcher decided that Michigan Motors was going to provide more food for thought than he had expected. Since MM had made no public statements about Ray Jensen, Ed Wahl was "directing" Plantagenet—not division manager. He saw that Berman had also registered this not-so-fine distinction.

After giving almost imperceptible nods of command to waiting secretaries, Madsen led his guests to the executive dining room, where their luncheon companions—the director of technical services and the assistant director of marketing research—were waiting. The conversation turned to turbines.

As the waitress produced butterscotch rolls, Glen Madsen asked a question about quality control. Unfortunately the director of technical services failed to field the ball. His attention had been diverted by the bellowing from a table in the center of the dining room.

"Buck's back," said the director of technical services. "Buck Holsinger, you know. A great storyteller." He stopped, belatedly aware of his imprudence.

"Yes," said Thatcher cordially. Incredibly, Holsinger's story seemed to be both bawdy and about disc brakes. "I see that jail has not dampened his spirits."

Madsen gave in.

"Buck says he met some great guys in jail," he drawled as another roar rose from Holsinger's companions.

"What does Ray Jensen say about jail?" Thatcher inquired.

That did it. Thereafter turbines were the topic of conversation.

"Now," announced Madsen. "Now we're going over to look at Plantagenet."

The director of Technical Services and the assistant director of Market Research detached themselves from the party with military precision. Their replacements struck Thatcher as identical in name, position, and general appearance. The regrouped party then proceeded outdoors to a chauffeur-driven Plantagenet Royale. In three minutes, feeling as if he himself were being swept along on an assembly line, Thatcher found himself being ushered into the sprawl of buildings where MM produced its high-priced line, the Plantagenet. The move, only about a mile from the front office geographically, was farther in spirit: Plantagenet's lobby was cinder-box utilitarian.

"This is where they steal guns," he pointed out to Berman in an undertone.

Berman, never particularly ebullient, had been depressed by turbines. "I don't blame them."

A welcoming committee materialized as soon as the front-office party appeared. Among the dignitaries was Frank Krebbel. With a civil hope that Thatcher and Berman had enjoyed a useful and informative lunch, he led the way to the receptionist.

"Mr. Wahl and Mr. Jensen, please," he said.

But despite this impartiality, the telephone produced only Mr. Wahl. Mr. Jensen was somewhere in the building, but he could not be reached. Thatcher noticed a quick exchange of glances among the men clustered around him. Both Madsen and Frank Krebbel remained expressionless.

"Ah, here's Ed," said someone sounding mildly apologetic.

Wahl, who lumbered out of a nearby cubicle almost immediately, was cut from a different pattern than his fellow executives. More rough diamond than whiz kid, thought Thatcher. But like everybody else in Detroit, he displayed a profound technical interest in cars and a touching, if misplaced, belief that everybody shared it.

"You'll want to see the Super Plantagenet we've just built for that sheik," he declared. "Mabel, if you find Mr. Jensen, tell him we're downstairs."

He turned and led the way down a steep flight of stairs.

"There she is!" he shouted, standing back to let the official party precede him into Plantagenet's echoing low-ceiling basement garage. "The most luxurious car ever made—if I say so myself."

An incredible expanse of tawny bronze enamel that approached cruising yacht proportions stood before them. There was a general surge of admiration and expert comment.

"Here, take a look at this," Wahl shouted, throwing open a gargantuan rear door to reveal an imposing display of genuine leopard skin. Leaning inside with no difficulty, although he was a bulky man, he pushed a button. Promptly a small teak bar (with gold bottles and ice tray) glided out of an arm rest while the strains of a popular song filled the room.

"When do we ship her, Ed?" Krebbel asked.

Wahl stepped back to admire his handiwork. "We're trucking her to New York early tomorrow morning," he said regretfully. "The Arabs are arranging the ocean transport. I hope to hell they know how to bed her down." He patted the Plantagenet's satin flanks soothingly.

Glen Madsen added his congratulations, then, with a glance at his watch, suggested they had better get on with the tour.

"That's right," Krebbel said, starting for the door. "We want everybody to make the cocktail party on schedule."

"Cocktail party?" Thatcher inquired apprehensively as he followed Krebbel upstairs.

"You'll want to meet our people," said Krebbel in another one of Michigan Motors' positive statements. "Too bad Ray Jensen didn't turn up. I asked Orin to tell him you'd be here. Well, Glen, will you just go ahead? I can't join you, but I'll see you this evening."

With this, Krebbel departed. His example was emulated by the junior executives, who melted back to their appointed rounds, leaving Thatcher, Berman, Madsen and Wahl outside the heavy metal doors.

"I can see that Michigan Motors believes in organization," Thatcher said caustically. Just then Wahl pulled open the doors and shattering pandemonium broke upon their ears.

"Don't worry," Wahl bellowed. "You get used to the noise!"

This too proved to be a Michigan Motors refrain.

"Terrible noise, isn't it?" Four hours later the noise in question was not the rumble of assembly lines, the whir of metal grinders, or the explosion of stamping presses at

Plantagenet, but a genteel din at the Bloomfield Hills Open Hunt Club.

"Yes," said Thatcher to his companion, a middle-aged woman with disordered gray hair. She had attached herself to him as he escaped from two Engineering Department zealots.

"You're that big banker from New York?" she said, hooking a martini from a passing waiter.

Thatcher admitted that he was and looked around for rescue. None was in sight. He missed his companion's next words.

"I beg your pardon?"

"I said things are awful at the company." The lady was having trouble articulating, so she paused before remarking conversationally, "It's that louse Ray Jensen." Then she teetered back on her heels and blinked owlishly. Thatcher's stubborn silence did not disturb her. Possibly she was used to companions dumb with embarrassment.

"It would be just like them to give him back his job," she continued. "Why the hell he doesn't drop dead and——"

"Audrey!"

Thatcher looked up hopefully. Another woman, well dressed and scrupulously groomed, favored him with a smooth social smile. "I'm Diane Holsinger, Mr. Thatcher," she announced graciously. "You've been introduced to Mrs. Wahl?"

Thatcher started to make the appropriate, if inaccurate, rejoinder, but Mrs. Wahl was impatient with civilities.

"Well, Diane, how does it feel to have your husband out of jail?"

She had sobered up enough to be deliberately offensive.

By not so much as a flicker of an eyelash did Mrs. Holsinger register this hit. She betrayed nothing more than indulgent tolerance.

"It's wonderful to have him home again," she said warmly. Then, deftly broadening the scope of her remarks to include Thatcher, she laughed lightly. "Being married to a businessman is an adventurous career, Mr. Thatcher. You have to be ready for anything."

While grateful to be spared a round of wifely bickering, Thatcher found the lady's self-control rather formidable. Audrey Wahl did too.

"Ed didn't go to jail," she countered nastily, "so don't give me that crap about all businessmen. And don't give me that superior look, either, Diane."

"I wonder if Ed is around anywhere," Mrs. Holsinger said, raising her well-modulated voice. Since a young man immediately detached himself from a nearby group, Thatcher was left to conclude that Mrs. Wahl was a familiar problem at Michigan Motors.

". . . not that poor old Buck is to blame," Mrs. Wahl continued implacably. "He doesn't have enough brains, Ed always says. It's that bastard Ray Jensen. You notice he isn't here, Diane? For that matter, I wonder where Celia is."

Mrs. Holsinger evinced some irritation at this description of her husband (who was in the far corner telling one of his famous stories) but managed to produce an understanding smile in Thatcher's direction.

". . . of course I can guess how she and Glen must be feeling. I don't know what they'll do about her divorce now—"

"Audrey!" said Mrs. Holsinger sharply.

"Audrey!" Ed Wahl repeated, appearing in the wake of the young man. Without embarrassment he greeted Thatcher, then put a muscular arm around his wife's shoulders. The movement bearing her away was forceful and practiced.

Thatcher expelled a sigh, put down his glass, and prepared to move on. Mrs. Holsinger had other plans.

"A problem," she confided.

"I'm sure it is," said Thatcher agreeably. "I think I see . . ."

He was outmatched.

"Of course I'm terribly sorry for Audrey, but you can see she's under strain. And of course there's always a reason for drinking. . . ."

She was right. Later that evening, in the comparative comfort of his cell at the Telegraph Motel, John Putnam Thatcher poured himself a stiff nightcap while he dictated a preliminary report, to be brought to the attention of Charlie Trinkam and Walter Bowman. It was not likely to soothe the convalescent.

4 • Merging Traffic

THE FOLLOWING MORNING Thatcher abandoned Arnold Berman to his fate—a conference with Glen Madsen in the Economic Planning Section—and played truant. Summoning the Plantagenet Sceptre placed at his disposal, he directed the driver to downtown Detroit, where he had hurriedly made an appointment at the Detroit Savings and Trust.

Discontentedly he stirred in the stifling luxury of his transport and looked out the window. A brilliant sun, a clear May sky—and beneath them merciless streams of traffic pouring in and out of the city, like so many mechanized lemmings.

"This is the Ford plant we're passing, Mr. Thatcher," said Mack through the speaking tube necessitated by the distance between them. Presumably he was accustomed to chauffering illiterates, Thatcher thought irritably; on its home ground the Ford Motor Company was not hiding its light under a bushel.

"Coffee, sir?"

Thatcher denied him the opportunity to push several buttons and produce boiling liquid from some cunningly camouflaged percolator—standard equipment, no doubt, in the Crown Jewel of Motoring. Mack registered disappointment; like everyone else Thatcher had met at Michigan Motors, he had a deep personal affection for cars. "She cruises," he had earlier confided, "at a hundred and twenty!"

Lacking passionate attachment to the automobile, Thatcher did not reply; instead he disapprovingly noted the colossal traffic backup at Michigan Avenue and First Street. Not that Detroit and its environs depressed him, although no right-minded observer could describe them as full of charm; no, it was the corporate world of Michigan Motors. Detroit Savings, thank God, could be relied upon to produce bankers—not hard-driving executives, dynamic managers, team men, and whiz kids. Or their wives.

Or Department of Justice men nosing around, for that matter.

"Here we are, sir," said Mack, gliding to a halt in Cadillac Square.

"I'll be ready at two," said Thatcher, extracting himself from cushioned depths.

Mack touched his cap smartly and retired to lead the Sceptre to some opulent pasture.

As Thatcher had anticipated, Detroit Savings and Trust proved a relief. Although intimately connected with the automobile industry, it did not produce executives with booming cheerful voices; it even escaped the brown business suit that is the uniform of the Midwestern business executive. Thatcher spent a refreshing morning dealing with knotty problems concerning Treasury funds— Detroit Savings being a Sloan correspondent—and lunched pleasantly at the Union Club, where Willis Ferry expanded into mild indiscretion and told him that Michigan Motors was the gossip of the industry. Bets were being placed on the future of the returned jailbirds, particularly Ray Jensen. "Heads," said Willis Ferry, "are going to roll." He considered this for a moment, then added, "Of course, around here, heads are always rolling."

Thatcher was feeling almost equal to his afternoon appointment with the MM Board of Directors by the time Mack deposited him back at the Kodachrome-print beauty of the Executive Building. He paused. Now that he came to think of it, the no doubt expensive (and possibly Oriental) architect had achieved an effect reminiscent of *Fortune*'s more poetic treatments of modern American industry.

Thatcher thought of the textile mills of the Merrimack Valley and stood for a moment, comparing them with the stage set before him: self-conscious latticed elegance in the buildings, a sun-dappled Plantagenet pulling away from the fountain, improbable carpets of greenery flanking the long pool which shimmered under the blue sky. He had to shake his head when a familiar figure emerged from behind an ornamental bush, hailing him warmly.

"Thatcher! John Thatcher! Well, isn't this great! I've been hoping we'd run into each other. I heard you were here, and I wanted to catch you for a talk about old times.

But we've been pushed in my shop! These Detroit fellows really set a hard pace, and it's a big change from the Sloan. You know, Thatcher, there have been times when I almost regretted making the change—that's speaking with absolute frankness. But I suppose we all have days when we feel like that, don't we? I miss the Sloan, but Michigan Motors really gives a man like me more scope, if you see what I mean. Going inside? Good, I'll walk along for a minute, although I'm rushed. You're looking very fit. . . ."

Lincoln Hauser, one-time director of publicity for the Sloan Guaranty Trust and now, it developed, director of public relations for Michigan Motors, burbled on, occasionally flashing a confident muscular smile to a passing functionary.

"I take it you're happy here, Hauser?" Thatcher inquired courteously, recalling that this idiot had once had the effrontery to suggest that he call him Link.

"It's great," said Hauser. "A lot of responsibility, of course. You know, my first big job was to handle the publicity about"—he looked around furtively and lowered his voice—"about the price-fixing case! There was a challenge for you! But if I do say so myself, we did a grand job. It's not like the conservative days at the Sloan, Thatcher. Here people really see the value of créative PR— and I've got a top-notch staff! We keep on our toes— seize the opportunity! Think fast! Take the ball and carry it down the field—"

"I didn't know you were an athlete," Thatcher interjected, eyeing his companion's weedy figure and black-rimmed glasses. Hauser, however, was in full flight.

"Now take the Super Plantagenet—although between the two of us I would have liked a more romantic name—well, we've just learned, just this morning, mind you, that the sheik has arrived in Boston for a prostate operation. What do you think of that?"

Thatcher could think of no reasonable comment.

"Don't you see what it means?" Hauser demanded. "The car—the special car that was going to be shipped to Arabia or wherever it was going to be shipped. They were going to truck it today, but now everything is changed. The sheik's son is arriving tomorrow to take possession and drive it back to Boston! Think of the opportunity! Crown Prince Bulbul—a romantic Saharan nomad—arriving to take possession of the world's finest car, a car worthy of the brave Bedouins! Well! We had just one day to arrange things—but we've done it! My boys have been hustling—but we've arranged to have the car posed beside the Mighty Michigan Motors Pool! We've got photographers coming out this afternoon to take pictures. We've got a model agency to send over girls tomorrow morning for the presentation! We've alerted the newspapers, the magazines— And listen to this, Thatcher! Not only do we have a man from *Life*—we have a man from *The New Yorker!*"

"No!" said Thatcher, impressed.

"Tomorrow morning," Hauser continued raptly, "when Crown Prince Bulbul in his flowing robes arrives, we'll have a presentation worth millions of dollars. Glamour, pictures—the car of the future!" He stood stock-still, then with reverence added, "And we did it on the spur of the moment!" He was overcome with admiration until duty recalled him. "Well, it's been good to see you, Thatcher—and talk about the quiet old days at the Sloan. But I'll have to be ready when the Super Plantagenet arrives—there it is!—I'll have to hurry off."

He suited action to word, striding toward the far side of the Michigan Motors pool where two men were just pulling up in the Super Plantagenet. Thatcher sighed. He had cherished reprehensible hopes that this fantastic vehicle might ultimately prove too unwieldy for movement. Rousing himself, he proceeded through the virtually invisible glass doors to the lobby. He was at the elevator when he heard his name called.

"John!" From a distant corner Berman waved energetically. He was surrounded by bespectacled men carrying scratch pads, charts, and the other paraphernalia of a meeting.

"If you wait a minute, John, I'll join you," he called and launched himself on a round of farewells.

Ever obliging, Thatcher waited. Idly he glanced through the panes of glass framing the lobby. Across the pool in the distance he could see a workman in overalls alighting from the Super Plantagenet, which he had just positioned accurately along the gleaming expanse of water. Hauser, rounding the building at a trot, beckoned commandingly. The driver, no doubt experienced in avoiding the demands of the Public Relations Department, merely hurried off in the opposite direction, abandoning his mechanical wonder to the PR man who had accompanied him and to the cameramen and publicity people now converging toward the patio.

A low moan heralded Berman's arrival. "I can take just so much of this," he said lugubriously.

"A full morning?" Thatcher inquired with amusement.

"Madsen marooned me with that bunch." Berman reviewed his tribulations and offered a specimen. "They brought their papers to the dining room."

Thatcher was bracing. "Well, then, your worst sufferings of the day are over. Mine are still before me. Which reminds me, hadn't we better be getting up to the board room?"

"No." Berman immediately turned away from the elevators and walked toward a couch by the reception desk. "Madsen's going to pick us up here. Anyway, we still have about ten minutes."

He disposed himself comfortably and began to unwrap a cigar. Thatcher recognized the symptoms. A fatalistic melancholia had settled over his companion in which escape from Michigan Motors seemed impossible unless exit routes were close at hand. Thatcher sat down.

When Frank Krebbel emerged from the interior of the building to pause at the desk, he found his two guests sitting side by side in pensive silence. One of them had his eyes fixed on the doors. A more imaginative man might have been embarrassed (and a more frolicsome one might have started some close harmony for "If I Had the Wings of an Angel"). Krebbel merely completed his instructions to the receptionist before turning to greet them.

"Tell them to give me a second-shift driver. He'll have to drive me home after the dinner, and I'll want the limousine to bring me in to Plantagenet tomorrow morning. Hello, Thatcher, Berman." He apologized for the business appointment that was keeping him from the afternoon meeting. "But French will be able to tell you anything you want to know." He waved his attaché case at the limousine that was pulling up in the driveway. "I've got to get into town now, but I'll see you at the chamber of commerce dinner tonight."

Enviously Berman watched his progress toward the entrance, then suddenly stood as he saw the woman for whom Krebbel was holding the door. After she exchanged a few words with MM's president, Berman called to her: "Celia! Over here! John, you haven't met Celia Jensen, have you?"

"No," said Thatcher. He did not add that he had heard

about her. Surely this must be the inebriated Mrs. Wahl's "Celia."

Arnold Berman introduced Ray Jensen's wife. Her charming smile did not completely conceal traces of worry and strain. Tiny blue veins shadowed the pale clear skin at her temples, and dark smudges lay under her wide-set hazel eyes. But there was a latent sparkle in those eyes and a warm curve to her generous mouth.

"Celia went to Cornell with Esther," Berman explained. After a moment's silence he added reflectively, "Different sororities, of course."

Mrs. Jensen laughed affectionately. "Arnie, you're still impossible, but it's such a relief to have you here. I only wish Esther could have come too. You don't know what it's been like and . . . Anyway, I haven't seen her for ages."

"You ought to come and visit us," he replied earnestly. "Why don't you go back with me? Esther would be tickled pink."

"Oh, Arnie! You know I'd love to." She smiled but suddenly her lips quivered. "But I can't now. Maybe later in the summer."

To Thatcher's mind the conversation was becoming undesirably emotional. Apparently Mrs. Jensen agreed with him because, almost immediately, she cast about for a calming topic.

"Oh, I see they got that car here after all."

"What car, Cele?"

"The Super Planty." She pointed to the pool. "Everybody at Plantagenet is behaving like a madman."

"Oh?" Berman asked alertly. "Been over at the division, Cele?"

"Yes." The gaiety faded from her voice. "I've been looking for Ray. I haven't had a chance to talk to him since he got back last Monday—and this situation is maddening." She flushed slightly. "You know, we closed down the house . . . before the trial. I've been staying with my sister. Well, when I saw Frank Krebbel's Drake pulling into the parking lot, I thought I had finally run Ray to earth. But up in Ray's office, Ed Wahl said No. Frank had been looking for him too. And Frank just told me that Ray isn't here, either. Nobody seems to know where he is."

"Playing hard to get," Berman muttered when her voice broke.

The interruption recalled Celia Jensen to her anecdote.

"While Ed and I were talking, the door flew open and one of the engineers roared in, shouting that the Super Plantagenet was being stolen!"

"Thirty thousand dollars' worth of car?" said Berman. "Stolen?"

Mrs. Jensen laughed. "I thought Ed was going to explode. Then we went racing down to the garage with half of the office behind us—just in time to see the taillights disappearing out the door!"

"I've always had my doubts about MM management," Berman informed Thatcher.

Celia Jensen ignored him. "Ed went absolutely wild. Before any of us could stop him, he was pounding after it, yelling and shaking his fists. And I was the only one who could laugh—since everybody else works for Ed. But it *was* funny."

An unhealthy state of affairs, Thatcher thought, when a group of sane adults remained respectfully grave while an out-of-condition middle-aged man tried to overtake a five-hundred-horsepower titan.

Mrs. Jensen explained the public relations coup, adding that when one of Lincoln Hauser's minions had belatedly told Ed Wahl about PR's plans for a grandiose Friday presentation of the Super Plantagenet, she momentarily feared for the man's safety.

"Hauser, and I suppose the people who work for him, do have that effect," said Thatcher. "At the Sloan we didn't give him quite the scope he has here, but I always felt he would make a first-rate horse thief."

Berman then expressed himself simply but at length: he didn't know about public relations, Waymark-Sims confining itself to simple tombstone ads in *The New York Times,* but he did know that he had no high opinion of executives who ran after cars, and, since he was with friends, he might add that he wasn't crazy about presentations of said cars to Crown Prince Bulbuls, either.

"Still," he concluded, "I suppose we'd better be getting upstairs, John. Glen's late."

They made their farewells to Mrs. Jensen, with Berman adding a fraternal kiss, then again proceeded toward the elevator. Just as Celia Jensen crossed the lobby, Glen Madsen hurried into their view. He stopped short for a moment, then ignoring both Berman and Thatcher, almost ran up to intercept her. Whatever he said when he reached her side was inaudible to the men at the elevator, but Madsen's intensity as he put a hand on Mrs. Jensen's arm was revealing.

Arnold Berman was releasing one of his mournful sighs of comment when there was another interruption.

A breathless young man hurled himself into the lobby.

"Mr. Madsen!" he called from the doorway. "Have you seen the driver?"

Reluctantly Madsen looked up.

"What driver?" he snapped.

"The one who drove the Super Planty over here. I was in the car with him—but he's just taken off," the young man cried, wrenching off black-rimmed glasses to lend force to his words. He was, Thatcher realized, one of Lincoln Hauser's henchmen. "We want to photograph someone in overalls near the car."

"I haven't seen him," Madsen said savagely, keeping his proprietary hand on Celia Jensen. "Why the hell don't you just put on some overalls yourself!"

The young man paled, but a passing secretary kindly told him that she thought she had seen the man in question going around the far side of the building. The young man darted off in pursuit.

After a brief but impassioned remark of some sort, Mrs. Jensen resolutely followed him. For a moment Madsen stood watching her. Then he turned to join Thatcher and Berman.

Berman made no effort to dispel the awkwardness of the whole episode.

"Where is Ray Jensen, Glen?" he asked bluntly.

"God knows!" Madsen replied. Then, with visible effort, he made a commonplace remark about the Super Plantagenet.

John Thatcher felt duty bound to make some push to be helpful, although under the circumstances it was difficult to hit on anything that would be.

"You MM people certainly emphasize limousines," he remarked.

Automatically Madsen informed them that MM policy was to publicize the Plantagenets for prestige purposes, while the Lancasters and the Buccaneers buttered the company bread. Accordingly top executives drove Plantys on company business, but they were encouraged to drive any MM car at other times. Even the president of Michigan

Motors was often seen driving himself in his modest
Drake. . . .

As Madsen spoke, Thatcher wondered how much Arnold Berman knew about Madsen and Mrs. Jensen. On the
other hand, how much more was there to know? The encounter he had just witnessed was eloquent.

When they reached the board room, Lionel McC.
French revealed the qualities that had made him a leading American businessman. "I can see we're all looking
forward to this meeting," he said. So far as Thatcher could
tell, he was perfectly sincere.

The interminable afternoon featured French, a silent,
bleak-eyed Glen Madsen, and assorted members of the
MM Board on one side of a long table, pitted against John
Thatcher and Arnold Berman on the other.

"Now," said Berman, smoking furiously to give vent to
his emotions, "about your depreciation system."

He elicited a detailed financial statement and several
speeches before the principals adjourned for the day.

"You won't forget the chamber of commerce dinner
tonight, will you?" asked Glen Madsen as they eddied out.
He was again the conscientious host. Conscientious to a
fault, thought Thatcher. With unflattering sincerity Thatcher replied that there was no need for Madsen or Michigan Motors to exert themselves any further on his behalf.

"You'll be interested," said Madsen, revealing a kinship
with all of Michigan Motors. "And we're stopping in for
drinks with the Wahls."

John Thatcher protested no further. Obviously during
their sojourn in Detroit he and Arnold Berman were
helpless in the grip of the powerful forces that mold industrial hospitality. By eight thirty that evening they had
been transported downtown to the dinner, sharing a table
with Madsen, Ed Wahl (whose wife had confined herself
to tomato juice during their brief visit), and Buck Holsinger. At the head table Frank Krebbel was reaching the
peroration of an unimaginative, if optimistic, assessment
of the Michigan Motors situation.

Thatcher, lost in private thoughts, noticed Wahl lean
over to ask Buck Holsinger something.

"No," replied that extrovert in round, full-bodied tones.
"No, I haven't been able to track Ray Jensen down, Ed,
but I can tell you one thing—"

"Never mind, never mind," said Wahl hastily.

". . . Ray Jensen will turn up tomorrow," Holsinger continued cheerfully. "When all the pictures of the Super Planty are being taken, guess who'll turn up trying to hog the publicity? Who'll try to throw his weight around? Who'll try to grab the credit and push you out of the limelight, Ed? Ray Jensen, that's who."

"For God's sake shut up, Buck!" Glen Madsen sounded taut as their table became the object of considerable curiosity. Ed Wahl's face had reddened unattractively, but Buck Holsinger, who had helped himself freely to the predinner libations, was not to be deterred.

"Yes, our friend Ray," he said. "The man who always stands up for his friends. The man who covers up for them when they're in trouble, the man who plans to come right back to Michigan Motors and take over!"

At the head table Frank Krebbel was coming to a conclusion. "On the basis of past performance," he read in his rather monotonous voice, "we see room for nothing but confidence in Michigan Motors' future."

John Putnam Thatcher could not find it in his heart to agree with him.

5 • Body Work

BY FRIDAY MORNING both Arnold Berman and John Putnam Thatcher were determined to wind up their conferences with Michigan Motors and escape to New York. This would entail a hard day, but as Berman said, it was well worth it.

These plans were neatly torpedoed. As soon as they arrived at the Executive Building they realized that Friday would not see much work done. Michigan Motors was triumphantly *en fête*. Japanese lanterns were bobbing in the trees, and a temporary dais hung with bunting had been erected in the midst of hundreds of folding chairs. From somewhere a menacing crackle suddenly resolved itself into a stentorian intoning:

"Testing — one — two — three — testing — one — two — three."

All this activity centered about the sleek Super Plantagenet poised in majestic immobility next to the reflecting pool where it had been stationed the previous day. The pool was doing the occasion justice. Instead of the leaden liquid surface so often presented by standing water, or the glassy mirror of a motionless summer afternoon, today the pool was a beautiful blue, stirred into hundreds of little ripples by the spring breeze which was whipping the flags overhead. The car's chrome grillwork was picked up by the water so that silver highlights danced over the crinkly blue of the surface.

"Well," said Buck Holsinger, materializing from the crowd to lead Thatcher and Berman firmly to the front row. "Everything's ready except that the brass hasn't shown up yet."

"We were hoping to see Madsen," protested Thatcher, fighting fate.

"Well," said Holsinger doubtfully, "he's here all right. Over there with Hauser. But I think he's pretty busy."

Thatcher followed his host's gaze and repressed a shudder. Glen Madsen was involved with a little group on the sidelines where Lincoln Hauser happily presided over the press. Issuing sharp commands, waving his arms, strutting about like a turkey cock, Hauser was having the time of his life. A prudent man would stay safely in the shelter of Buck Holsinger's orbit.

Arnold Berman, who had also resigned himself to a wasted morning, surveyed the crowd with a jaundiced eye.

"This been going on for long?" he asked disapprovingly.

"For hours. One of the guards told me that some people got here at seven o'clock this morning. Why," said Holsinger producing the clincher, "even my secetary got here on time! Haven't seen her since, of course. She must be around somewhere."

Locating any particular secretary would have been difficult. The clerical staff of Michigan Motors was brightening the scene with gay cotton dresses as they maintained a busy air of activity by passing back and forth, in and out, never very far from the focal point of attention. Chances to see a crown prince don't come every day. Some mysterious system of communication had been established, however, which allowed a young woman to interrupt a conversation every now and then by brightly announcing that Mr. So-and-so was wanted on the phone. Michigan Motors dressed up to meet its public.

"And not just the secretaries," Holsinger continued on a less impressed note. "Most of the wives are here too. I guess they want to see what a prince looks like. Diane left the house before I did this morning."

He waved casually across the pool to where his wife, resplendent in a rose silk suit, was talking intently to Orin Dunn. Dunn was shifting uncomfortably.

"Makes a nice outing for everybody," said Berman, trying hard to get into the spirit of things.

"Yes, but it's still tough right now. You have to admit . . . Hey, Thaddeus, come over and meet some people."

Thaddeus Casimir (UAW Local 7777, AFL-CIO), known to Thatcher only from his photographs, dropped into a seat and allowed himself to be introduced. He looked what he was—Labor's Man of Distinction.

"Well, Thad, this isn't your sort of rumble. You're supposed to be against crown princes and sheikdoms. What are you doing? Keeping an eye on the opposition?"

Thatcher, who had been privileged to hear some of Buck Holsinger's views about his stay in jail, was not surprised at this camaraderie. A man who could take the inmates of a federal prison in stride was not going to be thrown off by a mere union official.

Casimir's answer was brief and just as friendly. "Yes, but I'm supposed to be very much for cars. As a matter of fact I'm taking part in the presentation."

"Can you beat that? What do you have to do with it?"

"I represent labor." Casimir smiled slightly. "Tell me, Buck, who's going to represent Plantagenet, Ed or Ray Jensen?"

There was a brief silence as Holsinger eyed Thaddeus Casimir with some annoyance. Casimir, in turn, examined his square-tipped fingers.

"Mr. Wahl seems remarkably busy," suggested Thatcher kindly. Buck Holsinger, whatever his virtues, was not up to a sparring match with Thaddeus Casimir. Gratefully everybody turned to watch Ed Wahl direct the labors of several workmen in natty coveralls emblazoned with "Plantagenet" in Italian script.

"He's trying hard, that's all," said Holsinger grumpily. "Well, I see people are beginning to arrive. I'd better go over there." With a friendly nod Holsinger rose, and strode away to integrate himself into the welcoming committee now surrounding the first of a long line of black limousines sweeping up the driveway. Only a cynic would have called this an escape. Thaddeus Casimir, Thatcher was willing to wager, had been born cynical.

They watched Holsinger greet the men just struggling out of a shining limousine. Then Casimir uttered a short exclamation. "There are Coningsby and Shattuck from the board of directors." He paused meaningfully. "And Stuart Eberhart, the ex-president."

As aisles formed among the spectators for the dignitaries ascending the dais, Casimir continued thoughtfully: "You know, Eberhart's the man that the judge said was responsible for the price fixing. Now they've put him up on the platform, and they've got old Buck Holsinger giving everybody the glad hand. If they let Ray Jensen muscle in on Wahl for this presentation, it must mean they're going to take them all back. I don't think Frank Krebbel is the man to pull something that raw. He gave in to French about inviting Stu Eberhart, but I bet he draws the line right there. If you ask me, Ray Jensen isn't hiding out so he can steal everybody's thunder at the last minute. Jensen's not here because he's licked, and he knows it."

Thatcher maintained diplomatic silence in the face of a speech he regarded as deliberately designed to elicit comment. Even Berman heroically bit back a commentary on the management astuteness that could keep such a decision not only from the world but from Ed Wahl as well.

Undeterred by the general lack of response, Casimir went on. "Of course, Ray might have so much inside information about the company that Krebbel doesn't have any choice. But if that's the way the wind blows, things are going to look very ugly indeed."

Having made the Wall Street interests aware of the union position, Thaddeus Casimir bestowed a valedictory smile on them, and moved off to be photographed.

"Nasty," said Berman softly.

"But suggestive."

Berman shrugged. "Hell, I didn't say he was wrong. No matter how you slice it, this sort of situation— Uh-oh. There's Celia. And something's up. She looks as if she'd had trouble. You don't think she's run into Jensen, do you? Do you mind if we have her with us, John? I don't like to leave her alone in this crowd."

Without waiting for a reply, Berman stood and beckoned imperiously towards Celia Jensen. But in the end he had to go to her. She was walking blindly through the crowd, a handkerchief pressed to her mouth, oblivious to the curious looks she was drawing.

"Oh, Arnie, I'm so ashamed, I don't know what to say . . ." she gasped as he led her to the chair.

"Now, Cele, don't worry about that. Just take it easy. And you don't have to say anything if you don't want to."

"But I've got to tell you. He's just lost control. I can't believe the things he's saying. I wasn't looking for him, you know. I just bumped into him. And he said you just have to decide what it is you want, and then go out and get it. But it's the way he looked while he said it. I tell you, Arnie, I'm frightened. I never thought things would be like this. . . ."

Berman, who was rapidly soaring in Thatcher's estimation by the massive lack of self-consciousness he displayed in dealing with a near-hysterical woman at a crowded business function, ceased giving vent to soothing noises and put a straight question.

"When did you meet him?"

"About a half hour ago. On the other side of the building. It's deserted, everybody's on this side."

"What set Ray off? Or was it just seeing you?"

His cross-examination had a beneficial effect on Celia Jensen. Straightening, she gave a final decisive sniff into the scrap of linen she held.

"No . . . that is . . . let's not talk about it anymore," she said. "Arnie—and Mr. Thatcher, oh, dear, I know I've behaved like a fool and I'm so sorry. Look, I think the crown prince is arriving."

From the last of the stately limousines Lionel French was emerging in company with a slim, dark-haired young man clad in slacks and a sports jacket. So much for Lincoln Hauser's flowing white robes, thought Thatcher with satisfaction. As the two men shuffled uneasily for precedence in an "After you, Alphonse" routine whereby Lionel French tried successfully to extend the courtesies due from host to guest and Crown Prince Bulbul tried unsuccessfully to extend those due from youth to age, there was a disturbance on the driveway. The driver of the limousine was reluctant to miss any of the glories about to unfold. Since he knew there were no more limousines to come, he delayed putting his machine into motion. A stubborn little red car which had crept up behind him impatiently tooted. Unable to believe his ears, he turned to give the insistent motorist a frosty glare. A moment later he was galvanized into such a frenzy of activity that he jerked his Plantagenet Sceptre—"Symbol of Achievement" —up the driveway in a manner singularly inappropriate to any professional driver at Michigan Motors. The cause of his alarm became apparent when the driver of the red Drake—"The Lively, Fun-loving Compact"—uncurled his length from beneath the steering wheel and stood revealed as Frank Krebbel. A titter from the crowd greeted the president's appearance. Nothing daunted, he gave a friendly wave to right and left and strode unhurriedly to the platform, where he assumed a seat next to the crown prince.

"I think that's ridiculous. Why can't he use a Planty like everybody else?" asked the querulous voice of a newcomer.

"Hello, Audrey," Celia Jensen greeted her cautiously. "You've met Mrs. Wahl, haven't you?"

Thatcher and Berman acknowledged the acquaintance with civility if not enthusiasm and found Ed Wahl's wife a chair. Mrs. Jensen's caution was unnecessary. Mrs. Wahl soon proved to be perfectly sober. As far as Thatcher was concerned, that was no net gain.

"Well," said Celia, returning to the original question, "Frank probably just came in from one of the plants."

"I know, I know," Mrs. Wahl replied irritably. "He told Ed he was going to start the day at Plantagenet before he came over here. That's not what I mean. He shouldn't be running around doing errands today. He should have been in the car with the crown prince. And," she said, coming at last to the genuine source of complaint, "Ed should have been there too. Why, Ed isn't even up on the platform! It's a Plantagenet they're presenting, isn't it? And Ed's in charge of Plantagenet, isn't he?"

Decidedly, Mrs. Wahl was no easier to get along with sober than drunk. But the whining note in her voice failed to hide the urgency of her desperation. Celia Jensen, still pale from her own outburst, took the bull by the horns in a manner which Thatcher, for one, regarded as rash to the point of folly.

"Audrey, you've got to stop hinting," she said tremulously. "Are you trying to say that Ray is going to make the presentation?"

"Ray? Oh, no. He's not going to be a problem anymore." Mrs. Wahl's lips pursed with secretive malice. "That's been taken care of."

"What do you mean?" Celia demanded.

"Just that the division isn't going to do the honors, that's all," said Mrs. Wahl sulkily. "Frank Krebbel's going to do the whole thing himself. I guess they're starting now."

Celia Jensen frowned worriedly, but before she could speak, a voice which now seemed to be in complete control of the microphone system announced the national anthem of the crown prince's domain. If they would all please rise?

A medley of weird wailing noises, clashing in monumental discord, broke forth. The audience obediently came to its feet and an expression of bewilderment appeared on Prince Bulbul's pleasantly noncommittal features.

"Ten to one they got the wrong music," said Berman disgustedly.

After at least seventeen verses of somebody's national anthem, there came a vast shuffling of feet as the audience reseated itself. Frank Krebbel thereupon delivered a speech which, under the circumstances, was very creditable. Skirting all reference to the division from which the Super Plantagenet emanated, he spoke of the pleasure

Michigan Motors took in the performance of this particular bit of work and its pride in being selected as the company best equipped to do the job. He neatly encompassed Thaddeus Casimir, the union, and the men-on-the-line in the group for which he spoke, gracefully alluded to the glorious future confidently anticipated by all those present for the crown prince and the kingdom which he adorned, and deferred all discussion of the specific merits of the Super Plantagenet until the demonstration to be furnished at a later moment by the Public Relations Department.

"Wear it in good health," muttered Berman.

Crown Prince Bulbul was not to be outdone. Regretting the absence of his father on whose behalf he spoke, he went on, in a flat American drawl, to apologize for his attire. Some regrettable delay in his flight from California where he was attending Cal Tech. Pleasantries followed on the informality to be expected from a Californian, the merits of Cal Tech as a rival insitution to Michigan Motors in the field of industrial innovation, and his own competence as an engineer. A truly Oriental display of gratitude for this splendid automobile which would be lovingly cherished by his father, and a careful remark about his own preference for a sports car—the MM Hotspur, of course—concluded his speech to the sound of ringing applause.

At this point the ceremony was handed over to the Public Relations Department, and everything began to go wrong. Lincoln Hauser, stepping firmly into the spotlight, enunciated a tedious series of statistics relating to the car's specifications, which were received at least politely until hasty reading rendered the car's horsepower as fifty. Guffaws from the engineers spread rapidly. Quelling this outburst, Hauser went on with renewed zeal to the demonstration part of his program. A long pointer, flourished didactically, displayed various excellences. The most imperceptive lecturer would have noted restiveness in his audience by this time. But Lincoln Hauser was buoyed up by the conviction that he was saving his show-stopper for the finale.

Having swung open the front door of the car to prove his point about ample leg room, Hauser let a tentative silence develop as he favored his listeners with a wild grimace of anticipation.

"And now, ladies and gentlemen," he shouted in the accents of one gone completely mad, "you have heard

that this model was designed to be completely armored
—impervious not only to bullets but to mortar shells as
well. Well, we are going to prove it!" He gestured commandingly, and a flunky rushed forward with an omi-
nous-looking object.

"This," he continued impressively, "is a machine pistol
which I hold in my hand. A pistol issued by the United
States Army and capable of piercing two inches of sheet
metal! Before your very eyes I will fire a burst at point-
blank range, and you will see that there is not a mark on
the bodywork."

At this moment a hushed silence should no doubt have
descended on the audience. Actually the press looked
bored, although several cameramen hoisted their cam-
eras obligingly. Buck Holsinger said, "Oh, my God" loudly
enough to reach the back rows, and Prince Bulbul, to whom
all this expensive bodywork now belonged, looked worried.

A brief staccato of firing, and it was over. Michigan
Motors was as good as its word. The shiny metal showed
not a dent, which was more than could be said for the
paint. Prince Bulbul (and assorted automotive executives)
let out a sigh of relief.

Triumphantly Lincoln Hauser swung open the rear door
of the limousine with a great sweep of showmanship.

And slowly, but very visibly, the bloodied head and
shoulders of a man crumpled forward until the entire body
lay outstretched at the feet of Lincoln Hauser on the expensive and roughened flagstones of Michigan Motors'
poolside patio. For a moment the whole scene was a fro-
zen tableau.

Then seventeen women screamed and Lincoln Hauser,
moving like a sleepwalker, backed away from the grisly
object beneath him. His faithful aide rushed forward, bent
down, and exclaimed in clarion tones: "But, sir, it's Mr.
Jensen! He's dead. . . . You must have killed him!"

Celia Jensen went white and slumped toward Arnold
Berman as Audrey Wahl threw back her head and let peal
after peal of shrill hysteria ring through the clear spring
morning.

6 • Automatic Transmission

A SHORT TIME LATER, the forces of order and decorum having asserted themselves, two recumbent forms were removed from the scene of battle. One was the late Raymond H. Jensen; the other was Michigan Motors' director of public relations. Lincoln Hauser had met the needs of the moment by fainting.

They were, of course, not the only ones to leave the poolside patio. A surprising number of spectators chose to make less dramatic exits. While he helped Berman revive Celia Jensen, Thatcher noticed Mrs. Wahl recover enough to insist that her husband take her away. And in the flow of colorfully garbed secretaries streaming toward the building, he was almost certain that he spied Mrs. Holsinger. Men were harder to identify, but at least half of them had melted away by the time a long black car, not a Plantagenet, deposited the advance guard of the Michigan State Police.

Total confusion ensued. The Public Relations Department tearfully invited one and all to assure themselves that the Super Planty's body was unmarred by even the slightest puncture. The situation was not improved by the simultaneous arrival of four eminent cardiac specialists from downtown Detroit. More than one MM employee had drawn the inevitable conclusion from Lincoln Hauser's collapse and acted accordingly.

"Happens all the time," said Buck Holsinger with the cheer which neither penal servitude nor sudden murder could dispel. He then told Thatcher a long, complicated story about an automotive executive, unwell after a vigorous round of tennis, who had brooded over his infirmity until three o'clock in the morning. Sharp chest pains had then impelled him to summon his own specialist to treat his heart attack. He was suffering, it developed, from a rib cracked by a particularly vicious serve.

"There they go," Holsinger concluded as the medical

fraternity withdrew, no doubt already toting up the bill. "Now, we'll see some action," he added with gusto.

He was disappointed. The senior police official was taken in hand by Frank Krebbel, who gave him an accurate, detached description of the entire scene. Various technicians busied themselves with the interior of the Super Plantagenet and with the machine pistol theoretically capable of piercing two inches of sheet metal. Beyond demanding the names and addresses of the participants still present and accepting the statement of the company nurse that Mrs. Raymond Jensen was in shock, the police expressed no immediate need for witnesses. Thatcher and Berman satisfied themselves that Celia Jensen was remaining in the MM infirmary until her sister arrived and then sought relief at the cocktail lounge of the Telegraph Motel.

"This," said Berman, "is going to be a mess."

He was right. If Lincoln Hauser was incapable of capitalizing on the most newsworthy moment of his life, the same could not be said for the rest of the fanatics manning the communications media of North America.

By the time Thatcher and Berman could proceed to lunch, precedent was being broken and an industrious youth was hawking Detroit papers through the Telegraph Motel's posh dining room, the Wild Steer.

"Vehicle of death," read Thatcher, disapproving of the inevitable picture caption.

"It could be worse," said Berman fatalistically. "Any facts?"

"Not until the later editions," said the occupant of a nearby table, a parts dealer from Saginaw. "But they'll be bringing the papers in here."

He too was right. After a profitless afternoon spent communicating with their New York offices, Thatcher and Berman met again that evening in the Telegraph Motel's cocktail lounge, the Fuel House.

"Hugh thinks I should stick around over the weekend," Berman reported, helping himself to some salted peanuts. He gestured to the barman for their drinks and continued in an insubordinate tone, "He says that maybe we'll have to think about deferring the issue until the mess here is cleared up."

He looked inquiringly at Thatcher.

"That is roughly the line that Walter seems to have sold our Investment Committee," Thatcher replied. "Don't worry. With the market behaving the way it is, MM won't be issuing any stock. . . . Oh, there are the evening papers."

Fortunately reading material and liquor arrived together. Rapidly skimming a summary of the automotive excellences embodied in the Super Plantagenet, Thatcher found the meat:

State Police Captain William Georgeson announced that preliminary laboratory investigations indicate that the dead man was slain some time Wednesday. There was no possible connection with the burst of gunfire at today's ceremonies. Jensen's body was placed on the floor of the back seat after death. Experts as yet cannot determine whether Jensen was actually shot in the car. The police have established that the Super Plantagenet was on public display and unguarded for twenty-four hours prior to the discovery this morning. Access to the poolside area, however, is restricted to employees of Michigan Motors and their guests. The Super Plantagenet, constructed to specifications supplied by the customer, has been impounded by the state police and is being garaged at . . .

"Mm," said Berman, inspecting his drink. "That puts the finger on somebody in the inner circle, doesn't it? The car was unguarded for about twenty-four hours—in an area virtually restricted to our friends, the MM executives."

"And their guests—or families," Thatcher pointed out. Berman frowned but did not rise to the bait directly.

"Assume that Ray's body could have been dumped in the car only when there wasn't a crowd around it. Then it was only last night or early this morning. Remember Holsinger told us how early people started showing up today."

Thatcher nodded. "Of course Jensen's body could have been in the Plantagenet all the time."

Berman was doleful. "It's possible. But obviously the police are going to start digging around for motives."

"Of which there are many," said Thatcher.

Berman brightened slightly. "That's right. Plenty of people had good reason to want Ray out of the way—"

"Boy, you said a mouthful," said another neighbor, a car rental executive this time.

Plenty, Thatcher agreed mentally. Including Mrs. Ray

Jensen, who was still too unwell to answer the most so-licitous inquiries.

Another drink turned Arnold Berman's attention to a new subject. He dug into a pocket.

"You've seen this?"

It was a document he had obtained during a brief and abortive foray into the MM controller's office that after-noon. It was not the newspapers alone who were trumpet-ing the details of the Jensen murder, Thatcher saw. An incautious memorandum had been hastily issued for inter-nal circulation by somebody at Michigan Motors. After urging members of the MM family to refrain from dis-cussing "sensational aspects" of the death of Vice-Pres-ident Ray Jensen, whose passing was mourned by all, the industrial relations man went on to rebuke the security staff for laxity in preventing the theft of firearms. "The police have informed us that the murder weapon was a service revolver of the same make and caliber as those issued to MM plant guards. Such a revolver was stolen from the guard headquarters at the Plantagenet building last Tuesday. If proper precautions had been taken by the personnel involved, this entire tragedy might have been averted. Control procedures will be tightened immedi-ately, and we ask the cooperation of all employees. . . ."

"I'll look forward to seeing what Casimir has to say," Thatcher commented. "Ready to go in to dinner?"

(At that moment the union was readying a counterat-tack to be launched Monday morning, not restricted to in-ternal circulation. Lashing out at the idiocy which could suggest that Jensen's murder was simply due to the avail-ability of a weapon, the memo accused the industrial rela-tions staff of being ready, eager, and willing to lay any blame it could on hourly employees. It was not certain that the missing gun was the murder weapon. A murderer was responsible for this terrible crime—not the innocent victim of a theft. A victim, moreover, whose pay was being docked for having lost company property. After an inflamed discussion of the question of financial liability for stolen equipment, the writer concluded by inquiring nastily whether management had seen fit to ask itself who had the most to gain from Ray Jensen's murder.

"Not bad, Sid. Not bad at all," said Thaddeus Casimir dispassionately.)

Thatcher felt that under the best of circumstances the prospect of a weekend spent in the outskirts of Detroit was not one to cheer. Accordingly he made another effort to extricate himself.

"I'm sorry to ask you to stay, John," Bradford Withers, president of the Sloan Guaranty Trust, harrumphed over the phone at him later that evening. "But I was talking to George . . ."

In sum, the Sloan Guaranty Trust wanted a man on the ground when the smoke cleared—if it cleared, thought Thatcher, replacing the receiver. He had his doubts. Happily he also had a goodly endowment of curiosity. This at least rendered his plight less galling than it might have been.

Nevertheless he was left prey to ill-informed speculation about Jensen's murder in every public room of the Telegraph Motel and from every available news medium. By Saturday evening, pundits on all major networks were analyzing domestic affairs, international relations, and the moon probe in the light of the Jensen murder. But it was the prerogative of the bulky Sunday newspapers to feed the public's appetite for sensational detail, despite the silence of the police and most of the principals.

After one affronted glance, Berman plunged off to inquire after the well-being of Mrs. Jensen, now in seclusion at her sister's home. He returned some hours later more downcast than ever. (During this period Thatcher had been comparing newspapers and attitudes. Washington's front pages said, "State Department to Intercede for Bulbul," while Chicago throbbed to the human drama: WHAT DARK FATE STALKED RAY JENSEN? asked a heavy headline. Mrs. Jensen was described as the tearful and beauteous young widow. Boston was simply querulous: "What's going on at MM? Was Jensen's murder tied in with the price-fixing conspiracy? And what's the Department of Justice still investigating out there?")

Thatcher pushed at least twenty pounds of newspaper across the table, looked up, and saw Arnold Berman enter the lobby. "We've been invited to dinner by the Frenches," Thatcher said.

Berman flinched.

Thatcher relented. "I said that we were busy with Ferry, downtown."

Exhaustedly Berman dropped into a chair. "God, I need a drink. Hugh may have to invest in drying me out after this. Have you seen the statement that French made to-day? Everybody loved Jensen like a brother, some maniac found his way into the Michigan Motors compound, everything will be back to normal within a week."

"Well, what can he say?"

"He could keep quiet, couldn't he?" Berman growled, raising a finger for service.

"Apparently not," Thatcher rejoined. "Dismiss silence, and you're left without much to say for the facts that have to be faced. First of all, the gun was stolen at Plantagenet last Tuesday, the day before Jensen's murder. That does make it look as if somebody at MM planned to kill Jensen at least twenty-four hours in advance."

Berman nodded and drained his glass. "I know, I know. And they have to explain how Jensen could be missing from Wednesday to Friday without anybody reporting it. They can't very well issue a publicity release saying that Jensen was such an SOB that everybody assumed he was lying low to build up tension. Or even that he was such a bastard that they were damned grateful that he wasn't around. But I still wish French would just shut up."

With a good deal of comprehension Thatcher regarded his harassed colleague. His own Sunday, sequestered in the businessman's-elegant Telegraph Motel, had exposed him to the endless conversation of MM customers, suppliers, and other industrial satraps. But Arnold Berman, after a long telephone conversation with his wife Esther (who was, Thatcher gathered, as energetic as she was voluble), had manfully gone off to proffer comfort to the bereaved widow.

"Mrs. Jensen?" he asked cautiously.

Berman sighed deeply. "That's right. She's going to be in real trouble. No way to ignore it. You remember that business she blurted out—just before the presentation got under way?"

"I've been remembering it vividly for two days," said Thatcher truthfully.

"Well, that Wahl woman gave the police a souped-up version. She thought—the way you and I did—that Cele was talking about running into Jensen. And Cele, the little idiot, went along with that story. That was Friday afternoon, when the police first talked to her. Then when they realized how long Jensen had been dead, they got onto her again." Berman shook his head. "And now she's giving them some incredible story about quarreling with a maintenance man about where she parked her car. You can see how things look to the police."

"I'm not sure they don't look that way to me," said Thatcher.

Gloom settled on Berman. "Me too," he admitted. "But whatever Glen Madsen has been up to, Celia doesn't deserve more trouble. Frankly I don't think she can take much more, either. This last year hasn't been easy on her. She's pretty near the breaking point. And the police are going to be on her neck until she tells them the truth about what happened Friday morning."

He paused, oppressed by his own recital. Thatcher was glad that Berman had missed some of the public speculation about Glen Madsen and Mrs. Jensen that was running riot in the Telegraph Motel, but he could think of nothing to say that would cheer him.

"What I need," Berman announced defiantly, "is another drink."

The end of the weekend brought no perceptible improvement in the atmosphere, outside of an investment newsletter that the director of technical services called to their attention on Monday. The market letter started brightly:

Well, one of our stocks that got rained on last week was Michigan Motors, and I don't think it will dry out. In fact, I'm feeling bearish about all the auto stocks right now. Of course, people know that cars will go on being bought—but people basically react emotionally and not reasonably. Who wants money tied up in an industry where executives are either in jail or being shot up? I was talking with some of the people out in Detroit over the weekend, and they told me that one of the things they didn't like was the way Jensen dropped from sight while nobody missed him. Well, that's a funny sort of a team they've got out there. Now, if you're looking for a speculative stock on the over-the-counter market . . .

The letter went on to suggest that women being what they were, investment in high voltage generators was a sure thing.

By Monday night Hugh Waymark was beginning to have second thoughts about MM. A long telephone call culminated in arrangements for Berman to fly back to New York to brief his associates on current developments.

(At the same time, a prominent New York magazine was ripping out some of its front pages for a fast insert: "Our man Rodney not being available when the tidings from Detroit about Ray Jensen arrived, we paid a visit last Saturday to the Plantagenet display in the Grand Ballroom of the Hotel Biltmore. After verifying for ourselves the spacious dimensions of the back seat, sufficient for the accommodation of either legs or corpses, we were privileged to have a chat with Mr. James Pike, director of the exhibit. Mr. Pike, a small whirlwind of a man, has traveled more than sixteen thousand miles exhibiting the Plantagenet. We asked him if the crowds eddying about the long limousine were the result of recent headlines. Not at all, he assured us. . . ." For two columns Mr. Pike's staunch adherence to the company line was recorded— but so were the comments and questions of the bystanders come to see the kind of car in which automotive executives were put down.)

Berman was in a savage mood as he packed.

"You'll keep an eye on Celia?" he asked.

Thatcher, who had sociably come in to bid him *bon voyage*, replied that he would help as much as possible.

"I wish Hugh would make up his mind whether he's hot or cold on MM," Berman continued, thrusting a bathrobe into a corner of his suitcase.

Prudently Thatcher refrained from comment. Suddenly Berman looked at him accusingly. "And I wish I knew why you're staying, John. Don't tell me it's because Walter has sold the Investment Committee. The MM issue is a dead duck—and you know it as well as I do."

Thatcher preserved his dignity. "Naturally I'm curious," he said. "If American industry has just developed a new method for solving its executive personnel problems, it's my responsibility to keep the Sloan informed."

Fortunately Arnold Berman's attention was elsewhere.

Because over the weekend John Putnam Thatcher had developed a more fundamental curiosity. Who had killed Raymond Jensen?

He was surprised to discover that he had no intention of leaving Detroit until he found out.

7 • Under the Hood

By AFTERNOON of the next day Thatcher found his curiosity leading him into strange byways.

"So you are a friend of Mrs. Jensen's," said the matron on the couch disapprovingly. "I am afraid that she is low, very low indeed."

After a moment Thatcher decided that this remark was not a general moral indictment, but a reference to Celia Jensen's posture within the Protestant Episcopal faith. It was merely the latest in a series of brilliant *non sequiturs* which were giving his afternoon the flavor of an antic venture into another world. An involuntary glance of appeal toward his hostess produced nothing more helpful than a platter of tastefully arranged finger sandwiches.

It was no doubt a high sense of personal obligation to the absent Arnold Berman which had brought Thatcher (and a mystified Mack) eighty miles from Detroit to the gray stone rectory in Lansing which now housed Celia Jensen as well as her sister and brother-in-law. But no personal obligation would have led Thatcher to accept Mrs. Burns's invitation to tea while awaiting Celia's return if he had realized that this function represented the terminal activity of the monthly meeting of Saint Andrew's Altar Guild.

Before the full horror of his situation became clear, Thatcher had been imprisoned on a long, narrow sofa barricaded by a benchlike coffee table laden with fragile, and possibly precious, crystal dishes of comestibles. They now rattled dangerously as he shifted his knees.

"I beg your pardon, Miss Tickbourne?" he murmured politely to the angular spinster next to him.

Miss Tickbourne, it developed, harbored doubts which she was confident Thatcher could allay. Would an alb or a cope make the more appropriate gift for the rector? "Hand embroidered, of course," she reassured him.

"Naturally," said Thatcher. He added that so much

55

depended upon knowledge of the recipient that he was extremely hesitant to offer anything in the nature of a decisive opinion. Creditably done, he congratulated himself, for a man who didn't understand a word of what they were saying. He was spared further effort by an interruption.

"I understood," said Mrs. Prescott militantly, "that the committee had agreed on a cope."

Miss Tickbourne's eager face assumed a timidly mulish cast. "But a Eucharistic vestment . . . somehow it shows so much more feeling . . . and dear Father Burns is so sensitive to these distinctions . . ." she dithered.

"Father Burns!" snorted Mrs. Prescott, who was, Thatcher feared, the kind of woman who prides herself on calling a spade a spade. "That sort of talk may be very well under certain circumstances, but let me tell you, Lavinia, it is a very awkward way to refer to a married man." Turning a gimlet eye on her victim, she delivered the home thrust. "Almost indelicate."

Bridling, Miss Tickbourne took the offensive. Celibacy, she said, had never been required by Anglican doctrine. Except, of course, in the case of those in orders. And speaking of orders—here a new and sinister animation enlivened her voice—had she told them about the letter which had just come? Father John was such an inspiration. He understood her feelings so completely. She was sure she had brought it with her. She would just read them the bit about self-doubtings. . . .

Her two companions, instantly recognizing a habitual peril, leaped into action. Mrs. Prescott put one large capable hand on a platter of sponge cake and presented it menacingly before Miss Tickbourne's face. Mrs. Fulham broke into fluting conversation.

"We all know that Mr. Burns is sensitive. And Mrs. Jensen being his sister-in-law makes things so difficult for him just now. It was bad enough when she was living apart from her husband. But now! All this notoriety! Naturally the rector is very upset."

Thatcher glanced uncharitably across the room where the Reverend Lawrence Burns, the only other male present, was lounging against the mantelpiece, simultaneously balancing a teacup and mediating a dispute between two fluttering parishioners with what Thatcher resentfully characterized as unmanly aplomb. The Reverend Lawrence Burns looked fully capable of dealing with any amount

of in-law trouble. Indeed, thought Thatcher with no justification at all, he was probably enjoying the limelight.

Miss Tickbourne, torn between the delights of regaling
the company with a blow-by-blow account of her letter
and hearing the latest gossip, let herself be diverted.

"I understand that Mrs. Jensen refused point-blank to
rejoin her husband," she whispered in suitably confidential tones. "And only a few days before his . . . er . . .
death."

"But there had been a reconciliation," protested Mrs.
Fulham, a plump pouter pigeon of a woman who was
trying to believe the best of everybody in spite of heavy
odds.

"Just a sham," said Mrs. Prescott authoritatively. "It
was only for the look of things during the trial."

Thatcher abandoned the effort to ease his legs in the
narrow slit provided for their disposition. He had not anticipated that the ladies might prove a fruitful source of
information. Setting down his cup, he entered the conversation.

"I had not realized," he began cautiously, "that the dis-
agreement between Mr. and Mrs. Jensen was of such long
standing."

Three pairs of eyes assayed his probable intimacy with
the family and came to the same conclusion. Not too
close for comfort, but close enough to be interested.

Mrs. Prescott spoke dryly. "One might almost say that
their disagreements date from their marriage."

"I am afraid," said Mrs. Fulham sadly, "that Mr. Jensen was not what one would hope for in a husband.
Wrapped up in his business, you know, and not at all interested in a family life. And then, of course, there were
No Children."

Three heads bowed momentarily in token acknowledgment of the supreme conjugal failure. But Miss Tickbourne roused herself to the duties demanded of a church
stalwart. "Nevertheless, that is scarcely an excuse for a
wife to leave her husband. And whatever Mr. Jensen's
faults, there hadn't been any talk of a separation until
last summer."

Mrs. Fulham clucked unhappily, but Miss Tickbourne
swept on to her conclusion. "Until Mrs. Jensen met Mr.
Madsen!"

"Now there," said Mrs. Prescott, "I think we have a
great deal of smoke and very little fire."

"No." Surprisingly it was good-natured Mrs. Fulham who spoke, and with calm certainty. "Edgar played golf with Professor Belton the other day. And he said that Mr. Jensen went down to Ann Arbor to have it out with Mr. Madsen. They had a terrible quarrel. The neighbors almost called the police, and the whole university has been talking about it. So there must be something to it."

Thatcher was beginning to understand all too clearly why Celia Jensen had chosen to be out during the meeting of the Altar Guild.

"When was this?" he asked quietly.

"Sometime last week," replied Mrs. Fulham. "Just after Mrs. Jensen said she wouldn't leave Lansing."

Last week, Thatcher reflected. No wonder Raymond Jensen had not been in evidence at Michigan Motors. He had only returned from prison last Monday. The police thought he had been murdered on Wednesday. In the interim he had apparently traveled out to Lansing for one fight with his wife, then forty miles to Ann Arbor for another with Glen Madsen. Worst of all, both fights were common knowledge. When this became known to the police, the pressure on Celia Jensen would redouble to explain her cryptic remarks just before the discovery of her husband's body. Nor would she do much good with a series of ridiculous tales about quarrels with workmen in the parking lot. At the moment things looked bad, very bad, for Glen Madsen.

His review of the affairs of Raymond Jensen was interrupted by the arrival of a young woman clad in a black jersey, a black skirt, and black stockings. This ensemble was enlivened by a heavy chased-silver crucifix suspended on a long chain around her neck. She seemed bent on taking punctilious leave of everyone present. A handshake here, a few whispered words there, a cordial invitation to Thatcher to join them again, and she left the room accompanied by the rector, to whom she was speaking earnestly.

Her departure was a signal for the rest of the gathering. "Dear Mary Ellen has to get back to her children," explained Miss Tickbourne, assembling her belongings. "She comes to play the organ at our little service. Always so faithful."

Maternity, Thatcher reminded himself, takes many forms.

A good deal of complicated shuffling, regrouping, and

querying about cars followed before the Altar Guild made its exit and left the two men alone by the fire while Mrs. Burns removed the soiled crockery.

"Glad you enjoyed it," replied the rector to his guest's tempered thanks. "Let's see. You wanted to speak with Celia. I expect she'll be back shortly."

"Was Mary Ellen after you for confession again, Larry?" asked Mrs. Burns, returning.

"Well, as a matter of fact, yes," Burns admitted. "She wants to come in tomorrow, before school lets out."

"I really don't see why she can't make do with the General Confession, like everybody else."

Unhappily the rector answered, "Confession is an established prerogative of the Anglican believer. When the need is felt . . ."

"What's more," continued his wife, "considering that Mary Ellen is raising three children without help, taking care of a large Victorian house, and spending every free minute at St. Andrew's, it doesn't seem as if she'd have much material for you."

"There are sins of the mind, Louise," said her husband heavily.

"If we could just settle the ones of the body first, I'd be a lot happier."

Burns looked discouraged.

It was perhaps just as well that Celia Jensen now made her well-timed entry. Thatcher thought she looked ill.

After greeting him she sank down on the sofa, pulling off the scarf tied around her hair, while her sister examined her critically.

"All this slinking off doesn't do any good," Mrs. Burns announced. "You should have stayed in for the Altar Guild and seen some new faces."

Celia laughed shortly. "What? And deprive everyone of their chance to gossip?"

"Nobody gossiped," said the rector stoutly.

His wife and sister-in-law looked at him impatiently. "Oh, Larry! Not in front of you," they said in chorus.

"Did anybody talk about anything else?" demanded Mrs. Jensen.

"Yes," said Thatcher fair-mindedly. "Miss Tickbourne wanted to talk about somebody called Father John."

Mrs. Burns's tone was resigned. "Lavinia's been writing to the Cowley Fathers again," she explained.

"Is she going to publish?" asked Celia without much interest.

"For heaven's sake, Celia!" exploded her brother-in-law. "Why in the world should Lavinia Tickbourne publish her letters to the Cowley Fathers?"

"Well, everybody else seems to," said Celia reasonably.

Her much-tried relative abandoned the field. "In any event, Mr. Thatcher has not been waiting to hear us discuss the Cowley Fathers."

For the first time Celia Jensen seemed to realize that Thatcher's presence must be on her account. She looked at him inquiringly, and he explained Arnold Berman's concern. Mention of Berman evoked a wan smile.

"Oh, that is thoughtful of him. And you too, of course. But what is there anyone can do to help?" she said.

The Burnses hastily started to leave, but she impatiently waved them back into their seats.

"Do you think I'm going to reveal my secrets?" she asked almost angrily. "There isn't any secret. There isn't even anything to talk about. All I can do is grin and bear it."

Thatcher tut-tutted sympathetically, and the rector made an ill-advised remark about Glen Madsen dragging his sister-in-law's name in the mud.

"It isn't Glen's fault!" Celia fired up. "He's suffering as much as I am."

"Nevertheless you would never be in this position if you hadn't left your husband," said the rector, preoccupied with his own hobby horse. "Today everyone seems to think that marriage can be turned on and off like an electric light. Why, even the conference of bishops—"

"We're not talking about divorce; we're talking about murder," Celia broke in ruthlessly.

"Precisely!" barked Thatcher, quick to retrieve the conversation from the esoteric paths down which it was threatening to stray. "And I'm afraid that it's got to be talked about. To put it bluntly, you're not doing either Madsen or yourself any good by lying to the police. After all, the presentation was two days after the murder was actually committed. You're not achieving anything—except an air of collusion."

Thatcher paused for breath and looked closely at Celia. It would be worse than useless, he felt, to suggest that she try to disentangle herself and leave Glen Madsen to take his chances. Her loyalty to the man was transparent.

Meanwhile Celia Jensen had a surprise for him. "I'm not lying to the police anymore. I've told Captain Georgeson that it was Glen I was talking to on Friday at MM. I had to. Somebody saw us. And I've tried to explain to him, over and over again, that we were quarreling. That's why I was so upset. It wasn't anything important at all."

Thatcher shook his head. "You told Berman and me that he was out of control, that you were frightened at what he might do," he insisted, with guilty visions of himself as a bullying cross-examiner. "There must have been some reason."

Stubborn silence was his only answer. Thatcher played a hunch. "Was it because of the quarrel in Ann Arbor?"

Celia's eyes widened in dismay. "You know about that?" she whispered.

"It's common gossip. I heard it in this very room. If the police don't know about it yet, they soon will."

"But you don't understand," Celia protested. "It was Ray who was furious that night, not Glen. Because Glen just laughed at him when he started to threaten."

"Threaten?"

"Yes. It all started when Ray came to see me here. I suppose the Altar Guild brought you up to date on that too," said Celia defiantly.

Thatcher contented himself with a nod.

"Well, Ray said he wasn't going to sit still for a divorce. But I'd been to a lawyer, and I told Ray that I'd go to Nevada if I had to. That frightened him. Because in spite of all his toughness, that was where he was vulnerable. MM doesn't like divorce. With his job up in the air, he really didn't want to spend any time on my problems. It was one of the things he resented. That he was forced to worry about me when he wanted to spend full time at Michigan Motors. And of course the way our marriage had run, this was the first time he didn't have his way. When he left here, he must have decided to try and put pressure on Glen instead."

"I don't see how he could," said Louise Burns. "Glen was the one who was urging you to get a divorce."

"That's because you never understood how Ray's mind worked," said Celia in a flat, controlled voice. "He went straight for what he thought was Glen's jugular. He said that if I went to Nevada, he'd see to it that Glen lost his job. He'd let the front office know that his wife had been seduced by Glen. Then Michigan Motors would fire

Glen." Celia was twisting a small handkerchief between tightly clenched hands.

"And would they have?" asked Thatcher with genuine curiosity, trying (and failing) to visualize a similar scene at the Sloan.

"But Glen didn't seduce me!" Celia burst out.

The rector cleared his throat.

"Larry," his wife began dangerously, "this is no time for a lot of talk about sins of the mind."

A curious couple, the Burnses, Thatcher reflected.

"And anyway," continued Celia more quietly, "Glen didn't care about the job. He told Ray to do his damnedest. We were going through with the divorce. That's what infuriated Ray. He never contemplated such a reaction. As far as he was concerned, everybody lived and died for Michigan Motors."

Madsen's reaction might well have puzzled Jensen, Thatcher conceded. What was even more ominous, a jury of Detroit citizens might feel the same way. And it left one glaring fact unexplained.

"But if Madsen was so unmoved by this threat, why was he in a murderous rage two days later?"

"Because Ray did start a lot of gossip. And some of it was beginning to get back to Glen. Orin Dunn had just relayed some of the spicier bits." Celia leaned back against the sofa but continued speaking. "I think Orin wanted some kind of deal. He would help Glen—either squelch the gossip or stand behind Glen—if Glen would help him somehow. And Glen was livid with rage."

Just then the chimes of the doorbell sounded. As Louise Burns hurried into the hall, Thatcher spoke pensively, almost to himself: "There's one thing. If Jensen started this gossip as a result of his rebuff from Madsen, it may be possible to prove that Orin Dunn saw your husband alive after his return from Ann Arbor Tuesday evening."

Horror drained the blood from her face. "You mean the police may think . . . they might believe that Ray died *that* night?"

"If the time is medically possible, the thought will certainly cross their minds," Thatcher replied bluntly.

"Oh, no! They couldn't possibly—" began Celia hotly as Mrs. Burns returned.

"It's a Mr. Riley," she announced. "From the Department of Justice. He wants to talk to you, Celia." She looked doubtfully at her sister. "Don't you think it would be a good idea to see him? There's no point in antagonizing—"

"I won't!" cried Celia. "He wants to ask me about Ray's business dealings. Ray never told me anything, and now I don't care about all that." A tear was running down each cheek, but the light of battle gleamed in the hazel eyes above the handkerchief. "I don't care about anything but Glen! He didn't kill Ray—and even if he did, I'd still love him!"

Mrs. Burns started to expostulate, but Celia silenced her. "Don't look at me that way, Louise! You'd better understand that I'll stick with Glen even if he's guilty. I'll stick to him no matter what! Oh, I know you're just trying to do what's best for me. But you can't go on thinking of one person in a vacuum. That's what I tried to do with Ray." She laughed bitterly, and the tears flowed more quickly. "Oh, don't you see? I wasted ten years of my life. I can't give up my chance of happiness now. I won't! I won't!"

As she began to pound her fist on the arm of the sofa, Louise Burns hurried over to soothe her.

The rector, a man inured to feminine crises, moved as if somebody had pushed a button. He rose, muttered the word "tea," and padded purposively toward the back regions of the house.

Even a man deficient in social sensitivity would have realized that he had outstayed his welcome. Thatcher stated to the room at large his intention of taking an immediate departure. Distractedly his hostess replied, urging him to take Mr. Riley along.

In the front hall F. X. Riley was resigned. Celia's spasmodic sobs were plainly audible. At Thatcher's approach he rose and said, "I suppose she isn't going to see me."

"I'm afraid not," said Thatcher, removing his hat and coat from the closet. "She's too worried about her husband's death to have much time for his business difficulties."

"She sounds upset. I'm sorry," said Riley politely. "But the two may be connected, you know."

"Yes."

For a moment the two men measured each other silently in the small hall and recognized a basic similarity. Both were reapers of information, not sowers.

"I'm interested in Mr. Jensen's murder. And in Michigan

Motors," said Thatcher deliberately. "Sometime we might discuss the matter."

Riley's hat revolved slowly on one hand as he stroked its brim with a forefinger. "Yes. I'd like to do that sometime, Mr. Thatcher." He looked up suddenly. "We might come up with something useful. But I'd have to check some things out first."

Thatcher nodded briskly and wished him good day. But on the sidewalk he stood watching Riley walk toward his small black Rambler.

Celia Jensen said her husband thought everyone lived and died for Michigan Motors. Possibly Raymond Jensen, at least, had managed to do both.

8 • No Passing

JOHN THATCHER, hurrying off on his corporate-imposed round of gaiety, could only spare a moment's sidewalk reflection for F. X. Riley.

By the very nature of his role the Department of Justice man was in a better position to think about their meeting and its possibilities. A life spent gathering material for the proper enforcement of the antitrust laws has many hardships, but being relentlessly wined and dined by one's corporate host is not among them. On the contrary, long hours of solitary reflection unimpaired by expense account distractions can be confidently anticipated.

Special Agent F. X. Riley was spending his evening in the laundromat. He tilted his chair back against the wall, scowled at the clipboard on his knee, and listened to the bank of dryers whir round and round. Two things hampered his usual intensive concentration. One was the subliminal working of an internal timing device which told him that his dryer had exactly seventeen minutes to go. The other was a faint undercurrent of excitement; it had been in existence since his chance encounter that afternoon with John Thatcher in the rectory of St. Andrew's.

Days spent trying to explain the intricacies of antitrust regulation to Captain William Georgeson of the Michigan State Police were convincing Riley that the world, outside the Department of Justice and the Federal Trade Commission, was devoid of men capable of understanding the implications of the late Raymond Jensen's activities. When Riley described the desperation that Jensen's return might have induced, Georgeson shook his head knowingly and said he'd take passion every time. Not surprisingly, sight of a Wall Street banker had been a tonic. Here was a man who could not only understand Riley's information, but add to it.

No false modesty clouded the special agent's evaluation. He knew his technical data and sources were second to none, but he knew also that Thatcher must have insights into the personality stresses of MM's front office that were rigidly concealed from the Department of Justice. For instance, Riley knew that while he had been contenting himself with a solitary hamburger at a nearby Howard Johnson, the long black Plantagenet Sceptre, last parked near St. Andrew's, was conveying John Putnam Thatcher to a dinner party given in his honor by Mrs. Holsinger. And it spoke volumes for the social disorganization at Michigan Motors that the wife of a one-time loser was acting as semiofficial hostess for MM! Riley could even make a good guess at Thatcher's frame of mind on that journey. (In fact, Thatcher was trying to drum up some interest in the coming event by wondering how Diane Holsinger's gentility would measure up to the challenge of Mrs. Wahl's party behavior.) But Riley would never know what went on at that party. Gaps in his exhaustively detailed knowledge of the workings of Michigan Motors Corporation were bad enough; existence of a fund of information complementing his own was more than an irritant—it was a challenge!

Riley knew the loyalties binding both men made a full interchange impossible. The representative of the Sloan Guaranty Trust was clearly not a man to condone criminal activity, whether directed against the Sherman Act or the Sixth Commandment, but neither was he a man to disclose knowledge obtained in the course of duty. Nor could Riley make free with the information so laboriously garnered by the Department of Justice. A broad exchange was out.

But what about a narrow one? Well, if narrowing was needed, Riley was the man to do it. Abandoning the sheaf of statistics, he automatically noted that his dryer now had fifteen minutes to run, rescued his hat from the marauding advances of a wandering toddler, checked a hasty remark to its mother, and drew forth a much-folded diagram of the management organization at Michigan Motors.

This chart had been isssued by the company over fifteen months ago. No replacement had ever appeared, a token acknowledgment of the fluidity of the situation. On paper, Stuart Eberhart still reigned supreme at the top of the pyramid. On the staff level, only Frank Krebbel had survived the deluge. The heads of the Law Department, Public Relations, Government Relations, and Commercial

Marketing had all been swept under in the aftermath of the government's indictment. On the operating level, things were more complex. Utility Vehicles had come through relatively unscathed. Passenger Vehicles was dominated by the twin colossi of Jensen at Plantagenet and Holsinger at Buccaneer. Riley battled with the reluctant folds of the diagram in an attempt to review the line-up of assistant division managers. Suddenly the chart disappeared under a falling drift of white material. Somebody was scattering laundry over him. He grabbed the cloth and prepared to deal more effectively with the toddler.

But there was no child in sight. Only the back of a woman emptying the nearest dryer.

"Ahem!" said Riley.

"What? Oh, did I overshoot the basket? I'm so . . . why, Mr. Riley!"

"For heaven's sake, Miss Price!" The chair legs came down and the special agent arose. "I didn't recognize you at first. Here, I guess this is yours."

Susan Price blushed. Gravely Riley examined the object he was extending to her. With the exception of forget-me-knots embroidered in its lacy hem, it was as chaste as a slip could be. It compared, he thought, rather favorably with most of the lingerie that had come his bachelor's way.

"Thank you," she said with reserve.

"It's quite a respectable slip," said Riley reassuringly.

Susan grinned appreciatively. As she gathered her possessions she continued, "I know it seems silly. After all, every week I scatter my underwear around in front of strangers. But you don't expect to meet people you know. What are you doing here anyway?"

"My laundry," he explained simply. "They said it would take three days at the hotel and I couldn't wait."

"You never can," remarked Miss Price without approval. She had noticed the chart and clipboard on Riley's chair. "And I see you're not wasting time. Doing your homework for tomorrow's snooping?"

Riley stiffened. A more experienced man would have remembered that useful advice: *Never explain; never apologize; just counterattack!* Instead he appealed to reason.

"Well, you have to admit that MM's given plenty of grounds for snooping," he said.

"Everything was fine until you and all the others came sneaking around, trying to stir things up! Now it just gets worse and worse. We have you, and the police, and Captain Georgeson. And everybody's beginning to look hunted and suspicious. Why can't you just leave us alone?" she cried out. "Oh, what's the use? You don't even understand what I'm talking about."

Angrily she turned and stalked back to her laundry basket, the unhappy Riley trailing in her wake. His progress was suddenly impeded by a middle-aged woman with her hair in curlers and a distracted expression on her face. She wanted to borrow a pencil to write a note about some imperfection in the dryer reserved for the treatment of blankets.

"You wouldn't believe it, but the binding just melted and glazed!"

"I'm sorry," muttered Riley, thrusting a ball-point pen into her hand and hurrying over to Susan Price. "Look here, you can't pretend everybody at MM is a lily-white innocent."

"Oh, can't I? What about that poor guy in Public Relations who rode along in the Plantagenet? They've been grilling him for days. As if *he* knows anything! He's only been at Michigan Motors for two weeks, and we never even saw him in the front office before. He was only following orders."

She punctuated this protest by viciously snapping a towel under Riley's nose. He shied, then recovered.

"And the gun?" he demanded. "I suppose that was another coincidence? Being stolen in a company plant."

"Oh, that gun!" she said in a goaded voice, spanking the now-folded towel. "You simply can't imagine the trouble that *that's* causing us. Mr. Casimir is claiming that it's all a management plot to implicate a union man—"

"That's right," contributed the victim of the blanket-drying machine. "Those big shots will blame it all on the Working Man, you wait and see. Here's your pen. Thank you very much. What I wrote will make them sit up and take notice. . . ."

The departure of this believer in class warfare left Susan to glare at Riley. "See!" she said hotly. "That's the kind of feeling that Casimir will cash in on. And on top of everything else, he's claiming the driver of the Super Planty wasn't one of his men, when everybody knows we're a union shop."

Riley nodded. For a number of reasons he could readily understand, the driver was resisting police pleas to step forward and demonstrate how civic-minded the average man is.

"But what's that got—" he began. Susan had just run her hand through the black bangs over her bright eyes. For the first time he noticed how tired she looked, despite the high color engendered by their dispute.

He lowered his voice. "But, you know, you can't pretend the trouble is that people are asking questions about the gun and the car. The trouble started because someone murdered Ray Jensen."

This change in tone had its effect. "I suppose you're right," she relented. "But you can't imagine what things are like in the office. It's awful." She stared somberly at the mass of yellow chenille remaining in her basket.

"Georgeson isn't hounding you or anything?" asked Riley anxiously.

A sudden quirk lifted the corner of her mouth. "Oh, no. It isn't anything like that. In fact, he's more polite to me than you are." She shook her shoulders as if to throw off a fit of dejection. "I suppose I'm looking back to the good old days when I worked for Mr. Jensen. At least you knew where you were."

Riley eyed her thoughtfully. "You know," he said slowly, "you've always been loyal about Jensen's activities, but I can't help noticing that you don't seem to be very much grieved by his death."

She was silent for a moment. "Yes," she admitted at length, "that's true. But it was terribly hard to feel close to Mr. Jensen, you know, even though I worked for him almost two years. He was completely dehumanized. Everything was routine and procedure. Of course it made working for him easy. And then there was never any doubt about his authority, so there weren't any of these squabbles defending his interests. But you can't mourn him like a friend." Absently she picked up a corner of the yellow chenille and hoisted it skyward in an ineffective attempt to straighten it. Then she added the final comment to Ray Jensen's epitaph. "And Mr. Jensen had been gone for over six months. At Michigan Motors that's a long time."

"Here, let me get that," Riley offered. He fumbled around for the other end of the bedspread. "Ed Wahl must be a very different type to work for."

"He's much nicer," Susan agreed readily, backing away to draw the spread taut. "Grumpier, but human. Of course he's more nervous, but that's only natural. He was over in Trucks for years, and he's not really a front-office type. Then it didn't help him any to get an acting appointment. And having people come back and start thumbing through his files was just about the last . . ." Her voice trailed off in sudden confusion.

"So Jensen was combing the division files," Riley mused speculatively. "You know, I would have thought he knew everything there was to know about Plantagenet."

In spite of herself Susan was drawn. "It wasn't just Plantagenet. It was *all* the files."

"He might have been trying to catch up on what happened while he was away." A short pause and then Riley continued with deliberate provocation. "Of course you didn't notice the time period he was interested in."

The grinding of Susan's teeth was almost audible. "You're wrong. On both counts."

"So he was going back through last year. What a situation!" Riley gave a low whistle of appreciation. "He must have been dead serious about finding the tipster."

"Mr. Jensen was dead serious about everything," said Susan shortly.

The Department of Justice gives good training. Riley knew better than to press his advantage. For a few seconds he was silent as they flapped and folded, advancing and retreating in a stylized grand promenade, until the bedspread lay in the laundry basket, a precise yellow rectangle. When he spoke, he chose his words with care. He had long since realized that Michigan Motors regarded the activities of the mysterious tipster with deep corporate shame.

"Yes, I can see how things were easier under Jensen," he said. "And of course he was going to be the next president. So that added to his prestige."

But there were limits to Susan Price's support of her late employer. "Well, certainly everybody expected him to become president. But you know, I'm not so sure he would have been as good as Mr. Krebbel. For one thing, he was never very interested in compacts. He'd been in Plantagenet so long he wasn't well-rounded. And then he could never handle people. Mr. Krebbel's wonderful at that." Her voice warmed with enthusiasm. "After the trial I didn't think anybody could organize the front office again. But he had everything running smoothly by the end of the year. Somehow he managed to make everybody feel optimistic, as if the worst was over and it was going to be better from then on. And this last month he's had to smooth down both Mr. Jensen and Mr. Wahl, and he's tried to keep Mr. Dunn from nosing around. He always tries to be tactful, which a lot of men wouldn't bother about. And," concluded Susan, bestowing the final accolade, "no matter how sticky things get, Mr. Krebbel never blames the secretaries. He knows we can't do anything about it."

Riley rubbed the bridge of his nose thoughtfully. Then he decided to opt for bluntness. "What was Dunn nosing around for? Did he want to see the same things Jensen was interested in?"

"Well, naturally he was interested in who did the tipping too. He . . ." Susan's voice trailed off. "That's funny. I never thought about it before. It's so natural to think of him as Mr. Jensen's shadow. You know, that's what they called him when he was assistant at Plantagenet. But he's not interested in the same files. He's always trying to get into this year's files."

Her dark eyes widened in speculation. "It wasn't only Plantagenet either. I know Eileen was practically in tears when he sneaked a lot of Lancaster budget material off her desk during lunchtime. She went to Mr. Krebbel about it. She was sure Mr. Dunn photocopied it. And Mr. Krebbel was just wonderful. That's what I mean about him. Said it wasn't her fault and not to be upset, the company didn't expect her to have to guard against that sort of thing, just to be careful when the Justice people were around— Oh!"

"Sure, Krebbel's wonderful," Riley agreed sourly.

Susan was piqued. "Well, he is. He treats secretaries as if they were people, and let me tell you, in a front office that's something."

"It's easy enough for him to be agreeable now," said Riley out of some dim perversity aroused by Susan's fervor. "He's on top."

"That shows how prejudiced you are! He's always been that way. Why, last year when he was still controller, he was terribly nice to me. I rushed out to my car one night and threw some packages into it, and then I had to go back for my gloves. When I came back again, for a minute I thought my car was gone. I'd mixed up Mr. Krebbel's Drake with mine. Well, of course, he discovered the packages, and he didn't know what to do with the twenty shamrock cupcakes I had for a party that night. But the next day he brought me a cake with an inscription: 'For the Day after St. Patrick's.' Wasn't that sweet?"

"Just grand."

Susan sighed and looked around for inspiration. "If those green-and-white shorts are yours," she said meaningfully, "you'd better empty your dryer. It's done."

Riley swiveled around in surprise. Conversation with Susan Price, he decided, was impairing his professional efficiency. In the space of fifteen minutes he had become jealous of Frank Krebbel and lost his internal timing device. He marched over to his laundry. After a moment Miss Price joined him.

"Here," she protested, "that's no way to do it. Everything will get wrinkled." She reached into the untidy pile, abstracted a T-shirt, and reduced it to submission.

Riley cleared his throat, settled himself on both heels, and started a speech. "It's all very well for you to blow up every time somebody speaks slightingly of your precious MM, but you have to admit that there are some very queer things going on there."

"There are queer things going on in every company," she said, dangling an unmated sock from her finger.

"Not the kind of queerness that ends up in somebody stealing a gun and shooting."

She swung the sock lightly to and fro. Suddenly Riley gave a low growl and grabbed it from her. "Dammit, will you be serious! This is no joking matter."

"Yes, it's very serious," she said obediently. "And I really don't understand the things that are going on. Mr. Jensen was easy enough to figure out. But Mr. Wahl is so nervous these days. And Mr. Dunn's creeping around. He was always a snoop, of course, but now there's an intensity about him that almost frightens me." Her voice was very grave. "It's as if he himself were scared stiff of what he's doing, but determined to go through with it."

Susan shuddered. Riley put a steadying hand on her shoulder.

"Excuse me!" A harried mother, clutching a small child who in turn clutched an ice cream cone, had appeared on the scene. "Would either of you have two nickels for a dime?"

"I'll see," said Susan, reaching for her bag.

"Harry, watch that cone! Don't let it drip on the gentleman's trousers."

The gentleman, reddening slightly, removed his hand

from Susan's shoulder and his trouser leg from Harry's reach.

Susan delved unsuccessfully. "I'm afraid I can't find any. Mr. Riley?"

A general turning out of pockets ensued while the mother chattered happily. "They have all these machines for giving you quarters and dimes. But they know bleach costs a nickel. So why don't they . . . Oh, thank you so much. That helps a lot. You really need bleach to take out the stains."

Her departure left them staring at each other with some constraint. Suddenly Susan poked her head into the dryer and twisted it about alarmingly. With a triumphant yip she re-emerged bearing a sock.

"I knew it must be somewhere." She turned back to the laundry.

Riley took a deep breath. "Now, Susan, I'm sorry about—"

Miss Price had an unerring eye for essentials. She interrupted ruthlessly. "Mr. Riley, if you're going to call me Susan, perhaps I'd better know your first name."

Silence.

"Well?" she challenged.

"It's Fabian Xerxes," said Riley stiffly. "Father was a socialist."

Susan was thoughtful for a moment as she patted the last of the pile into place. Then she giggled slightly. Riley raised an affronted eyebrow. She sobered.

"It's quite a respectable name," she said in a very passable imitation of his own voice.

For a moment he was blank, then he grinned. A dimple appeared on Susan's face. He reached out a long arm and drew her laundry cart next to his own.

"A drink? Dinner? Movies?" he suggested.

"I think there's something I should tell you first."

"Yes?"

"My name is Susan B. Anthony Price. Mother was a feminist."

9 • Hairpin Turns

HAPPINESS CAN FLOWER amidst hamburgers and washing machines. At the moment John Putnam Thatcher had no inkling of this, of course, but he was living proof that caviar canapés and eighteen-year-old Scotch do not guarantee freedom from appalling discomfort. The only thing to be said for his present circumstances was that Mrs. Holsinger had solved the problem of Audrey Wahl in the most efficient way possible. By not inviting her.

But this exclusion could have been based on grounds other than personal. Thatcher, always sensitive to atmosphere, realized within a few minutes after his entrance that the economical Mrs. Holsinger was making her dinner party serve more than one purpose. On the one hand, she was establishing her right to entertain Thatcher as a company hostess. On the other hand, she was gathering together the remaining *outs,* namely her husband and Mr. and Mrs. Orin Dunn, and any *ins* who might be prevailed upon to receive them back into the MM fold.

Lionel French was the most significant member of this second group. The chairman of the board treated his hostess with a playful deference which confirmed the suspicions born in Thatcher's mind while his car traveled up the long driveway leading to the Holsinger home in Grosse Point Farms. That driveway had suggested broad acres. Delicate probing confirmed his diagnosis.

"Di Holsinger? Oh, yes, she's one of the Chicago Bredons. Meat packing family, you know."

Thatcher did indeed know. The Bredons had a chapter to themselves in every standard history of the great American fortunes. Even a remote collateral would have an impressive net worth.

Then surely, he suggested, the Holsingers could in no way be dependent upon Michigan Motors.

Lincoln Hauser, his informant, was pained. "Well, not

financially. But money," he reminded Thatcher reproachfully, "isn't everything, you know."

Clearly diplomacy was in order. Of course money wasn't everything. One was perhaps inclined to forget that, immersed in the parochial concerns of Wall Street. Banking, Thatcher heard himself fearing, did tend to emphasize the sordid side of life. But here in Detroit, at the mainspring of American industrial development—

"Exactly!" beamed Hauser. "Out here it's achievement that counts. Not how much money a man has."

Thatcher kept a straight face. By now something of an expert on the native habitat of the automobile executive, he tried to isolate the distinctive quality of the Holsinger residence. It might have been the period pieces, casually placed and so well maintained as to imply irrefutable authenticity. But Thatcher knew he was not knowledgeable enough about this sort of thing to respond instinctively to its presence. It must be something else. Of course—no wall-to-wall carpeting, only the faded majesty of Oriental rugs and the polished gleam of dark parquetry, bespeaking ample domestic help. He scanned the room. Unless he was mistaken, the big one under the sofa grouping was an old Kirman, the Queen Anne library table rested on an Ispahan, and the Bechstein in the music corner was set off magnificently by the grandeur of a Bokhara. And it was very unlikely that he was mistaken. His late wife had been a lover of fine rugs.

Meanwhile, Hauser continued to explain to him that their hostess was a simple toiler in the vineyard of industrial progress.

"You couldn't go further wrong than to think Di is just another parasite. Why, you should have seen her when Buck came up with the Drake. She was starry-eyed! That's what she wants. The sense of accomplishment."

Thatcher felt obliged to demur. "Offhand, you know, one would expect it to be her husband who had the sense of accomplishment."

"A-h-h-h!" purred Hauser slowly, with the air of a man springing an extraordinary subtlety. "But Di was the woman behind the man behind the compact! Just think of it."

Thatcher's eyes glazed slightly as the tidal wave swept over him. Dimly he distinguished references to pioneer women, to the effete East, and, if he could believe his ears, to "here in the West where a man can breathe." He wondered if Hauser had the remotest conception of the topography of North America. Any minute he'd be hearing about the Father of Waters.

"And," said Hauser, concluding his eulogy, "Diane's not the woman to throw her weight around. She always makes it clear that, at Michigan Motors, she's operating as Buck Holsinger's wife."

Thatcher was left to speculate on what Mrs. Holsinger made clear when she was in downtown Detroit, not to mention Chicago. At that moment plain, straightforward Di Holsinger put her hand on Lionel French's arm to attract his attention. The chairman of the board inclined his head.

"I was just letting Thatcher know how highly we all think of Diane," explained Hauser as Buck Holsinger joined them to announce the imminence of dinner. Holsinger's conviviality faded when his attention was thus drawn to the twosome across the room. His reddened cheeks assumed a slight purplish cast; then he set down his drink, muttered abstractedly, "You'll show Thatcher the way, won't you, Link?" and bore down upon his wife.

It would be interesting, thought Thatcher, to know how much of Diane Holsinger's modesty in the automotive world could be attributed to unexpected displays of marital authority by her husband.

The dinner gathering was not large enough to disintegrate into splinter groups. Conversation was general and, it soon became apparent, so was exposure to a display of truculence by Orin Dunn.

Although Thatcher, the guest of honor, had an inalienable claim to the seat on his hostess's right, she had not let Lionel French stray any farther from her ambit than the seat on her left. The elevated position of the Frenches was reinforced by placing Mrs. French, a dowager of the old school, next to her host, where she could enjoy the dubious distinction of receiving Buck Holsinger's confidences on life and high times in federal penal institutions.

While a maid circulated vegetables in heavy Victorian silver dishes, Thatcher's hostess inaugurated an unexceptionable conversation concerning the amenities of Detroit, the climatic extremes of the Great Lakes region, and the inexplicable failure of the Moiseyev dancers to stop on their last tour. But no conversation centering on the regional characteristics of Detroit can long avoid the automobile industry. When Thatcher's attention was momentarily diverted by Mrs. Dunn, Diane Holsinger used the interval to introduce the subject of displaced auto executives. Two returning parolees, summarily dismissed by their employer in a blaze of righteous indignation, had just been hired by one of the smaller auto companies. They were taking with them a catastrophic amount of secret trade information.

"A shocking situation," rumbled French, loudly enough to draw his host's attention.

"What's that?" Holsinger queried sharply, abandoning Mrs. French in the middle of a stately anecdote about the conductor's behavior at a spirited performance of the *Capriccio Español* by the Detroit Symphony.

"Lionel," said Mrs. Holsinger placidly, "is disturbed about Gleason and Tom Halliday."

Buck Holsinger was not sympathetic. "There's nothing to get excited about," he growled. "The boys have to take care of themselves. Nobody's got any right to say they shouldn't. Hell, we're all in the same spot."

His wife's lips tightened slightly, but before she could reply, Orin Dunn took the floor.

"Who says we're all in the same spot? That's not the way it looks from where I sit. Was Jensen in the same spot?"

"Now, now. *De mortuis*, and all that," French said.

"*De mortuis*, hell! Jensen steps off the train, and he's in Krebbel's office for two hours. I want to talk to Frank too. Do I get in? We got here over a week ago, and he still hasn't found time to see me." Dunn's eyes glittered resentfully.

Lincoln Hauser, exercising his infallible instinct for doing the wrong thing at the wrong time, promptly poured oil on the flames.

"You're forgetting Ray's position, aren't you, Orin old boy?" he said in a spirit of bright helpfulness. "After all, he was senior management. It's only natural that Frank wanted to talk to him right away."

"Senior management!" Dunn shrilled. "He was so senior he was responsible for the whole damned price-fixing mess. How do you think I got mixed up in it? He put the bite on me for sales. Then, when the pressure was on, he squealed like a pig. First he railroaded me into this fix, then he sent me up the river!"

Thatcher pondered the influence of six months' confinement on Dunn's vocabulary while other faces at the table registered disapproval.

"Ray Jensen did not . . . er . . . squeal," said French reproachfully.

"The hell he didn't! If Jensen had had his way, I would have taken the rap alone. My God, when the feds first came around—"

"Now, Orin . . ." began his hostess.

But Dunn was in no mood to be shushed. "Do you know what he said to me last week? He said his future plans for Plantagenet didn't include me. He said"—Orin's voice cracked alarmingly—"he said my jail record would be a handicap!"

"Now that," said Buck Holsinger weightily, "is just about the limit."

Orin Dunn laughed harshly. "Don't think I'm through yet. Oh, sure it'd be convenient for everybody if I shut up like a good boy. Do you expect me to forget that, if it hadn't been for those photostats of the code, I was going to get thrown to the wolves all by myself? Do you expect me to take that lying down? Well, I didn't work for Ray Jensen for five years without learning a thing or two. They've got some surprises coming to them." His voice began to rise ominously.

Buck Holsinger was not a man easily shaken by incipient hysteria, but the dinner party was deprived of his views; after some preliminary throat clearing Lionel French began an address in his best public platform manner.

"We all know that Frank Krebbel is very fair. Like everyone else at Michigan Motors, he is fully aware of the contribution to the company's welfare made by the timely introduction of the compact. Furthermore, he is always interested in hearing the views of others, and of having an opportunity to thrash out any differences of opinion which may exist. I have every confidence that any decision he may reach will reflect the best interests of the company and of the public."

This pontifical enunciation would have had wider appeal, Thatcher reflected, if any of the interested parties had been concerned with the problems of either the company or the public. But even Mrs. Holsinger looked unpersuaded, while Orin Dunn was openly rebellious.

"That's fine," he snarled. "So he takes into account that the compact was a good thing—and maybe even the sales of Plantagenet too—and *then* he decides it's in the best interests of the company to kick us out. I suppose that's expected to satisfy us."

"That won't happen," prophesied Diane Holsinger. "Not if it's handled properly. But you'll have to pull yourself together, Orin, if you want to make a good impression on Frank."

The lady was an arrant optimist, Thatcher decided. Nobody could possibly form a good opinion of Orin Dunn. Least of all, a man of Frank Krebbel's patent good sense.

"I realize you're upset," she continued, "but you mustn't let it affect your judgment."

A new voice intervened. "Of course, he's upset," said Mrs. Dunn in throbbing tones of rich understanding. "Orin has been under a terrible strain. First there were weeks and weeks of pressure during that terrible trial . . . and the tension of being on public view. Then there were six months in jail with common criminals. Just imagine what an ordeal it must have been for someone like Orin. And then to come back to a murder! And all of this without a single word of complaint. Naturally it's been almost more than he could bear. And, darling," she murmured. turning to her unfortunate spouse, who was turning a splotchy crimson as he convulsively swallowed whatever remarks were on the tip of his tongue, "I think it's *good* for you to get some of this off your chest. It can't be healthy to repress your natural feelings. I'm sure that you must feel much better now that you've told us frankly what you think." She smiled kindly at her companions.

Paralyzed silence.

"Well," said Buck, letting out his breath warily and eyeing Dunn with the first stirrings of sympathy, "I don't deny you had a raw deal, and I hope things work out."

His wife followed his lead. "Yes, we all hope so."

She was not completely accurate. What John Putnam Thatcher hoped was something quite different.

Three of the men drank their brandy apart from the card table.

"If you ask me, that young man is unbalanced." Lionel French's tone was distinctly petulant.

Lincoln Hauser burbled something about instability in the brilliant, creative minds of the automotive industry.

Thatcher twirled his snifter silently. Things had come to a pretty pass if Hauser represented the forces of common sense and balanced judgment.

"I have the greatest respect for Diane Holsinger," announced French, "but I am at a loss to understand what she sees in him." He looked at his companions inquiringly.

Thatcher said that it was no doubt his transient status which prevented his speaking with authority about the virtues of Orin Dunn with which his colleagues must necessarily be acquainted. Even Hauser looked suspicious at that one.

"Not that I regret having prevailed on Frank to see the boy. Everyone should have his day in court." Conscious, perhaps, of the infelicity of this metaphor, French expanded his remarks. "That is to say, it's only right he should have an opportunity to explain things from his point of view."

"I thought his complaint, or at least one of them," said Thatcher, "was that Krebbel hasn't seen him."

"Not yet. But he's going to, tomorrow morning. After all, the boy's been haunting the executive offices for days now." French sighed mightily. It was obvious that Michigan Motors' front office was not the happy refuge it had once been. "It's time his status was . . . er . . . clarified."

Hauser, professionally looking on the bright side of things, pointed out that it could be worse. At least Mrs. Dunn would not be present at the meeting.

John Thatcher immediately lost himself in the vision of Mrs. Dunn explaining to Frank Krebbel that jail intimacies were particularly trying for a man of Orin's sensitivity.

Lionel French poured himself more brandy. "I had hoped that Buck would come along. The cool deatchment of an older head, you know. . . . Invaluable. These occasions can be pretty difficult. In fact, I don't see the point of the meeting without Buck. So why does Diane insist on it?"

"Perhaps," suggested Hauser, "she is interested in Dunn's future because they are all in the same boat."

Thatcher was amused by Lionel French's expression. Clearly French yearned to tell Hauser that it was impossible for a Bredon to be in the same boat with a Dunn. That, in fact, it was hard enough for her to be in the same boat as a Holsinger. Instead he was reduced to plaintive and disjointed mumblings.

"Nonsense . . . she's always taken an interest in the careers of the young men at Michigan. . . . Feels a sense of responsibility. . . . But why does she bother with Dunn?"

Why, indeed? Thatcher asked himself. It might simply be that Diane Holsinger, finding her husband lacking in a desperate determination to hang on at MM, could command the qualities she required only by trying to drive Holsinger and Dunn in tandem. But it could also be that she and Dunn were already in unholy alliance because of past activities. And in that case it would be interesting to know what they were up to . . . and what they had already done.

10 • Unimproved Surface

THE NEXT MORNING was unmarred by masculine tantrums or iron-plated feminine graciousness. Recent events proved this was a blessing not to be despised at Michigan Motors. Nevertheless the agenda was not promising; John Putnam Thatcher was part of a conference in downtown Detroit with the company's largest truck dealer. The subject was federal highway expenditures and their impact on MM's Service Vehicle Division. Retreating behind an expression of serious attention, he examined the gathering.

On the whole they were a sorry lot.

The truck dealer was having difficulty functioning as buyer rather than seller. He had a tendency to explain the excellences of his product to the men who made it.

Glen Madsen presented a complex report on tax burdens at a machine gun pace that left some of his slower-witted listeners gaping. Despite his efficiency he sounded as though his thoughts were elsewhere. In view of Celia Jensen's disclosures at the rectory Thatcher could understand this. Madsen was a man in danger of imminent arrest.

Frank Krebbel had arrived after the others; held up, he said briefly, by an extended meeting with Orin Dunn. He did not elaborate. The president of Michigan Motors listened to a slightly confused discussion of cost projections and frowned with calm professional censure. Krebbel remained contained, if undeniably sobered, in the midst of the aftereffects of Ray Jensen's murder.

Thatcher let him pass.

The rest of Michigan Motors' executive staff was responding to the difficulties of the current situation by assuming an air of impenetrable soggy peevishness. Division manager and junior accountant alike exhibited a glum self-pity that contrasted unfavorably with the bouncy bonhomie normally characterizing the front office.

"I have another appointment," said Frank Krebbel at

82

the end of the discussion. "You boys can talk out the details at lunch." Snatching up the ever-present attaché case, he was gone, leaving Thatcher to the mercies of the Service Vehicle Division.

It was too much for Thatcher. He was going to eat at least one meal free of the megrims of the automobile world.

"Good God!" he exclaimed with great presence of mind. "I'm late for an appointment too. Didn't realize it was after one. I'll have to run for it."

With that he effected an exit hasty enough to miss the usual interminable discussion about which car should be placed at his disposal. Felicitating himself on this escape, he was on the street and feeling the pangs of hunger before he realized that a cooler head would have first ascertained where his confreres were dining. With restaurants in every major American city bidding for the expense account trade, you weren't safe unless you sat at a counter or carried a tray.

Thatcher decided to play it safe. Turning down a side street which promised a rapid descent in the social scale, he put five blocks between himself and the enemy before coming to a halt at a busy commercial corner where a sign proclaimed: GUIDO'S CAFETERIA.

"And a small price to pay," said Thatcher to himself upon entering. Guido's was very non-Michigan Motors. The balcony, to which a busboy directed him after the usual encounter with the stuffed pepper spesh-ull and the two eggs ov-uh, provided further reasons for self-congratulation; it was dim and muted. Thatcher deposited his tray at a table with a solitary occupant and addressed himself to a roast beef sandwich. Guido's was simply a road version of the Chock Full o'Nuts on lower Broadway, which often provided him with refuge under similar circumstances. John Putnam Thatcher was a banker and a realist. The first statistics on the population explosion had convinced him that in the future privacy could be achieved in but one way—camouflaged withdrawal into the herd.

His wandering gaze, examining this particular herd, was arrested by the sight of his table mate's lunch: it consisted of a large cereal bowl containing an unidentifiable substance, flanked by two smaller dishes, both empty. His companion became aware of the scrutiny.

"It's jello and cottage cheese. One dish of each and I mix them together," he said defiantly.

"Er . . . quite so," replied Thatcher in expressionless tones.

Mollified, the other continued his confidences.

"I'm on a diet. Can't stand either one. If you mix them together, it confuses things."

"I can see how that would be true."

His neighbor scraped up the last of the gelatinous mess and pushed back his chair as one who has fought the good fight.

"Helluva thing, diets," he said in parting. "At night I eat unsalted turnips."

Of course, mused Thatcher, it explained Metrecal. There were circumstances under which any man might lose interest in natural food products. Perhaps he shouldn't have squelched Walter Bowman so sharply on the subject of concentrated food tablets. Munching his second sandwich, Thatcher explored the problems of dieting and high finance, only dimly aware of a late luncher who deposited his tray on the table and disappeared into the gloom, presumably in search of the water cooler.

What percentage of the population could be expected to hail tablets as a happy release from the bondage of turnips and buttermilk, no doubt mixed together? A water glass descended on the table, indicating its owner's return. Thatcher turned to the nearest evidence of the eating habits of modern America. Common, garden-variety food, he saw with relief, the humanitarian triumphing over the financier. The pot roast spesh-ull, to be exact.

Thatcher's eye traveled upward to examine the healthy owner of this healthy meal. He found himself looking into a pleasantly neutral face, characterized by nothing more remarkable than a retreating hairline and old-fashioned rimless glasses. Looking, in fact, into the face of Frank Krebbel.

Silence held the president of Michigan Motors and the senior vice-president of the Sloan Guaranty Trust in a protracted moment of social shock as they stared at each other over the crumb-strewn cafeteria table.

Then Thatcher disgraced himself.

Unwisely clearing his throat to venture some hopeless platitude, he got as far as: "Hello, Krebbel. It's a small . . ." and dissolved into laughter.

For a medium-sized man Krebbel had a surprisingly

fortissimo guffaw. Holding on to the table, he rocked and swayed in an abandon of mirth that drew glances from surrounding tables. Glasses and silverware danced a merry accompaniment until he leaned back limply.

Removing his glasses to wipe his eyes, Krebbel congratulated his companion on orienting himself in Detroit so rapidly. "Took me years to find this place. I've never met a soul until now."

Thatcher told him all about the Chock Full o'Nuts on Broadway, including specific directions for finding it. Krebbel wrote them down.

"I haven't seen anything so funny since Wahl chased that damned car," said Krebbel, restoring handkerchief to pocket as a sign of recovery.

"What was that? I remember I heard something about it."

Krebbel retold Celia Jensen's story with a wealth of detail, including a rather unkind description of Wahl going through the motions of an Olympic track star and achieving the pace of an agitated hippopotamus. Ed Wahl was clearly not one of his chief's favorites.

"He's really not up to the weight of that job. There's no point not telling you. If you haven't figured it out, you soon will."

Maybe so. What Thatcher *had* figured out was that Frank Krebbel was a shrewd operator. He had recognized this chance meeting as an opportunity for a "soft sell" under spontaneously informal circumstances that no company hospitality could ever duplicate—let alone MM hospitality.

"But," he was continuing, "Ed Wahl is as clean as a hound's tooth on that conspiracy rap. He wasn't within a mile of it. When I took over, I knew I was going to have to mop up everybody who'd touched it. And don't think it's been easy. I don't mind admitting I would have had real trouble about Stu Eberhart if the judge hadn't given me some help. But look where that left me. Practically everybody on a top level in passenger cars had to go. Ray Jensen, who was our real fair-haired boy, turned out to be the ringleader of the whole thing. Dunn and Holsinger went to jail with him. As soon as I started digging around, I saw we had to pressure Wheaton—he was in Lancasters —into early retirement. Holsinger's back-up man saw which way the wind was blowing and took himself off a month after the trial." Krebbel ticked off the delinquents on his fingers. "You see what I'm driving at? Six months ago every single one of our car divisions had a major shake-up."

"That's quite an array of vacancies," Thatcher agreed. "You must have reached everybody involved in the conspiracy. But wouldn't taking Jensen back undo everything?"

Krebbel was firm. "There was never any question of taking him back."

"There was certainly a good deal of talk about it," said Thatcher dryly.

"Unavoidable," Krebbel said. "The real question was how to make his severance palatable to the board. Until I licked that one, there couldn't be any public announcement. Privately, of course, I let him know my decision. He was a last-ditcher by nature. He didn't know when he was beaten."

"Very awkward," commented Thatcher.

"Yes, it wasn't an easy situation," Krebbel agreed. "For me, for Ed, or for poor Ray."

It was a situation that would have become more awkward if Jensen had lived. Thatcher did not say this aloud.

"But," continued Krebbel, "I want you to see that these drastic reforms make us a real potential investment for the Sloan."

"Yes?" said Thatcher, in effect inviting him to get specific.

"Wahl is a good example of what's happened at Michigan Motors. Six months ago he was assistant manager of Trucks. He was good at the job. In the normal course of events he might have become manager before he reached retirement age. That would have given a nice boost to his pension and a little bit of glory for his last five years in harness. Instead he's been catapulted overnight into our prestige division. He has to sell in a market totally unlike the one he's used to. I said that he's not up to the job, and he isn't. But he will be! And it won't take very long. And in spite of this kind of situation in every one of our car divisions, we've been doing very well. You know the financials for the first quarter as well as I do," he reminded Thatcher. "Sales in Plantagenet and Buccaneer are booming. The Lancasters are a problem, but that's true for every medium-priced car in the country. Our models are going over fine this season. In another year the industry will be talking about the Big Four, not the Big Three. And we've done it with a scrub team in the face of constant howls from the unions, the federal government, and our own stockholders."

This speech was the more effective for having been delivered with the neat precision which characterized most of Frank Krebbel's statements. In a world of backslappers he achieved emphasis through understatement.

"And you say Wahl is typical?" asked Thatcher.

"He's an extreme example, I admit. In the other divisions we managed to upgrade some of the middle men. Years before they had the necessary seasoning, of course."

It sounded, thought Thatcher absently, as if they marinated them. Even Krebbel was not immune to the prevailing jargon of American management.

"It's an impressive record." He paused a moment before going on to voice skepticism. "But after all, your difficulties have been shared by your competitors. And they're not doing badly."

"Nobody was as hard hit as Michigan Motors."

"That's true. But they all had to adjust to personnel changes and to a good deal of outside criticism. Plus, of course, foregoing the very substantial advantages accruing from the conspiracy."

Krebbel frowned. "I'm not sure I agree about substantial advantages. MM can do as well without price fixing. That's always been my position. If we had all the facts, it may have cost us something to play that game during the last couple of years."

"That may be so," said Thatcher peaceably. He had no intention of arguing the merits of price fixing, price leadership, or competitive pricing. That was not his mission in Detroit. "Basically I wonder if six months is long enough to judge the effectiveness of . . . er . . . unseasoned management. The momentum of your previous management may be carrying you along. It might be the booster effect of a good year for the consumer that's kept your sales growing. You can't tell what's going to happen in the next six months. Particularly when you have a murder thrown in."

"I don't agree." A thin note of stubbornness underlined Krebbel's dissent. "Except about the murder, of course. The results there are unpredictable. We're having a board meeting next week, you know. And I'm pretty sure that we'll decide to defer the new issue. With the market sliding this isn't a good time to raise money under any circumstances. But this is only a temporary delay. It has nothing to do with basic conditions. We'll be calling on you again . . . and soon."

Thatcher examined his companion with genuine interest. "You think the murder is only a temporary embarrassment?"

"Of course," said Krebbel with emphasis. "That unfortunate delay in firing Jensen confused everybody. Just because he was hanging around the company, people think he was still involved with it. That's nonsense. Ray Jensen ceased to be a part of Michigan Motors when the Department of Justice indicted him. None of our people had anything to gain or lose by his murder."

Thatcher resisted the temptation to wish Krebbel joy of his opinion.

"Are you sure that you're being realistic?" he asked quietly. "After all, Ray Jensen could have given the Justice Department a lot of information. There must be people at Michigan Motors who would have suffered if he had made more disclosures."

"The people who could have been hurt by Jensen," said Krebbel emphatically, "have been dealt with. We have nothing more to hide."

Thatcher could not believe this. MM might have dealt with them, but what about the Department of Justice? Ray Jensen, Orin Dunn, and Buck Holsinger were not the only Michigan Motors executives privy to the price-fixing conspiracy: presumably the rest of them entertained the usual prejudice against penal servitude, whether or not still formally enrolled on the roster of the company's employees.

"It's an interesting situation," he said aloud. "One tends to forget that while a good many people were damaged by the trial, others benefited, didn't they? On the basis of what you've said, you can see that there have been several unexpected promotions—"

"That's not a view we encourage at Michigan Motors," Krebbel cut in austerely. "But I wish I could convince you. . . ."

He did his best to do so during the rest of their lunch.

But Krebbel abandoned Michigan Motors' earning potential as they were finishing their apple pie, which was better, Thatcher noted, than what had often been presented to him by a white-coated waiter amidst all the paraphernalia of luxury.

"I know you're concerned about the effects of Jensen's murder. And I've admitted that it's an unpredictable factor.

But remember, we're in the full blaze of publicity right now. After tomorrow it will die down, and then I think you'll agree that things are coming back into proportion quite quickly."

"Tomorrow?" asked Thatcher. "What's happening tomorrow?"

"Jensen's funeral. Didn't you know? The police have finally released the body."

"Oh." Thatcher thought for a moment how this would impinge on his own plans. "I had been hoping to meet with your treasurer tomorrow and review your revolving loan agreement."

Krebbel shook his head. "I'm afraid not. He'll be at the funeral. Most of us will be out for a good part of the day."

Thatcher resigned himself. He should have known. Good intentions and days replete with hard work seemed doomed at Michigan Motors.

"As a matter of fact," said Krebbel, "I was going to suggest that you go out to Ann Arbor with Madsen."

Thatcher was wary. "Ann Arbor?"

"Yes. They're holding a colloquium this year on the automobile industry. MM's turn is tomorrow, but because of Jensen's funeral, French and I have to renege. Of course we could call the whole thing off. But they got some great turnouts from Ford and Chrysler, so I've asked Madsen and Wahl to go. But that's still short. We're in something of a bind. . . ."

"You just want another body, eh?" Thatcher commented.

"Yes, I'll be glad to go if it will help."

"Splendid. That'll be a load off everybody's mind." Krebbel made appreciative noises.

Not until he was asking the motel's switchboard to call him in the morning did this conversation recur to Thatcher. Krebbel had smoothly managed tomorrow's interment so that neither Glen Madsen nor Ed Wahl be present. That was understandable. After all, their feelings for the departed would be no secret to most of the mourners. But Thatcher was beginning to absorb the MM *Weltanschauung*. Tact—in whatever form—was suspect. Krebbel was far more likely to be engaged in some esoteric maneuver to protect Michigan Motors, such as weeding out the company's most promising candidates for Death Row. In which case he, Thatcher, was going into the wilds of Michigan with a select, but not necessarily congenial, group.

Immediate departure for the Sloan was beginning to look more and more attractive. Thatcher returned his attention to the switchboard operator. Walter Bowman wanted him to phone; there was the daily package from Miss Corsa. This package contained whatever mail, in Miss Corsa's view, required on-the-road action. The one today seemed to be filled with clippings and reports. Puzzled, he riffled through figures on New York City real estate taxes, office space dedicated to government use, the vacancy rate in Manhattan, and the height of the Chrysler Building (1046 ft.). At last he unearthed a memo slip. The formality implicit in its printed heading quickly collapsed before the personality of its author.

To: J. P. Thatcher
From: C. F. Trinkam
Subject: WORLD TRADE CENTER

John—

Withers wants you to look at this stuff. God knows why. It's about the new World Trade Center. Couldn't make out what's on his mind. Probably some of his pals at the Dntn-Low.Manh. Assoc. have been after him. The infighting between the Port Authority boys and the N.Y. Real Estate Board is beginning to hot up.

If you ask me, they deserve each other.

CHARLIE

Cheered by this communication, Thatcher decided to look on the bright side of things. He would return Bowman's call, even though it was one o'clock in the morning —and serve him right too. As for tomorrow's outing, however dangerous his associates, at least it did not involve further inspection of mechanized vehicles.

11 • Abutters Only

As THOUSANDS of curiosity seekers were filing into the Cathedral Church of St. Paul on Woodward Avenue to hear the funeral services for Raymond Jensen, the investigation of his death was leading representatives of three major forces in the American way of life down markedly divergent paths.

The sovereign state of Michigan, in the person of Captain William Georgeson of the state police, was on the trail of information about the murdered man's personal life.

"I want you to talk to the sister-in-law, Mrs. Burns, as soon as she's back," he instructed one of his subordinates. "Gallagher is going to check up on the neighbors."

"What about Madsen?" asked Kelly.

Georgeson smiled a big man's patient smile. "I talked to him yesterday," he said. "And I'll be talking to him again, don't worry."

F. X. Riley, on behalf of the might of the Justice Department, was deep in consultation with Susan Price.

"But why can't we go out together three nights running? What's so special about three?"

"It's not that there's anything special about three," said Miss Price stubbornly. "It's just that I don't want to rush things. We have plenty of time."

"How do you know how much time we have? What if I get called back to Washington?"

Susan gasped.

A watching brief for Wall Street, an important underwriting firm, and the Sloan Guaranty Trust was being held by John Putnam Thatcher, who was inclined to put this kind of gloss on his inquisitiveness. With barefaced dissimulation Thatcher had agreed with the convalescent Walter Bowman, via two expensive and inconvenient telephone calls, that the Sloan should keep an eye on Michigan Motors. He had further assured Bradford Withers, president of the Sloan, that only the press of important business in Detroit was delaying his return to New York and a sliding stock market.

Now he was paying the price for such self-indulgence. Sandwiched between Ed Wahl (bored) and Glen Madsen (preoccupied), he was in a crowded lecture room at the University of Michigan listening to Professor John V. Ellery discuss "Marketing and Financial Aspects of the Automotive Industry." In prospect were comments from Madsen and Wahl as well as reports by the assembled academic dignitaries.

The Interdepartmental Colloquium, according to a small brochure thrust upon Thatcher as he entered the lecture hall, espoused "a fruitful, interdisciplinary exploration of the social, economic, legal, and political problems raised by large-scale industrial development."

Thatcher reminded himself to find out if Harvard were going in for this sort of thing.

"Calling upon specialists from many disciplines," was presumably a reference to the gnomish little man who had been introduced to Thatcher as "Dr. Brimmer, Psychology," and to four professors from the law school who smiled modestly as Professor Ellery droned on.

"Ford Foundation put up the money," Glen Madsen had explained as they drove out.

"Bad cess to them," Thatcher had replied.

The automotive industry, it appeared, had agreed to cooperate with this worthy venture some time ago, and indeed scheduled an impressive series of pilgrimages to the groves of academe in an admirable, if doomed, attempt to induce the academic world to recognize the social awareness, liberal-mindedness, and disinterested professionalism of the American businessman.

". . . representatives of financial institutions," Ellery was saying offhandedly. Thatcher stirred and looked around the smoky room; he wondered just how much the man knew about financial institutions. Certainly he was not the sort that the Sloan Guaranty Trust would have on the premises. As if to confirm this uncharitable thought, Professor Ellery began drawing diagrams on a blackboard. In the row in front of Thatcher, three Nigerians started taking notes. In addition to the psychologist, now smiling menacingly, and to the lawyers, there were a large number of young-old balding men, in double-breasted suits, also taking notes. Two sharp-featured, dark-haired women scowled at Professor Ellery; an old man (in a green eye-shade) dozed in the corner. Among the forty or fifty people present Thatcher saw no one who looked the way he thought students should look. Considering Ellery's remarks —"with kinked demand curves and monotonic cost functions"—this was probably just as well.

Next to him Glen Madsen shifted impatiently and jotted a brief note. Kinked demand curves apparently meant something to him. But after the professor regretfully sat down and Madsen rose to take his place, Thatcher was less impressed by the vigor and coherence of his delivery than by the sense of nervous energy deliberately held in check. It was like watching a man hold a brace of high-bred trotters to the pace of a team of work horses.

"So you feel that the elasticity of demand facing Michigan Motors' Viscounts is less than unity?" one of the young-old men interrupted to demand.

Madsen did. Thatcher watched him turn to the board and sketch a rather messy graph. Why was he generating an aura of conflict? Simple depression Thatcher could have understood. But was there an element of hope underlying Madsen's apprehension? After all, Celia Jensen was now free. Ray Jensen, the barrier to so much of Madsen's happiness, was gone. Not, presumably, in a way that anybody could approve, but definitely gone. Suddenly Madsen had every prospect of happiness. Unless it was even simpler. Unless Madsen was concealing an upsurge of exultation. Was he thinking, in effect: "I've done it! They haven't arrested me. I've gotten away with it"?

Thatcher glanced to his left. Speculatively Wahl was watching Madsen in action. Thatcher wondered what he was thinking.

Madsen was succeeded by Ed Wahl, who described himself as "just an ordinary guy" who didn't understand "what you professors are up to." He then proceeded to give a detailed description of the sales dealership situation in Plantagenets. The Nigerians stopped taking notes.

"Now," said Professor Ellery with an element of the sinister, "we're going to throw the meeting open to comments from the floor."

The fruitful interdisciplinary exploration of the problems raised by large-scale industrial development produced, to Thatcher's way of thinking, a surprising range of questions; no doubt what the Ford Foundation had in mind. Professor Ellery and Glen Madsen were subjected to rapid-fire, highly technical queries from the young men in business suits; Madsen acquitted himself brilliantly in a ceremonial little exchange centering on an article written by somebody named—if Thatcher heard correctly—Evsey Lumar. He and Professor Ellery were politely differing about the findings reported there, when the psychologist hitched himself forward and, in a Viennese accent, asked a question that went to the heart of what he described as the "socio-economic nexus of the suprapolitical corporate enterprise." Unfortunately nobody understood him. The lawyers, with charming rue, mentioned the Sherman Act. Everybody laughed intelligently—including the representatives of Michigan Motors. There was even one question directed at John Putnam Thatcher.

"Now if I were investing," said a round-faced pipe-smoker in superior accents, "I'd be pretty interested in capital coefficients in industries where the demand is inelastic. Do you bankers ever think about that sort of thing?"

Considering the provocation, Thatcher was mildness itself. "We've discovered," he said, "that if you persist in interesting yourself in capital coefficients and inelastic demand curves, you are rarely in a position to invest."

The meeting drew to a close at five thirty. After suitable courtesies among the principals, Wahl, Madsen, and Thatcher finally left the building. Sunlight was slanting off the trees and illuminating the top of the Baird Carillon that dominated the square. Sally Wahl, a handsome blonde who looked the way John Thatcher thought a student should look, waited outside. She greeted them prettily, admitted that she was majoring in botany but confided that she was engaged so that it didn't matter, and bore her father off to relieve him of his ready cash in decent privacy.

Thatcher and Madsen started toward State Street, where Madsen's Hotspur was parked. They had arranged to stop at Madsen's house for a drink.

"I took my doctorate here," Glen Madsen said, pointing out buildings of interest to no one but an alumnus.

Thatcher expressed polite admiration as they got into the car.

"Yes," said Madsen reminiscently, "I came up here when I got out of the Army. Took my undergraduate work at Texas earlier." It was either the nostalgia of homecoming (Thatcher had seen hard-bitten corporation lawyers

weep at their Harvard Twenty-fifth) or a determination to
avoid more engrossing topics that led Madsen on: "I
was doing some pretty good research when MM asked me
to head up their economics section. . . ."

"There's much to be said for industry," replied Thatcher bracingly, recalling Professor Ellery. "The academic
life has a marked soporific quality."

"Mm," said Madsen, unconvinced.

"Do you think of going back to the university now?"
Thatcher asked out of the kindness of his heart. Madsen
was clearly in the mood for confidences; Michigan Motors, at a guess, did not afford him many such opportunities.

Madsen, it developed, did think periodically of giving up
his business connections and returning to research, either
at the university or at some foundation. He liked the pay
at Michigan Motors, but the work was becoming limited,
and he did not find the personal contacts congenial. Grosse
Point Farms and the Bloomfield Open Hunt Club were
not his milieu: he lived nearer to Ann Arbor than was
fashionable; he liked to keep in touch with the people he
had known in the graduate school. So he wondered . . .

Thatcher, who had heard this speech at least one hundred times before, maintained a silence which could have
been interpreted as sympathetic.

"I used to think I might want to teach," Madsen continued. "Now I wonder if I'll get the chance."

Thatcher pondered this reply as they pulled into the
tree-shaded driveway of a rambling white house whose
twin porches and front doors proclaimed the old-fashioned
duplex.

"It's me, Mrs. Creamer," Madsen called from the hallway. "Cleaning woman's here today," he explained as he
ushered Thatcher inside.

Somewhere in the back of the house a vacuum cleaner
ceased its laborings. Slippered feet shuffled along the floor,
and a turbaned head appeared in the doorway.

"I thought I heard you, Mr. Madsen. You may as well
know the worst." The face fell into bloodhound lines of
sadness. "They're in there, in the living room."

"Who's in there?" Madsen demanded, although Thatcher
thought he must already know the answer.

Mrs. Creamer became, if anything, more lugubrious.
"The police," she whispered hoarsely. "And those McKennas, they've been filling the police with a pack of lies."

Visibly startled, Madsen swung toward the living room just as Captain William Georgeson appeared.

"Ah, Mr. Madsen. I've been waiting for you. And it's Mr. Thatcher, isn't it? Come in, come in."

Georgeson was a big man, made bigger by his uniform. He filled the doorway as he smiled a bland, insincere smile and gestured his invitation.

"Pushed their way in, they did," Mrs. Creamer complained, her old eyes squinting with dislike as she turned and shuffled back down the hall.

"Just a few little things . . ."

"What the hell!" The naked fury in Glen Madsen's voice was an explosion of pent-up emotions. "What the hell right do you have . . ."

"Madsen," Thatcher began warningly, but the younger man's control had snapped.

"I said what are you doing here? Do you have a warrant? If you don't, get out!"

He strode past Thatcher, past Captain Georgeson, who was no longer smiling, and moved into the living room, where a uniformed man stood confronting him.

"Did you hear me!"

Madsen hurled his briefcase onto the sofa and, with his shoulders hunched suggestively, advanced toward the officer.

"Now look here," the police captain started to bluster.

"Georgeson," Thatcher intervened with calm authority. "Before this situation gets out of hand, you'd better clarify your position. On what basis are you here?"

The dry, unimpassioned voice had its effect.

"What basis do I need?" Georgeson snapped. "It's Madsen's duty to help, and he knows it."

Madsen started to interrupt, but Thatcher silenced him. "Keep quiet, Madsen," he said decisively. "Well, Georgeson? If you're asking for cooperation, that's one thing. If you have a warrant, it's another."

"All right, all right," said Georgeson sullenly. "So I'm asking for cooperation. I just want to ask you a few questions, Mr. Madsen." The title was sarcastic.

"For God's sake!" Madsen burst out. "You've been doing nothing but asking me questions!"

Both he and Georgeson were bulky men with the kind of big open faces that reflect anger quickly. Looking at them as they scowled at each other, Thatcher was momentarily tempted to turn on his heels; physical violence, which

seemed perilously close, might clear the air. However, he
had rashly promised the absent Berman to act as tower of
strength to Mrs. Jensen. There was no doubt that this currently involved keeping Glen Madsen from making a bigger
fool of himself than he already had.

"You offered me a drink, Madsen. I'll take you up on it,"
he said crisply. Then, ignoring Georgeson, who was looming near the door, and his patrolman, whose hands rested
lightly on his leather belt, he proceeded into the living
room and sat down.

"Scotch, if you have it. With a touch of water," he
added.

For a moment Madsen remained poised. Then with a
short, angry laugh he disappeared through an archway
into his dining room. There was a great racket of slam-
ming drawers and clanking glasses.

"Just some questions," Georgeson repeated, sitting
down. Almost immediately he ceased being an ominous
physical presence and became an overweight public official.

Thatcher was too wily a fox to breathe a sigh of relief
as the emotional temperature dropped several degrees.

"Help yourself if you want, Georgeson. Then ask your
questions and get out."

Madsen's voice was still raw, but the hand tendering
Thatcher his drink was steady enough.

"Thanks," said Georgeson briefly. He fell silent. Somewhere in the back of the house Mrs. Creamer was continuing her chores with defiant noise.

"You had a fight with Ray Jensen last week." Georgeson
was stating a fact, not asking a question. "A big fight.
You threatened him. The two of you started in here,
then you spilled out into the driveway, trading punches."

Narrowly Thatcher watched Madsen over the rim of his
glass. The heavy satisfaction in Georgeson's voice would
have goaded a man more equable than Glen Madsen. But
Madsen did not betray emotion.

"Yes," he said. "I had a little fight with Ray last week."

"Not so little," said Georgeson quickly. "You told him
you'd kill him if he came back. Told him to leave Celia
alone—"

"Keep her out of this!" said Madsen before he could control himself. But Georgeson's watchfulness steadied him.
He took a drink, then went on, "Anyway, Ray and I tan-
gled last Tuesday."

Georgeson smiled once again. "I have witnesses who

say it was Wednesday, Mr. Madsen. That makes you the last person to see Jensen alive, doesn't it?"

Glen Madsen's face went white. Was it with shock, Thatcher asked himself?

"It was Tuesday," Madsen said. "I know who your witnesses are. You mean the McKennas, across the street. Well, they're mistaken. They're old, and they do get confused about things. Ask the Singers next door. They'll tell you it was Tuesday night."

Georgeson grunted a little as he shifted. "Good friends of yours, the Singers. Apart from your good friends, can you prove it was Tuesday?"

"Can you prove it was Wednesday?" Madsen countered.

"That's what my witnesses say. Now, they claim you were fighting about Jensen's wife. . . ."

Again Thatcher saw Glen Madsen's mobile ugly face darken with involuntary anger. Remorselessly Georgeson continued, trying to make Ray Jensen's murder the end of the old story of a man and another man's wife.

But if Madsen's short replies did nothing to disabuse him, Madsen scored nonetheless. However damaging this disclosure of a fight with Ray Jensen, it was not as damaging as it might have been. A confrontation on Tuesday night was bad enough, but Jensen had been seen alive at Plantagenet on Wednesday.

And while the unknown McKennas claimed the fight was on Wednesday night, they were old and liable to err. Georgeson knew this, and once again hesitated.

This hesitation, Thatcher could see, was the only thing keeping Glen Madsen from immediate arrest.

Captain Georgeson put it in so many words.

"Well, that's it, for now. We're going to check this out, Mr. Madsen. We're going to check on you and Jensen's wife until we're blue. And I just hope you've been telling the truth, for your sake."

Suspicion, and perhaps dislike, shone from his small eyes. Then he was gone, leaving the slumped Madsen staring blindly after him.

"It really was Tuesday," he said at last. "Although I can see how you might have your doubts."

Thatcher was astringent. "It's to be hoped that somebody beside those Singers can testify to that effect."

"People get mixed up," Madsen said vaguely. "And it's over a week ago. . . ."

"Now listen, Madsen," Thatcher began.

"Oh, I could have killed Ray. If ever I hated anybody, I hated him," Madsen continued conversationally. "Whoever did it was a real benefactor. Ray was a sadist. He liked to make Celia suffer. For her sake, I put up with it. But Ray pushed me a little too far. . . ."

Thatcher had some experience in dealing with people in shock.

"Madsen," he said tartly, "take my advice. Forget the reasons you wanted to kill Ray Jensen. That's Georgeson's job. Let him do it. What you should do is spend some time thinking of the many reasons why you couldn't have killed him!"

Thatcher's vehemence startled Glen Madsen out of his reverie and into protest. "But I didn't do it!"

"In a real sense," Thatcher told him sternly, "*that* is quite irrelevant!"

12 • Rotary Ahead

THERE IS A CERTAIN FINALITY about funerals, even those of murder victims. Six feet of sod had succeeded where six months of prison had failed; Raymond Jensen was at last neutralized as a vital factor in the affairs of Michigan Motors. For a good many people this fact prompted a brief stock-taking.

In the secluded comfort of the Detroit Club, Lionel French and Stuart Eberhart, chairman of the board and president emeritus, respectively, unfurled after-lunch cigars and resumed their conversation about the company.

"Yes," French said, "I think we can look forward to some peace and quiet at last."

Eberhart snorted. "You're easily satisfied! What if Ray implicated me in writing? It would have been just like him to keep some real dynamite up his sleeve."

"Nonsense. In the past six months the Justice Department has been over Jensen's papers with a fine-tooth comb," said French with unabated cheer. "The only danger was what he might tell them. And that could have been worrisome. He was making some pretty wild threats the other day, you know."

Eberhart clipped off the tip of his cigar savagely. "Vindictive, that's what Ray was. No gratitude at all. I gave him his start. And yet the minute he got out of jail, he made a dead set for me."

"It wasn't personal, Stu. He was just looking for some leverage."

"That's one name for blackmail!" snapped Eberhart. "You seem to forget it could have landed me in jail."

"Oh, I agree, I agree. But say what you will about Jensen, you have to admit that he ate, drank, and slept Michigan Motors. That's why you picked him. And that's why he went crazy." French mentally reviewed the past before adding regretfully, "He would have been great in the front office."

"He was unbalanced!" said Eberhart shortly.

"Well, that may be what it takes. In any event we don't have a thing to worry about. Riley must realize he won't get any more evidence, now that Jensen's gone. You'll see. Things will start to die down in a week or two."

Eberhart said it was high time, and the two men went on to debate the relative merits of some potential acquisitions. French was inclined towards a palomino stud farm in the Upper Peninsula, while the less dashing Eberhart still favored orange groves in Florida. As they prepared to leave, they were respectfully approached by two local advertising men with condolences for the tribulations of Michigan Motors and the death of its most publicized vice-president.

French rose to the occasion.

"A loss," he said, shaking his handsome head gravely. "A great loss, indeed."

Dead, Ray Jensen was acknowledged to be a loss. Many an observer would have been tempted to make the same assessment of Orin Dunn—on the hoof, as it were.

Lying limp in a hammock overlooking his expensive patio, he stared dully at the maid announcing Mrs. Holsinger on the phone.

"For God's sake, can't they leave me alone anywhere?" The maid did not respond.

"Oh, all right. Plug it in out here."

Exuding displeasure, the maid retreated in search of the phone. She had never been enthusiastic about the installation of jack outlets all over the Dunn property; now that her connection with the family was about to be terminated, she saw no need to conceal her feelings on that or any other subject.

For Orin Dunn's interview with Frank Krebbel had ended his association with Michigan Motors. He was preparing to relocate in the West. It was not a prospect to cheer.

He shifted his weight restlessly. Diane Holsinger would be difficult; there was no point in kidding himself about that. But then everyone was being difficult. His resignation, presented yesterday, had been accompanied by all the awkwardness inherent in the situation. Ed Wahl, consulted first out of deference to his position as head of Plantagenet, had wished Dunn well with offensive unconcern. Frank Krebbel, although accepting his withdrawal with the dexterity of a man performing a familiar task, had not bothered to conceal his surprise that Dunn should regard the formality as necessary. His old cronies at Plantagenet, over whom he had been lording it in high style a short year ago, were visibly skeptical at his sudden zeal for the aircraft business in Southern California.

And this morning his discomforts had assumed domestic form. Taking his family to the swimming pool at the club, secure in the knowledge that no adult male associated with the automotive industry would be lolling about on a weekday morning, he had been forced to watch his wife being brave.

"Yes. Orin and I are leaving." Her chin came up proudly. "We think that it's the best thing we can do for the company."

Simple justice should have caused Orin Dunn to honor her performance. Not every woman can be noble in a swimming pool. But Dunn was in no mood for simple justice. And now, in the privacy of his home, he was being hounded by Diane Holsinger—on the very site of his former barbecue triumphs. Orin Dunn had always prided himself on a steak sauce of his own creation.

The maid handed him the receiver.

"Hello, Di," he began cautiously. "Yes, that's right. . . . I've taken a job at Santa Barbara. . . . Well, I don't know why it should be such a surprise."

The phone crackled ominously and at some length.

"No, of course it isn't what you planned," he expostulated. "Do you think it's what I'd planned? . . . Be reasonable, Di! Do you think I'd do this if I had any choice? . . . For heaven's sake, be careful what you say. You don't know who might be listening."

The phone said that he had the brains of a peahen.

"Dammit, whose fault is this anyway?" Dunn roared in anguish. "You and your smart ideas about the Department of Justice. I've had a bellyful. . . . Of course I mean that you handled things wrong. I never should have gotten mixed up in this. . . . The trouble is that I let you talk me into— . . . By God, you can't talk to me that way, you and that half-baked husband of yours. Why should I pull your chestnuts out of the fire? Di? Di? . . ."

At Grosse Point Farms Diane Holsinger cradled her princess phone, looked reflectively at the piecrust table set against rose shot-silk draperies, and came to a decision.

Without haste she descended the carpeted staircase leading to the lower floor and sought out her husband in his elaborate workshop.

"Buck," she announced without preliminary, "Orin Dunn is cutting his losses and running out on us."

Her husband looked up from the lathe, absorbed the news, and made a simple statement.

"Good riddance."

His wife tapped a foot impatiently. "Don't act that way," she urged. "And for heaven's sake, will you shut that thing off!"

Obediently Holsinger switched off the lathe. He examined his wife thoughtfully. Her fingers were clenched, and she was breathing rapidly.

"What's the matter, Di?"

She was silent for a moment. "It's Dunn," she said finally. "I may have told him too much."

"Always said he was a jerk. No telling what he might do," her husband grunted. This was a very charitable résumé, as Diane Holsinger knew full well. What Buck had really said was that she was a fool to get mixed up with Orin Dunn.

Holsinger continued thoughtfully, "But I wouldn't worry about his talking. Got his own skin to save. Even if he is leaving, no company likes a man who blabs."

His wife relaxed slightly. "You think he'll keep quiet because he's got enough of his own to hide?"

"Oh, yes." His eyes narrowed slightly in speculation. "Say, Di, has it ever occurred to you that Dunn may have been the guy who tipped the feds in the first place?"

"What?" Diane Holsinger was markedly shaken by the suggestion. "But he went to jail too."

"It would be just like him to mess the thing up. Naturally he wanted Jensen's job. And the real evidence was all against Jensen. If Ray hadn't talked, nobody could have touched Dunn."

"That's absurd, Buck," she said sharply.

But Holsinger was stubborn. "I don't think so. Sometimes you can't stay on top of these things. It would explain why he was so wild at Jensen. Naturally if Orin started the whole thing, he didn't expect it to backfire."

"Nonsense. Whoever informed on Jensen must have taken good care to see that it didn't backfire."

Something in his wife's voice made Holsinger look up quickly. But Diane refused to meet his eye.

Other people beside Buck Holsinger were inclined to think that the entire conspiracy investigation might have boomeranged on the informant.

"You know, Celia, sometimes I can't help wondering. Maybe it was Ray who started the whole thing off." Glen Madsen was seated on the sofa in Louise Burns's living room, very much against the wishes of Mrs. Burns.

"It's madness, Celia," her sister had protested. "You know how people are talking. This will just give them more to talk about."

"I know, and I don't care!" said Celia recklessly. Her face was drawn, but her eyes shone with rebellion. "I'm past thinking what people will say. I've got to see Glen someplace where we can talk. I can't bear to think of his going through this all by himself."

"People are talking about more than your private affairs," said Louise, with the aggressive candor of a minister's wife. "They're saying Glen murdered Ray because of you. Are you sure you won't be doing him more harm than good?"

But Celia's line was that things couldn't possibly be worse, and the police had all the evidence they needed about her feelings for Glen Madsen. Together they had overcome her sister's objections, and Madsen had been received into the house.

He was not looking well when he arrived, but two hours with Celia had their effect. Madsen, if not exactly cheerful, could turn his mind to some of the problems exercising the entire staff of MM.

Celia was not noticeably shocked at the suggestion that her late husband might have been involved in double dealing. But she had a higher regard for his efficiency than Buck Holsinger had for that of Orin Dunn.

"But, Glen, if he'd arranged the whole thing, surely he would have managed to get off himself."

"Maybe he unleashed something he couldn't control. Until he was on the stand, he could have thought he was going to get away with it. You remember how stunned he was when they started bringing out those photostats of his handwriting. He never dreamed that they had so much on him. Do you think . . ."

"Yes. What is it, Glen?"

He chose his words. "It's hard to be detached. That was a bad time for Ray. You'd left him, and of course he wasn't completely normal. But I could swear he had something else on his mind when the trial started. Maybe he'd gotten tired of waiting for Eberhart's job. He knew he was going to get it eventually, but he didn't want to sit around for ten years."

"You mean maybe Ray aimed the whole thing at Eberhart?"

"Sure. Remember, if Ray had opened up, the government would have had the goods on Eberhart. What if that was what Ray had orginally planned? But then, when he realized that he was caught in his own trap, he shifted tactics and decided to sit tight, hoping to come out of jail with something to sell. That would explain his behavior after he got out."

"You don't need any explanation for that," said Celia sadly. "That's just the way he was."

"No," said F. X. Riley. "You can take it from me that Ray Jensen was not the man who tipped."

He was instructing a freshly arrived subordinate in the intricacies of the great Michigan Motors case, now of sufficient dimensions in the mind of his department to justify increased manpower.

"Well, who did then?" asked that simple-minded youth.

"We don't know. It came anonymously. You'll learn that most good tips do. This isn't like Customs cases, where people work for a bounty. Of course often it's a competitor. This time it wasn't. We've always known it was somebody at Michigan Motors. And so has the rest of the industry. Naturally it doesn't lead to very good feelings."

"I'll bet it doesn't!"

"But the thing to keep in mind is that the tip was aimed at getting both the Plantagenet and Buccaneer divisions into trouble. If Jensen had been behind it, you can be damn sure he would have stayed away from his own division. And we never would have gotten his own notes on that March fifteenth meeting. It's a shame he was murdered."

The youth nodded. In his book it was a shame for anybody to be murdered. But it developed that Riley was proceeding along more selective lines.

"He would have talked, you know. In the end public pressure would have kept Michigan Motors from giving him what he wanted, whether it was a job or money. Then he would have come to us out of sheer spite. It's really a shame. A lot of information went down the drain with Raymond Jensen."

"I suppose they're relieved at MM. They must realize that as well as we do."

"Realize it! Hell, I wouldn't be surprised if that isn't why they murdered him."

Ed Wahl's new-found job security as head of Michigan Motors' prestige division was not making him any easier to live with. Always brusque in manner, these days he was nervous and short-tempered as well. Even Susan Price, prepared as usual to stretch a point in favor of MM's executives, had to remind herself forcibly that, whatever his faults in dealing with junior management, Mr. Wahl was invariably considerate to his secretary.

She watched the departure of a production manager, badly deflated from a rough going-over during which Wahl had alternated fits of bored abstraction with bouts of harsh cross-examination, and was relieved to have her employer raise a subject which could not fail to lighten his mood.

"You've heard that Mr. Dunn is leaving us," he said to her as she closed her dictation book.

Susan agreed that the word had gotten around.

"Well, we'll have to organize some sort of party. The usual thing. You'll see to it, won't you?"

She made a note. "Just the division people?" she asked.

"What the hell!" He drummed his fingers irritably before coming to a decision. "Make it the front office too. I suppose we have to act as if he's an assistant division manager."

Susan nodded. Her question had some point. The protocol at Michigan Motors for departing executives was well defined: assistant division managers got the front office; those below did not.

"And, Miss Price," added Wahl as she was leaving the room, "don't forget to put yourself on the invitation list."

Yes, there was no doubt that Mr. Wahl meant well. Not that he would ever measure up to Mr. Krebbel, as far as Susan Price was concerned. Catch him sending her a cake! But an invitation to the Dunn party was not to be sneezed at. As Wahl said good night to her, striding hat in hand toward the elevator, Susan Price speculated on the possibility of asking Fabian Riley to be her escort. Normally such an invitation carried with it unrestricted rights in the matter of companion. But, Susan sadly acknowledged to herself, the front office of Michigan Motors was singularly impervious to the charms of its own special federal investigator.

Ed Wahl, stopping by the club for his wife, was also enveloped in speculation—although not so agreeable in content.

"If we can just ride this out for the next couple of weeks, we'll be over the hump," he announced tightly. "That is, if those boys wise up enough to let things cool."

"What do you mean—over the hump? You're not going to let them take away the division now, are you?" his wife challenged. Her outing with the ladies had been teetotal, and she was not in the best of moods.

"For Chrissake! I've had the division sewed up for weeks. You know that."

"I know that's your story," Audrey replied nastily. "It doesn't seem to have done down so well at the company before Ray was shot."

Ed Wahl stared grimly ahead at the road, but his hands tightened on the wheel. "My story, and Frank Krebbel's! Try and remember that!"

His wife's discontented face moved restlessly as she hitched up the mink stole required of MM front office wives, regardless of temperature or season. "All right, all right," she muttered. "You know I'll back you up whatever you say."

"Whatever I say! But I'm telling you the truth!" he howled.

"Then why are you getting so upset? If you've got the division, what else can go wrong?"

"Plenty." His lips tightened. "You seem to have forgotten we're in the middle of a murder investigation. As if that isn't enough, we've got people nosing around to find out who tipped off the feds about the price-fixing ring."

"I thought they were trying to brush that under the rug."

"They were, until Jensen came back. He got them all stirred up. But if they have the brains they were born with, they'll let it die down now."

"Why should they?" his wife demanded perversely. "They ought to find out and get rid of him."

"You don't know anything about it," he barked. "A witch hunt doesn't do the division any good. We've got enough trouble as is. Much better to let sleeping dogs lie."

"That's the trouble with you. You're always ready to let things lie. Sometimes people have to stand up for things. But not you. . . ."

Ed Wahl took a deep breath. Audrey in this mood was as tenacious as a bulldog. But there was a diversion that had never been known to fail.

"Well, I'm not standing up for Ray Jensen's crusades." Then he made his gesture. "I tell you what, Audrey. It's still early. Let's stop off for a drink."

All sense of *malheur* evaporated, his wife responded warmly.

"You know, Ed," she said, coming to a sudden conclusion, "it's a damned good thing Ray got himself murdered."

"About this Jensen," said the union publicity man. "It's a shame he was murdered. So long as he was out at Michigan Motors, it gave a nice indignant air to our releases."

"Now, Sid," said Thaddeus Casimir reasonably, "we've been indignant for twenty years without any help from Ray Jensen."

The two men were putting the finishing touches to a statement which Casimir would shortly deliver at a press conference. The contract negotiations were not far off, and the union was beginning to beat the drum.

"Well, they're bound to ask you about the murder," persisted Sid. "And we've got to think up something for you to say."

"There's only one thing the union can say."

Twenty minutes later the occasion had arrived, and Casimir was rising to meet it.

"A loss," he said, shaking his handsome head gravely. "A great loss indeed."

13 · Men Working

As LIONEL FRENCH had observed, the death of Ray Jensen, however little mourned elsewhere, constituted a real loss to the Department of Justice. No one appreciated this loss more keenly than the three men seated in a Washington office two days after the funeral. Fabian Riley was reporting to his superiors.

"So we'll never know what he might have told us," Riley concluded.

"We may not know," said one of the others, "but we can make a damn good guess."

The gloom in the office deepened. There is never any shortage of good guesses in the Antitrust Division of the Justice Department. An entire staff labors mightily to no purpose other than the elevation of these guesses into hard facts and trialworthy evidence.

The man behind the desk flapped his hand as if to clear the air. "That doesn't help us any, Art. The point is that Riley, here, thinks that the whole murder may hinge on just this consideration. In which case, the department has a real interest in seeing that the investigation doesn't get sidetracked or bogged down because the local police don't have access to our knowledge."

"Well, Riley, if you're going to explain the ins and outs of that conspiracy to the Michigan police, I wish you luck. I had the devil's own time doing it for a Michigan jury."

Fabian Riley bit back an uncharitable comparison between Captain Georgeson and that bluest of blue-ribbon juries. Instead he contented himself with saying that the police thought the entire antitrust complication was irrelevant.

"I suppose they're just passing it off as a lucky coincidence," Art snorted. "We all know what Jensen was—ambitious, unscrupulous, and out for himself. But he never offered to make a deal. He just took his sentence like a lamb and sat tight on a whole wad of figures and names.

Now, you can't make me think he was doing that because of *noblesse oblige.*"

No, indeed, Riley agreed. What's more, he was willing to bet that Jensen had played his cards wrong. Michigan Motors, instead of being touchingly grateful, had been very wary of Ray Jensen. Buck Holsinger, a less forceful and less dangerous personality, might still be welcomed back to the fold. Orin Dunn was junior enough to dismiss. But Ray Jensen?

"They were going to wash their hands of him. And *that* he wouldn't have taken. He would have come to us and had his revenge."

"And very nice for us it would have been," sighed Julian Summers. "But it doesn't seem impossibly difficult to explain to a layman."

"Things aren't that simple," Riley stated.

"They never are at MM," said Art.

"You see, there are two sides to the coin. Jensen may have been killed because of what he knew. But it's also possible that he was killed because of what he was going to find out."

Raised eyebrows invited him to proceed.

"Jensen was trying to find out who the tipster was. The front office has been hoping to forget about it."

His listeners frowned in thought. "It would be awkward at this late date for MM to discover it was someone who profited from the cleanup," said Art.

"That's their problem." Summers was grimly amused as he turned to Riley. "But it's still part of our business. Now, the way I see it, I'm not going to be able to spare you from Detroit until this investigation either is concluded or seems hopeless. We'll give it another week, at the least."

Art intervened. "Quincy won't like that. He's been hoping to send Riley out to Denver for a month now."

"Yes, I know. I got another of his memoranda this morning reminding me that there are other industries in this country besides automotives. He'll just have to learn the facts of life about operating with limited personnel."

Quincy was a recent political appointee in the department, thirsting for a major kill. No one was wasting much sympathy on his troubles.

"There's just one other thing, sir," said Riley with unusual diffidence. "I don't know if you've heard of it, but there's been some talk about a new public offering."

"I thought they'd dropped that for the time being," replied Summers, giving proof of the efficiency of the department's economic intelligence section.

"Yes, they have. But in the meantime, they've had a banker practically living with the front office day and night. He could know a lot."

"What banker?"

"John Thatcher of the Sloan."

"Wall Street," said Art darkly. "You wouldn't get anything out of him."

"I wasn't thinking of violating any professional confidences. But he must have picked up a lot of personal detail."

"Forget it," advised Art.

"I don't know about that," Summers mused. "There might be possibilities. But you'd have to go cautiously." For a moment he looked directly into Riley's eyes. "I think I'll leave that to your discretion—bearing in mind, of course, the interests of the department."

He paused and then, apparently satsified with the ambiguity of these instructions, continued briskly to those orders which could be put into words: "Now, Riley, you can hand over the routine surveillance to that youngster we sent you. I want you to concentrate on liaison with the state police. . . ."

Fabian Riley was ready to bring all the vigor of an enraged—and balked—reformer to his task. He was perfectly prepared to place himself at the disposal of the Michigan State Police. And with him his enormously detailed information about the inner workings of Michigan Motors.

Unfortunately, he thought as he drove out to the barracks on Friday morning, the Michigan State Police did not seem inclined to capitalize on either of these powerful assets. He swung off Telegraph Road onto the extensive grounds, drove past the dormitory for the uniformed men, and once again entered the spacious, well-lit office that clacked endlessly with teletype messages about stolen cars and missing husbands.

Captain William Georgeson rated a small, well-designed private cubicle, soothingly decorated in beige. The Michigan State Police compound compared favorably to the shabbiness of the Department of Justice offices in Detroit, Chicago—and Washington too, for that matter. Fabian Riley would have traded the whole trim ensemble for one copy of *Standard and Poor's* and a man who could understand it.

Because he found himself, fifteen minutes later, saying, "I think you're wrong, Georgeson. Absolutely wrong."

Mindful of instructions to cooperate with the federal authorities, Georgeson let his gaze stray to the portrait of a bygone Michigan dignitary on the wall and emulated its patient smile. "All right, Riley, tell me where I'm wrong. Glen Madsen has fallen for Jensen's wife. Everyone knows it—the Holsingers, the Wahls—even the MM secretaries. He wants her to divorce Jensen so they can get married, and she wants to leave Jensen. In fact, she had left him before the trial. But Jensen won't go along. Now, you've got to admit that gives Madsen a great motive."

"Yes, I admit that—" began Riley, when he was waved to silence by Georgeson's fleshy hand.

"So Madsen has this motive. Then he admits he had a rough fight with Jensen. Probably the night Jensen was murdered. . . ."

"But Jensen was killed on Wednesday," Riley pointed out. "A lot of people saw him Wednesday morning—Dunn, for example. And Madsen says the fight was Tuesday night."

"Madsen claims the fight was Tuesday night," Georgeson parroted with vast irony. "But his neighbors aren't sure that it was Tuesday! They think it must have been Wednesday! Do you see what that means? Madsen and Jensen have a fight; Madsen goes after him—shoots him, then somehow manages to get the body into that Plantagenet. It was sitting by that damned pool! It would have been a cinch for Madsen to put the body into the back seat sometime Thursday—and there you are!"

Years of pursuing financial peccadilloes had sharpened Riley's eye for detail. "The neighbors," he said after a pause.

"Name of McKenna," Georgeson supplied. "Good, solid citizens. Respected in the community. No reason to dislike Madsen. . . ."

"Aren't they eighty years old?" Riley asked. He knew they were.

William Georgeson was not fond of contradiction and generally managed to avoid it. He was kept from retorting by a uniformed trooper who opened the door, admitting the nervous tapping of the teletypes. "Governor's on the phone, Captain," he said over the competition.

Georgeson expanded before their eyes. Abandoning Riley, he reached for the phone, clearing his throat. "Georgeson here," he said, his voice lower and more resonant than usual. "Yes, Mr. Governor. Yes, sir. . . . certainly, sir. . . ."

With the civil servant's contempt for the incumbent of elective office, Riley listened to Georgeson's eager monosyllables. His own goal—to apprehend a murderer and incidentally punish the criminal who had aborted Department of Justice information—was beginning to seem visionary.

"The governor," said Georgeson, when he had returned phone to cradle, "is interested in this case. He had ties with the automobile industry himself, you know. I told him that we're ninety-five per cent certain that Glen Madsen did it. He's got the motive—and the opportunity. And Mrs. Jensen's story is so fishy it could swim! The way I see it, she ran into Madsen, and he told her he had killed her husband. . . ."

Georgeson's side of the conversation with the Executive Mansion had been confined to "Yes, sir" and "No, sir!" Riley did not, however, waste time pricking bubbles of self-esteem; instead he reverted to his earlier argument.

"Look, Georgeson. You have to admit that all you've got against Madsen is motive—which I grant you—and a lot of circumstantial evidence. Sure, this Madsen–Mrs. Jensen mess is a strong motive for the usual murder. But this isn't the ordinary murder!" He tried to keep his temper from rising as he noted Georgeson's mulish look of obduracy. To keep from being interrupted, he went on quickly, "First, three executives from Michigan Motors were convicted of price fixing! Now, that's important—and you're forgetting it—"

"Listen, Riley, I don't like that tone of voice," said Georgeson, on whom the governor's call had acted like Benzedrine. "I'm not forgetting anything. We've checked up on Holsinger and Dunn—as well as Jensen. We've listened to everything you had to say. But what the hell! Big shots from the other companies went to prison, didn't they? They're not dead! You've got an ax to grind, I can see that."

"Don't you understand? Things at MM went to hell because nobody decided what to do with these three when they got out of jail!" Riley brought a bony fist onto the desk and glared at Georgeson. "Look, this was a company murder all the way! It was a company gun that killed Jensen! He was found on company grounds, in a company car! Half the top management at Michigan Motors wanted to get rid of him. He was a menace to Wahl—who took his job. He'd railroaded Orin Dunn into jail when he could have covered for him. He was shafting Buck Holsinger! For Chrissake! He might have been the guy who sent us the tip! In which case half the board of directors would have been gunning for him."

Georgeson was not unaffected by this show of feeling. "Watch your step, Riley," he rumbled, clearly tempted to extend one mighty arm and shake the younger man like a wet dog. "In the first place, Glen Madsen works at Michigan Motors! Don't forget that! He had access to the gun —he could get at Jensen on company grounds—and stow him into that Plantagenet!" Georgeson threw himself back in his chair and made an unconvincing attempt at jocularity. "I can see you're a specialist, and all specialists have one-track minds! I don't deny that all this business stuff is important. Hell! That's why the governor keeps calling! But just like you know about business—I know about murder! And believe me, nine times out of ten it's liquor—somebody gets tanked up and runs wild. But when the murder is premeditated—and whoever killed Ray Jensen had it all planned out—then I'll turn in my badge if it isn't sex or money!"

Satisfied with this peroration, he leaned back. Riley opened his mouth for rebuttal, then shut it. Currently he was not in a position to deny that love has a powerful effect on human behavior; it was, however, disheartening to see that his extended lecture on Michigan Motors had failed dismally. Captain William Georgeson could not grasp the fact that, in the last analysis, price fixing, politicking for new jobs, managerial squabbles, and early retirements are as much a matter of money as the most violent bank robbery.

Riley sighed. Georgeson, after a searching glance, interpreted this as admission of error. He said, "Oh, I'll admit that I haven't got enough on Madsen to pick him up, Riley. But he did it! We've got a lot of evidence about his affair with Jensen's wife; we have witnesses to prove that Madsen was hanging around the car on Thursday—"

"Everybody was," said Riley gamely.

Georgeson ignored him.

"He had a motive, the opportunity, and access to the

weapon. And he may have had help. That Celia Jensen. We'll never be able to touch her. But she knew all right —and she may have helped decoy her husband. . . ."

"Have you grilled her?"

Again Georgeson's face darkened. "Watch your language, Riley! We pulled her in for a few questions—and a sweet mess she made of them. First, she says, she saw her husband on Friday! Then—after the laboratory says he was killed on Wednesday—she says she didn't see Jensen on Friday. Finally, she admits seeing Madsen."

"If she knew that her husband had been killed," Riley pointed out, "she wouldn't claim to have seen him on Friday, would she?"

Georgeson, whom nature had blessed with an open Scandinavian face, assumed an expression of Machiavellian cunning. "That's just it!" he said triumphantly, "She wanted to be sure to make us think that she didn't know her husband was dead! So she risked that lie!"

Inured to the tortuous ways of financial fraud, Riley was nonetheless baffled by this logic and showed it.

"She's clever," said the policeman. "But all we need is confirmation . . . just one piece of hard proof. With these big businessmen we've got to be careful. We can't bring him in and break down his story until we have more to go on."

Riley, who had had some experience in being careful with big businessmen, rose to go, but Georgeson continued his confidences. "Say we find someone who saw them together! Near the Plantagenet—that would do it! We're interviewing every single man in the plant! Or the gun— we've already searched his apartment and his car—but if we had that gun, Riley, we'd have everything we want! Madsen's goose would be cooked!"

"Would you have a case you could give to the district attorney?" Riley asked, curious about law enforcement in Michigan as never before.

"With the gun," said Georgeson, "I'd have everything!"

Having exhausted the patience of the Michigan State Police, Riley turned to the last available source of information about the internal workings of the company.

That same afternoon found him closeted with Thaddeus Casimir, president of Local 7777, UAW, AFL-CIO. Here at least was one man who did not have to be convinced that avarice, brutality, and murderous passion could arise in corporate surroundings. The problem lay in persuading him to give a damn.

"Big business," Casimir was saying conversationally, "is a pretty selfish proposition. But I want you to understand this, Riley. We don't care if they start bombing each other in the front office—particularly when Jensen's the target—but my boys have their rights, and I'm here to look after them. The shop stewards tell me that they're still trying to sell the police on the proposition that one of our boys took the gun. . . ."

Riley broke in to say that neither he nor the federal government harbored the slightest design on those cherished rights. He was here merely because he was disturbed at his inability to convey to the police the facts of corporate life. He repeated Georgeson's suspicions of Glen Madsen.

"That's absurd!" flashed Casimir, jolted out of his detachment. "Glen Madsen, for God's sake! Sure, he was breathing fire when Jensen came back. But I don't blame him. Jensen was pure poison, you know. Anyone could have told you that there'd be trouble when the two of them got together. I wouldn't be surprised if Glen hauled off and punched him. But to shoot him and then get involved in a circus-act sneaking the body into the plant—that's laughable."

Heartened to find a Madsen supporter, Riley asked Casimir if he knew Madsen well.

"Sure. Glen does most of the background work on the negotiating rounds. He works with our people on the profit-sharing plan. Not that we have anything to write home about in the way of profit sharing. Nothing like what the boys at Kaiser have been getting. Have you seen how they're doing?"

Casimir showed signs of being distracted from the issue at hand. Riley said hastily that, yes, he had seen the figures in the *Wall Street Journal* and they were very impressive. It showed that cost cutting really could be effective and what about the driver of the Super Plantagenet? Had they ever found him?

"That'll shake up the steel industry," said Casimir with great gusto. "You've got to hand it to them. The driver? The guy who took the Planty to the pool that Thursday? No, they haven't found him and they're still hounding us. If this goes on," he said, reverting to his public manner, "I'll pull the men out! That driver business is a red herring. In the first place, I don't attach any importance to his refusal to come forward—in view of the persecution he's likely to encounter. In the second place, I'm willing to bet it was not an authorized driver at all. Probably just another one of Hauser's boys. They're all over the place. You notice they haven't made a big issue of the fact that a Public Relations man hopped in for the ride. Why all this fuss about the driver? It's just another instance of the flagrant bias—"

"Georgeson," Riley intervened desperately, "is convinced that murder stems from sex and money. And I suppose he's right. But you can't make him understand the different forms that money takes." He recapitulated Georgeson's statement of faith and his own failure to instruct.

"That's interesting." Casimir examined his square-tipped nails for a moment in silence. "But Georgeson's wrong, you know. It's got to be sex *or* money. People murder because they have a passion for something. The whole point about a passion is that it's single-minded. You don't go passionately chasing off in two directions. That's what makes the case against Glen Madsen stink. I suppose he's capable of murdering someone. They keep telling us we all are. But he couldn't kill Ray Jensen, because the two of them didn't care about the same thing. Glen would never kill because of Michigan Motors. Hell, half the time he's wishing he was back in research. And Ray Jensen sure as hell would never kill—or be killed—for anything else."

Riley let out a sigh of relief. What Casimir said made sense. Not, of course, that that gave it any value in communicating with Georgeson, he reflected bitterly.

"That's it. I've felt it all along. Jensen's death had to make sense to someone in terms of Michigan Motors."

Casimir looked thoughtful. "You've been here long enough to get the feel of the place. I'll tell you something, for whatever it's worth. There's been a sense of . . . of incompletion around here for months. Everybody's known it, and everybody thinks it's because they didn't decide about taking back Jensen and Holsinger. But I don't. I think the biggest mistake French made in his life was not letting Krebbel dig out the facts on who tipped off your people at Justice. And French is no fool. A lot of people think so because he's a windbag in public. But he can be plenty damn tough when he has to. But on this one he made a mistake."

Riley nodded slowly. "Of course we've been just as glad they didn't start digging around. But what makes you think it's so important?"

"Because the tip came from someone in the know, someone in the inner circle. Normally most corporate maneuvering is out in the open, and everybody knows who his enemies are. But this is a new switch. Here somebody moved underground and did it to bring the whole house of cards tumbling down. I don't know who it was, or whether it worked, or whether it backfired. But I do know that everybody up in the executive office has been living with this knowledge and pretending to forget. Everybody but Ray Jensen, that is. He was a vindictive man, and he never would have rested until he found out. That's why I say French made such a mistake. He could have trusted Krebbel to handle it smoothly—and to have the whole thing buried before those three got back. But Jensen wouldn't care where the chips flew. And there was nothing anybody could have done to stop him. If you ask me, that's why everybody's been sitting around biting their nails, waiting for him to get out. And I'd be willing to bet that that's why he was murdered."

As Riley had thought before, what Casimir said made sense.

14 • License Suspended

F. X. Riley found his conferences with Captain William Georgeson irritating and those with Thaddeus Casimir overpowering. Nevertheless he had the consolation of evenings with Susan Price. They took him to restaurants costing far more than his *per diem* rate and led him into heated, illogical arguments about MM's standards of commercial honesty. Curiously he found these evenings more than adequate compensation.

John Putnam Thatcher had no such solace. His days (when they did not entail strange forays) were occupied by conferences with MM's financial executives. His evenings were also spent in the bosom of the corporate family. Again he enjoyed the amenities of the Bloomfield Open Hunt Club; again he dined with Lionel French (who was reviving—tactlessly, it seemed to Thatcher). Mr. and Mrs. Wahl entertained him at a cocktail party that he hoped to be able to forget. Lincoln Hauser bore him off to the Kingsley Inn for an extended paean to the art of public relations in modern America.

Thus when the Sloan Guaranty Trust telephoned just before noon on Friday, he was not tempted to indulge any further his weakness for stagnant homicide investigations: "No, no, Miss Corsa. Tell Withers I am flying to New York tonight."

"And Mr. Bowman wanted me to ask you," said his secretary, checking a list, "if you think it would be advisable to schedule a special meeting of the Investment Committee tomorrow morning."

"On Saturday morning?" Thatcher asked, unfairly forgetting that he had contributed to Bowman's sense of urgency about Michigan Motors. "No, I don't think that that will be necessary. You might let him know, Miss Corsa, that it is highly unlikely that Michigan Motors is going to proceed with its financing just now."

"Yes, Mr. Thatcher," said Miss Corsa. Her disapproval

told him that she had seen through his pretenses, if Walter Bowman had not.

"Any important messages?"

"I've taken care of everything, Mr. Thatcher," she replied kindly.

It might be dog-eat-dog among the upper management at Michigan Motors, Thatcher reflected as he packed; at the Sloan Guaranty Trust there was only one threat to his position. Thank heavens Miss Corsa was as devoid of ambition as of all other emotions.

He was so cheered by the prospect of returning to his own front office (and incidentally his own apartment, blessedly deficient in motel decor) that he resolutely beat down a flickering sense of dissatisfaction. He knew no more about Ray Jensen's death now than a week ago, when that eminent executive slumped out of the back seat of the Super Plantagenet. "A week wasted," he told himself censoriously. "You've found out about the Michigan Motors underwriting in some detail," he offered in expiation. This held no water. He had known more than enough about Michigan Motors to make a correct investment decision before he left New York. But Thatcher was not the man to brood over past errors. Escape was at hand; he greeted Mack with real anticipation as the lordly Plantagenet Sceptre rolled up to transport him, for the last time, from the Telegraph Motel to Michigan Motors.

It developed, as they proceeded, that Mack felt he had to ask a personal question, seeing as how Mr. Thatcher was leaving that night.

"Ask ahead," Thatcher invited.

"At this bank you own," said Mack. "You've got a car?"

"A Plantagenet, of course," Thatcher said with grave benevolence, unhesitatingly sinking the pearl gray Rolls Royce with which Bradford Withers dazzled visiting Levantines.

Mack beamed.

This merciful tempering of justice brought its own reward. As the Plantagenet glided alongside the Mighty Michigan Motors Pool, Thatcher sighted a crumpled cigarette wrapper floating brazenly on its pristine surface.

Instructing Mack to be ready at four o'clock ("If that will get us to the airport?" he incautiously inquired, eliciting Mack's fervent promise that the Sceptre would perform as never before to assure him of the five o'clock plane), Thatcher entered the lobby, reviewing the minimum courtesies demanded in this last round of conferences. Glen Madsen, who had a special claim to civility, he had already called. Madsen had sounded harassed. Mrs. Jensen, predictably, was not in. Thatcher, who had been driven to reading the local press by his extended stay in the area, could well believe that anybody invariably described as "the grief-stricken young widow" might choose to disappear. That took care of his real obligations: Mrs. Wahl and Mrs. Holsinger were getting nothing more from him than flowers.

This left, as an irreducible minimum, Frank Krebbel. With luck he might escape the rest of the front office. There was that assistant treasurer . . .

Thatcher was engaged in this uncomplimentary review of the Michigan Motors family when he saw Fabian Riley in the lobby. A sense of something left undone, of some source untapped—which would have been recognized at once by Riley—stirred. He checked it and stepped over to say good-bye.

Riley replied that he was sorry to see Thatcher depart. Then, unable to resist the temptation to talk to another financial specialist, he described Georgeson's suspicions about Glen Madsen with considerable acidity.

"Damned fool," said Thatcher. He was not referring to Captain Georgeson. He understood why the police suspected Madsen; he was merely surprised that Jensen's anomalous position at Michigan Motors had not received more scrutiny.

When he remarked as much, Riley agreed. "But Georgeson has gone overboard for a personal motive. The only thing Madsen can be grateful for is that there isn't enough evidence for an arrest."

On this sober note they parted. Thatcher ascended in the elevator, his sense of well-being evaporated.

He found that his final exchanges with Frank Krebbel were not going to be the pleasant dialogue of luncheon at Guido's Cafeteria. Ed Wahl was in conference with his chief.

"Sorry you're going," said Krebbel when he heard Thatcher's plans. At last he was beginning to show signs of the strain he had been living with since the murder.

Mendaciously Thatcher agreed that it was too bad the press of duty recalled him to the Sloan. He expressed formal regret for the difficulties surrounding the Michigan Motors financing and his belief that after these temporary awkwardnesses were over, MM would grow and prosper.

Ed Wahl, less perceptive than Krebbel, launched a last-minute attempt to sell John Thatcher on the Sloan's participation in this hypothetical stock offering. He too showed signs of stress—bloodshot eyes and unhealthily high color.

Thatcher became aware that ordinary stress was the least of Wahl's problems. He was riding an uneasy course between nervous anxiety and incipient arrogance. He was now firmly ensconced as division manager of Plantagenet; this might explain the arrogance. But not the fear which so clearly accompanied it.

". . . get a copy of those reports for you," said Krebbel, interrupting Wahl. He stabbed a desk button and his secretary materialized. "Miss Shaw, will you get those projected sales figures the division managers sent in? I'd like Mr. Thatcher to have a copy before he goes."

Miss Shaw withdrew, and Thatcher assumed the look of a man who has been promised a pearl of great price. The three men spent the next few moments in conversation dominated by Wahl's ill-timed sales pitch.

". . . and the Planty is a beautiful job," Wahl announced.

"How does Consumers Union like it?" Thatcher inquired provocatively, eliciting an amused glance from Krebbel.

Consumers Union, it appeared, had rocks in its head.

Wahl was about to embroider this when Miss Shaw appeared, reporting that the Division Managers' Projections (Preliminary Report) were not in the file.

Krebbel frowned slightly. "We didn't route it on to Holsinger, did we?"

"I don't know," said Miss Shaw. "I'm sorry, Mr. Krebbel. But with all the excitement, I seem to have forgotten to log it."

"You haven't seen it, have you, Ed?" asked Krebbel. His division manager looked confused. "Listen, Miss Shaw, why don't you call around the divisions? If we can get hold of it, I'd like Mr. Thatcher to have a copy—"

"That's quite all right," interrupted Thatcher hastily. "I assure you it's not necessary."

"Don't give it a second thought," said Wahl before Krebbel could speak. "No trouble at all. Is it, Miss Shaw?"

Miss Shaw, quite naturally, agreed. "I'll try to locate it," she said and withdrew before Thatcher, his uneasy eye on the clock, could protest. If this was the new

Wahl, shored up by position and security, he preferred the old Wahl. So, he suspected, did Frank Krebbel.

But the president of Michigan Motors was too suave an executive to take offense at the usurpation of his position as host to Thatcher and employer of Miss Shaw. Favoring Wahl with an appraising glance, he remained silent.

Thatcher resigned himself to ten minutes more of conversation. After twenty minutes he braced himself to plead flight time. But before he could speak, Miss Shaw erupted into the office.

"Yes?" said Krebbel stiffly.

"Mr. Madsen had it," breathed Miss Shaw.

"Good. Well, if you'll just run off a copy . . ."

"It was in his files," she continued dreamily.

"Fine," said Krebbel.

"And they went to get it, and they found a gun!" Miss Shaw's eyes widened at the recollection.

Speechlessly they stared at her as she put a hand to her cheek.

"Millie was looking through Mr. Madsen's Annual Reports and there, stuffed at the back, was the gun."

"Well, for Chrissake!" said Wahl. "So that's it, after all. Sally told me they had a fight in Ann Arbor."

"Now, wait a minute, Ed. Don't go jumping to conclusions," said Krebbel with forced calm. "You've got no proof that this has anything to do with Jensen. Glen may keep a gun in his office for all sorts of reasons."

"Baloney!" replied Wahl tersely. "I know how you feel, Frank, but this is too big to soft pedal. You're going to have to call the cops."

Before Krebbel could reply, the division manager received unexpected support.

"You don't understand, Mr. Krebbel." Miss Shaw sank onto a nearby couch. As she removed her hand from her pale cheek, red fingermarks were outlined as if she had been struck. "Millie said we shouldn't say anything until we checked. She called personnel and read them the serial number. It's the same gun that was stolen before Mr. Jensen was shot!"

"The damned fool!" Ed Wahl shouted. "But you don't have any option, Frank! Half the plant knows by now."

Krebbel was white. "Yes," he said, almost under his breath. "I don't have any choice. Not now."

No, thought Thatcher, Ed Wahl was making very certain that Krebbel had not the slightest option.

The ensuing two hours were a nightmare. Georgeson, informed of events over the phone by a reluctant Krebbel, had crisply listed a number of impossible demands. These included keeping Glen Madsen ignorant of the afternoon's dramatic discovery, holding incommunicado everybody who did know about it, and not letting anyone near the relevant file cabinet.

For the first time, Thatcher felt the onset of a wave of sympathy for the much-tried management of Michigan Motors. It was apparent that most of Georgeson's injunctions were going to be violated as soon as possible. The least he could do was abstain from exacerbating the situation with an immediate flight from the state. Therefore the five o'clock flight to New York was taking off minus its most enthusiastic passenger by the time Georgeson put in a delayed appearance.

He was accompanied by a representative of the district attorney's office. Although he had postponed his own arrival to seek legal counsel, he took instant exception to similar conduct on Krebbel's part.

"Look here!" he stormed. "I thought I told you to keep this quiet. Now you've spilled the beans to Madsen and brought in your general counsel. That's a hell of a lot of cooperation we're getting from your office!"

Krebbel did not allow himself to be provoked. His voice was deceptively mild as he replied: "It is customary for a corporation to inform its general counsel of its legal problems, Captain."

Georgeson, turning an ugly red, was not going to take this, but his attention was diverted by the general counsel.

Victor Appleby smiled deprecatingly. "I see you have had the foresight to bring a stenographer along, Captain. Would you like to open the record of this interrogation with a statement of your objections to Mr. Madsen being represented by counsel?"

"Certainly not!" snapped the assistant district attorney, mindful of several recent Supreme Court decisions. He directed a look of rebuke at Georgeson and mounted a counterattack. "Captain Georgeson has no such objection. He was merely surprised by the nature of Mr. Madsen's representation. Are we to understand that Mr. Appleby is representing Mr. Madsen in his personal, as well as his corporate capacity?"

The genteel wrangle continued for several minutes, apparently affording considerable satisfaction to the lawyers.

In the meantime the principals measured each other. Georgeson, having refused the offer of a chair, was athletically flexing himself on his toes, glaring triumphantly across the room at Glen Madsen. The economist, drained of color and vitality, was huddled on the sofa, eyeing his tormentor hopelessly.

With the preliminaries over, Georgeson took command.

"All right, Mr. Madsen. There's no point in stalling. Obviously Mr. Krebbel, here, has brought you up to date on the discovery of the gun. And we've got plenty of witnesses covering every minute of that gun since it came out of your file cabinet." He waved to indicate the presence of Millie, Miss Shaw, Wahl, Krebbel, and Thatcher. "So there's no point in claiming we've pulled a fast one. O.K., now what's your story? How did it get there?"

"I don't have any story," said Madsen dully. "I've never seen that gun before in my life."

"Just something the fairies left behind, eh, Mr. Madsen? Who has the keys to that cabinet?"

An exhaustive survey of the security governing file cabiets followed. Madsen had a key. His secretary had a key. In theory, the cabinet was locked whenever the secretary was absent. In fact, a less rigid procedure was employed. The cabinet was left open when the secretary was absent for a few minutes.

"And I suppose just anybody could waltz in and loot your files without being noticed?" asked Georgeson with heavy sarcasm.

"No, I didn't say that. Of course it would have to be someone with legitimate business in my office." Glen Madsen avoided looking around the room. The statement spoke for itself. Only an insider could have acted that way.

Wahl raised his eyebrows and shook his head commiseratingly, heedless of Krebbel's frown.

Georgeson pressed on: "You say you don't know much about guns, Mr. Madsen. But the record shows you were on active duty from 1944 to 1945. . . . Tuesday night? We have witnesses who place that fight on Wednesday night. And Ray Jensen was never seen alive again. . . . What did he threaten you with? Or did you lose your head and just go berserk? . . . Who saw you on Thursday? Where? When? For how long?"

And finally: "All right, Mr. Madsen, you'd better get your hat and coat. We're taking you in."

The departing cavalcade was a sober group, with Victor

Appleby hovering beside his exhausted client. As the doors closed behind them, Ed Wahl gave a great sigh and said: "What a shame. But he was crazy about Celia, you know."

The statement was inoffensive, but the emotion it carried was not regret. It took a moment for Thatcher to identify, then it came. Wahl communicated, as clearly as if in so many words, overriding relief.

15 • Financing Arranged

FOUR DAYS LATER John Putnam Thatcher was at his desk on the sixth floor of the Sloan Guaranty Trust. Nevertheless, despite a barricade of junior trust officers and protective secretaries, he was remote from the convulsions in Detroit only geographically. On Friday the murder weapon had come to light in Glen Madsen's file cabinet. On Saturday Glen Madsen had been charged with first-degree murder. Michigan Motors was as much in the news as if it were suffering a major strike or attempting to raise prices. At the Sloan, at the Empire Club, even on the courts of the West Side Tennis Club, Thatcher found it providing the central topic of conversation with tedious regularity.

It came, therefore, as no surprise that his Tuesday morning conference with the Sloan's chief of research should deal with automotive matters.

"I don't deny that MM has its troubles," said Walter Bowman, making a handsome concession, "but they still have a great potential, John. I understand they've got the inside track on a big contract from NASA. Over at Waymark-Sims they're still optimistic."

"And Glen Madsen's arrest?" asked Thatcher.

"Madsen may have been arrested," Bowman said, "but you can't convince me that he's a murderer. . . ."

"I'm inclined to agree with you," said Thatcher, but Bowman swept on.

". . . the man simply isn't the type. But that's beside the point, John. The fact is, Michigan Motors is going to surprise you. I want us to keep an eye on it."

He continued in this vein at length, showing Thatcher that he was only incidentally concerned with homicide; Bowman's specialist eye remained unwaveringly fixed on the possibility of profit.

"Wait a minute, Walter," said Thatcher when Bowman came to a halt and began preliminary operations to hoist his great bulk from chair to crutches. "What's happened to Bay Vitamins? Phil Cook sent me a report this morning, and I don't like the look of things."

Bowman fell back, dissatisfaction on his normally jovial face. "Bay Vitamins!" he said in tones appropriate to typhoid fever.

Bay Vitamins, a small firm with a dramatic weight-reduction plan—so promising scarcely eight months ago—had encountered rough going. Among its formidable array of adversaries were the American Medical Association, the Food and Drug Administration, and *Reader's Digest*. The net result was that the Sloan's investment, modest to begin with, was daily growing more modest.

"Well, John, here's the story," Bowman began.

As he reviewed the debacle with Bowman, and considered salvage operations likely to appeal to the Sloan Investment Committee, Thatcher felt the familiar satisfaction of being back in harness. Miss Corsa had competently handled the routine documents flooding his desk during his absence, but when he arrived at his office Monday morning, he had found a backlog large enough to keep his thoughts from straying to Michigan Motors—and, more insistently, to Celia Jensen and Glen Madsen. Virtuously he determined to concentrate on business, not murder. Thatcher's report on Michigan Motors, dictated to Miss Corsa at nine thirty Monday morning, was a model critique of its financial situation (with pessimistic overtones) together with a fair summary of the Waymark-Sims position (exclusive of Arnold Berman's more intemperate comments). Thatcher had initialed the report, dispatched it, then resolutely turned to other work.

". . . I'll call Robichaux & Devane," Bowman said, referring to the underwriters who had sold Bay Vitamins to the Sloan. "But as things stand now, I recommend that we sell. Unless there's any possibility of a merger."

"We should cut our losses now," said Thatcher authoritatively, rejecting the comfort of wishful thinking.

Bowman sighed and struggled to his feet. "I suppose so. Oh, by the way," he added transparently, "I understand that Arnie Berman flew out to Detroit again."

Thatcher shook his head. "Only a personal trip, Walter. Berman is a friend of Mrs. Jensen's, and she's in some distress about . . . these latest developments. His trip has nothing to do with business."

"I see," said Bowman, all innocence. "I just wondered,

you know. Hugh Waymark is still all for Michigan Motors. I thought maybe Arnie was going to settle things. . . . Well, I'd better get back to work. I'll let you know about Bay Vitamins."

Thatcher watched him leave and again shook his head, this time at the tenacity of the financial man. Then, obediently implementing his plans to clear his desk, he returned to the encyclopedic document that had been forwarded to him by the indefatigable Everett Gabler, senior trust officer. Idly Thatcher flicked the pages of what appeared to be an exhaustive historical review of the Sloan's training programs. His eye fell on Gabler's comparison of personnel procedures in the Investment Division with those in the Trust Department; it came as no great surprise to him that Gabler found those of the Trust Department immeasurably superior. Skipping several pages, Thatcher reached the climax of the treatise, a searching analysis of personnel techniques of the future, entitled: "Projected Standards of Selection under Various Assumptions of Size of Staff over the Next Decade."

"Why am I reading this?" Thatcher murmured, pushing the buzzer for his secretary.

Miss Corsa, dictation pad in hand, presented herself.

"No, I don't want to dictate," said Thatcher. "Miss Corsa, what is the reason for this enormous report that Gabler has produced?"

"I'll ring for Mr. Gabler," said Miss Corsa, depositing a newspaper on his desk.

"Oh, no!" said Thatcher brutally before she could leave. Not only did he intend to avoid an extended conference with Gabler—and all conferences with Gabler were extended—he enjoyed extracting information from Miss Corsa. "Sit down, Miss Corsa. I want to know why Mr. Gabler sent me this thing. There must be a reason. I don't know what it is—but I have every confidence that you do."

Miss Corsa, very dignified, protested. "Really, Mr. Thatcher . . ."

"That won't do, Miss Corsa," said Thatcher at his sternest. "I respect the high professional manner with which you discharge your duties, and I realize that most of your vast information about the Sloan is not for my ears—please don't interrupt. But simply as a time-saving device, this time I am going to have to ask you to tell me what this Gabler business is about. You do not have to reveal your sources."

He was pleased to see Miss Corsa stunned by his flow of eloquence. "Come, come, Miss Corsa," he said, pressing his advantage.

Miss Corsa capitulated. Mr. Gabler had been summoned to Bradford Withers' suite last week, it developed, during one of that executive's descents upon the bank (between stints of deep-sea fishing in the Bahamas and slaloms at Gstaad, so to speak). Mr. Gabler had emerged from his interview rigid with indignation—so moved, in fact, that it had been two days before the secretarial staff learned the provocation: Mr. Withers had asked Mr. Gabler to consider the possibility of Sloan employment for a youthful connection graduating from the Harvard Business School in June.

"His nephew, Bud," said Thatcher appreciatively. He had been privileged to meet young Gilbert Withers Austin.

"Yes," said Miss Corsa repressively. "I understand that Mr. Withers thinks he might be useful in Rails and Industrials."

"Yes," said Thatcher with gravity. "Well, we'll let Mr. Gabler fight his own battles. A man with his experience should be able to slough this youth off onto Trinkam."

Miss Corsa unbent. "Mr. Trinkam has also been with Mr. Withers," she confided. *"He's* preparing a memorandum for your attention too, I understand. Is that all, Mr. Thatcher?"

Thatcher waved release and devoted a moment to the menace of Bud Austin—youthful, ponderous, and probably unavoidable. He came from a family with a high sense of public duty, of course. Possibly it might be wise to suggest that a career in government—say, the United States Senate—would be more worthy of his talents. After all, the concept of on-the-job training had expanded since Thatcher's apprenticeship at the bank.

The headline of the afternoon newspaper erased Thatcher's smile.

MM OFFICER CHARGED WITH LOVE NEST SLAYING, it screamed.

The two photographs on the front page showed Madsen surrounded by guards, and Mrs. Jensen, behind a large hat and dark glasses, as they had appeared at Madsen's arraignment. Celia Jensen had decided to come out from hiding, regardless of notoriety and scandal, in order to support her lover. Poor woman!

Of course she had Berman out there with her. But this was a time when a friendly call might mean a good deal. Thatcher's efforts to reach her before leaving Detroit had been abortive, the secretary at the Rectory being unwilling to reveal Mrs. Jensen's whereabouts. It was worth a try. Within minutes Miss Corsa had him connected with Louise Burns, who agreed that talking with Thatcher might be good for Celia and produced her sister.

"Oh, Mr. Thatcher! You know that they've arrested Glen for murder!"

Thatcher agreed that he knew and asked how bad things were.

"The lawyers are impossible. They started out by trying to persuade Glen to plead guilty on a manslaughter charge, to claim that Ray stole the gun and brought it to the fight."

Thatcher's brows contracted. If that were so, then the prosecution's case must be airtight. "That doesn't sound encouraging," he agreed.

"Thank goodness, they've changed their minds."

"Oh?"

"Yes, when they heard the outlines of the prosecution case at the arraignment. Apparently they feel that the shift in murder time is a good thing for Glen."

"You mean the police have abandoned the idea of a Wednesday night fight? I thought they were pushing that."

"They were. But there was a fraternity party down the street on Tuesday. Three of the students went to headquarters to say they saw the fight on Tuesday. It seemed so wonderful at the time. I thought all our troubles were over."

"I suppose the police now claim that the murder was an aftermath of the quarrel."

"Yes, they say Ray was shot out at the Plantagenet plant on Wednesday afternoon." She broke off as her breath caught on a convulsive sob. "They'll say anything, as long as they can accuse Glen. But at least the lawyers agree now that Glen should fight every inch of the way."

That, of course, was both good and bad. Either the lawyers felt this time shift indicated weakness in the prosecution's case or, alternatively, that it was hopeless to plead absence of premeditation when the victim had been killed the next day rather than in the heat of battle.

Thatcher did not relay these doubts to Celia Jensen. Instead he expressed muted joy at this turn in events, sympathy for the participants, and an eagerness to be of service in any way possible.

After hanging up, he returned to the newspaper for a closer perusal. If the murder had taken place at Plantagenet on Wednesday afternoon, he reflected with a start, it must have coincided closely with his own tour of the plant. Then the body had been bundled into the Plantagenet—and he well recalled its gleaming isolation in the basement garage—or wait! Thatcher reread the paragraph; these journalists were masters of inexact language: ". . . shot Jensen Wednesday, May 16, at MM's Plantagenet plant, concealed the body in the back seat of the Super Plantagenet. . . ."

Thatcher scowled. It seemed hard to believe that anybody in his right mind would take the chance of shooting Jensen in a well-lighted plant where two shifts worked regularly, then lugging his body to the car. True, the car was so grotesquely long that it afforded opportunities for concealment, but still . . .

What if Jensen had been killed in the car?

The more Thatcher thought about it, the more convinced he became that this must have been how it happened. Surely the police had laboratory proof by now. It made the whole thing more plausible; two men, wishing to talk privately, casually seating themselves in the Plantagenet. A quarrel—a shot—somebody slumped down . . .

But then, Thatcher reflected, following this train of thought, what about the two men who drove the Plantagenet to the Michigan Motors pool on Thursday? And the crowds that milled around it?

"Pfa!" he said irritably, tossing the paper onto his desk.

"What are you pfa-ing about, John?" inquired an interested Charlie Trinkam from the doorway. "Miss Corsa told me to come in."

"Come in, Charlie," said Thatcher, wrenching his thoughts from Glen Madsen. "I warn you that I am in no mood to waste time talking about Withers' nephew. . . ."

"No, no," said Charlie hurriedly. He had taken his own reading of Thatcher's expression. "I can handle that. It's this Maryland Fund Report," he said, handing Thatcher a blue-jacketed file. "They've just hired a new chief of research, and I want you to tell me if I'm crazy, or if he is."

Silence reigned, except for Miss Corsa's distant typing,

while Thatcher scanned the document that Trinkam proffered. Unexpectedly it provided comic relief.

The Maryland Fund, if its report could be credited, was convinced that disarmament was around the corner; in consequence, it was initiating a program of selling all stocks and bonds remotely connected with rockets, missiles, airplanes, communications, and military contracts.

"And the strange thing," said Thatcher when he digested this, "is that this may be a good time to sell. I don't like the looks of the market, Charlie. These people may be covering their pessimism."

"I don't like the market either," Charlie said, "but if you'll read on, you'll see that the Maryland Fund is investing heavily in discount houses, prefabs, and textiles."

"Good Lord!" said Thatcher. "What's happened to them?"

What had happened, explained Charlie, was that the Maryland Fund had hired a new research chief. Before hiring him, however, they had subjected all the candidates to psychological tests.

"Well, you know what that means," said Charlie. "Everybody from Wall Street registered strong homicidal tendencies, so they hired this nut boy from Boston. . . . He's above average in normalcy, I understand. . . ."

"We'd better warn our people," said Thatcher just as Miss Corsa buzzed.

"Mr. Withers on the phone."

"I thought he was going to Switzerland," grumbled Thatcher. "Hello, Brad? Fine, good. . . . Yes. . . . Yes, I'm free for dinner. . . . What? Oh, good, I'll see you both. . . ." Charlie Trinkam was silently interrogative as Thatcher glowered at the phone.

"I am dining with Brad and Hugh Waymark," Thatcher responded irascibly. "You know what that means, don't you? It means that eternal dunderhead Waymark has corralled Brad—who did go to Switzerland, by the way, but unfortunately came back—and now Brad is convinced that Michigan Motors is the buy of the century."

Prudently Charlie agreed that this was a net addition to the considerable difficulties of running the Trust and Investment divisions of the Sloan Guaranty Trust. He took his departure without giving his opinion, which was that, on the whole, he too was inclined to think well of Michigan Motors.

Thatcher was left to simmer in his own wrath. His essential fair-mindedness only contributed to his irritation. Despite antitrust convictions, murder investigations, and executive arrests, it was still possible that Michigan Motors might have a good financial year. The stock market, particularly in this long slide, was unpredictable.

If in the general decline of the glamour stocks Michigan Motors, old, established, and expanding, appealed to buyers being burned by whiz-bang outfits, then the Sloan Guaranty Trust might well profit from participation in the new issue.

Things being what they were, John Putnam Thatcher found the prospect completely distasteful.

16 • Overtime

DINNER AT KEEN'S CHOP HOUSE with Bradford Withers, president of the Sloan Guaranty Trust, and Hugh Waymark, a senior partner of Waymark-Sims, did not allay John Thatcher's premonitions.

"On Monday her husband showed up at the chalet." Withers poised knife over plate and assumed the expression of an indignant bloodhound. "On the chairlift she never said a word about expecting him!"

Waymark shook his head sadly. "Terrible," he said. "Still, I envy you, Brad. Skiing must be great exercise. Out of the question with my tricky heart, of course."

Although his well-schooled features remained bland, Thatcher was conscious of burgeoning resentment. The conversation of his colleagues depressed him. Not that he deplored the anecdotal ribaldry of the one—all of Brad Withers' chance-met women had husbands speeding to their side—or sympathized with the ailments of the other—after all, Hugh Waymark had never seen fit to go skiing during the fifty years preceding his heart attack.

No, it was simply that he had good reason to mistrust this small talk. Withers' jollying him along could mean only one thing, Thatcher knew.

The dinner conversation had commenced with a spirited overture on the atrocities contemplated by the Port Authority. ("The real estate boys have just about had it. . . ." "Twin towers with a hundred and ten stories, for God's sake! You know what that'll do to the vacancy rate around City Hall? . . ." "Of course they're playing their tax edge for all it's worth.") Withers' experience on the *piste* had served as flourish; now his running mate was introducing the major theme.

"Heard from Berman today," Waymark remarked casually.

"Oh, yes? And what did he have to say?" asked Withers.

"He expects MM to be going through with its new issue.

135

Things are really shaking down out there since Madsen was arrested."

Thatcher was noncommittal. "That seems natural."

"Of course everybody realizes, now, that Jensen's murder had nothing to do with the company. Just a simple case of one man after another man's wife."

"Terrible, terrible," muttered Withers, momentarily forgetful of alpine chairlifts.

"So you see," continued Waymark persuasively, turning a deaf ear to his supporter, "MM has really been an innocent bystander. You can't hold them responsible if one of their men goes out and commits a crime."

"That's exactly the defense they used in the price-fixing case," Thatcher was provoked into retorting, "and much good it did them."

Waymark pushed his pilsener glass to one side and addressed himself seriously to the task of placating the head of the Sloan's Investment Division.

"Now, John," he said, "you know it's not the same sort of thing at all. If a man goes out and fixes prices, he's acting in the company's interests, but murder—well, that's something else entirely."

Thatcher broke in to say that, as nearly as he could tell, Jensen's murderer might have been acting in the interests of humanity. Waymark tut-tutted this frivolity, and Withers helpfully reminded them that every company expects its management to infringe antitrust laws. Thatcher allowed himself a fleeting vision of Bradford Withers at the head of a vast marketing organization, then turned to the business at hand.

"Very well," he said, "I grant you, if Madsen is the murderer, it is remotely possible the stock won't be affected."

"What do you mean 'if'?" complained Withers. "The police have arrested him."

"Did Berman have anything to say about it when you spoke with him?"

"Arnie said the situation was very fluid," Waymark temporized.

Thatcher reminded himself to call Detroit and get Berman's opinion firsthand. Waymark was far too experienced to act as a conduit for information detrimental to his product. In the meantime all Thatcher could do was fight a delaying action.

"Even so, we're just where we were four weeks ago,"

he said, "which still doesn't make Michigan Motors an ideal investment."

"No, we've got more information now." Waymark leaned back with visible satisfaction. "When you went out there, all we had was the first-quarter report. Well, they've just shown Berman the sales figures for April and May. Now, you know, Arnie's never been enthusiastic about the whole MM setup. But even he admits you couldn't ask for anything better. Sales are booming."

Thatcher closed his eyes. It was of course typical of Michigan Motors that, at this juncture, they should turn in a spectacular sales performance. Undeterred by notoriety, management dissension, and murder, somewhere a band of dedicated salesmen was doing its job and doing it well. It was the kind of factor one could all too easily forget in the insulated environment of a front office. Frank Krebbel, while prepared to use a light hand in dealing with the machinations of his immediate subordinates, obviously reserved his real efforts for the business of designing salable models and then selling them. As a potential investor Thatcher honored this judicious selectivity. It might, after all, be necessary to reconsider the entire Michigan Motors situation.

Waymark was far too wise to disturb these internal communings. He refreshed himself with a quaff of Wurtzburger and a warning motion for silence at Withers.

After a moment of suspense Thatcher shook his head and looked at his two companions irritably.

"Yes," he said, "that makes a real difference."

"Knew you'd see it our way," Withers congratulated him. "It's the opportunity of a lifetime."

"In any event," said Waymark, with a caution he knew would recommend itself to Thatcher more than his chief's enthusiasm, "I think you'll agree that it might be worthwhile taking another look at MM. Why not go back to Detroit? They're digging out all their information for Berman, anyway."

In future days Thatcher was to maintain that his return trip to Detroit was the result of pressure from on high and in no way attributable to personal dissatisfaction with the publicly accepted solution to the murder of Raymond Jensen.

Vice-presidents of the Sloan Guaranty Trust do not simply hurl themselves onto the nearest available airplane when they decide to go to Detroit. Particularly when the market is falling rapidly enough to give men under forty-five a new insight into the nature of 1929. Thatcher's next day was devoted to an intensive review of the Sloan's market position, with all the ancillary effects that this sort of activity entails.

First, and most important, the Sloan made a major move into the bond market. Second, and even more inevitable, frayed tempers appeared on the sixth floor with increasing frequency as the day progressed. Everett Gabler was reduced to speechlessness by a call from a client, even testier than himself, who made a practice of keeping his funds briskly circulating in short-term Treasury notes, and took this occasion to congratulate himself. Charlie Trinkam, the soul of camaraderie, was driven to snarling at an alarmed visitor that people who insisted on investing in United States Steel had to take Roger Blough as they found him. At four o'clock Walter Bowman exploded from his lair to defend the Research staff against a series of unusually acrimonious accusations; he found Gabler in a mood to take on all comers. The ensuing scene, conducted before a spellbound audience of two stenographers and four visiting Japanese dignitaries, was destined to find its place in the institutional folklore of the Sloan.

John Putnam Thatcher, in addition to trying to control the energies of his pugnacious subordinates, spent the day working his way through a monumental agenda. Seven o'clock found him sitting in his office during a temporary lull, recalling his intention to telephone Arnold Berman. He eyed the door to his outer office appraisingly. Relations between himself and Miss Corsa had hit a new low at five thirty when he presented her with fifteen pages of handwritten statistical manuscript and the news that the resulting typewritten product must be hand-delivered that evening.

It was not the work. Miss Corsa, a virtuoso of the typewriter, was ever willing to sacrifice herself to the call of duty. There was, it appeared, a technical snag.

"But, Mr. Thatcher," she protested, "how can I get anybody to proofread at this hour?" Her tone made it clear that simple consideration on the part of her employer—with regard to a problem she had often been required to bring to his attention—would have enabled her to secure the services of an assistant well before closing time.

On a normal day Thatcher would have advanced an apology, and that would have been that. This, however, had not been a normal day.

"Surely you can find someone to do it with you," he said briskly. "There are still people around. I can hear the typewriters."

Miss Corsa bridled. "They are staying because they have their own work to do," she said unanswerably. "And all these numbers have to be proofed."

She looked at him meaningfully. Attempts on the part of secretaries to inject menial tasks into the lives of their nominal superiors are never-ending.

But Thatcher was both experienced and wily. "Then you'll just have to find somebody on another floor," he said, washing his hands of the entire affair. Nothing in the world would induce him to go through that report once more. It had been occasioned by a panic-stricken call from the trustees of a large corporate pension fund. The conversation had resulted in a demand for an instantaneous analysis of their extensive portfolio, coupled with a hysterical threat to leave the market entirely. Just where they planned to go was not clear.

Thatcher examined his phone longingly. It would be simpler to call Detroit himself than to deal with an unappeased Miss Corsa. On the other hand, she would certainly view any such antic behavior on his part as an act of aggression amounting to open war. Therefore he advanced toward the door. Mere prudence suggested that his request be delivered in person rather than over the intercom. Happily he could hear a reassuring drone from the outer office, which indicated that some helot had been dragooned.

He cleared his throat. "Er . . . Miss Corsa?"

Miss Corsa looked up. So did her companion. Thatcher beheld an apparition, surely not more than sixteen years old, decked out in lavender eye shadow, bobby sox, and an elaborately curled mop of luxuriant black hair.

"This," said Miss Corsa, "is Miss Tourene, who has kindly agreed to help me. This is Mr. Thatcher."

The apparition shifted its wad of chewing gum.

"Pleased to meetcha," it said cordially.

"We're very grateful for your assistance," replied Thatcher with *empressement*.

"It's nothing." An airy wave of the hand relieved Thatcher of all obligation. "My boy friend isn't picking me up until eight, anyway."

"Splendid," said Thatcher heartily. "When you have a moment, Miss Corsa, perhaps you could get me Mr. Berman in Detroit."

"Certainly, Mr. Thatcher." Miss Corsa could be relied upon to maintain his prestige in public.

Well, if it was a matter of prestige, the least he could do was keep his end up. Pausing in the doorway, he bowed ceremoniously—once to his secretary and once to her improbable assistant.

The apparition grinned appreciatively. Then, the formalities over, she returned to the work at hand. As Thatcher closed the door, he could hear her rasping voice:

"In the fourth column here, it should be nine hundred and seventy-three, not nine hundred and forty-three. . . ."

Clearly, that report would be delivered tonight, come hell or high water. Thatcher was still recovering from his exposure to Miss Corsa's ruthless press-gang tactics when Arnold Berman came on the line.

"John? Hugh Waymark called today. He said you'd be coming out again."

"If the sales figures are as good as he claims," replied Thatcher cautiously.

"Oh, the sales are all right." Berman's voice conjured up a host of considerations which were not.

Thatcher was in no mood for equivocation. "Well, then, what's wrong?"

"Jensen's murder," said Arnie bluntly. "I don't think Madsen did it, and I wouldn't be surprised if the whole thing blew up again."

"You've been talking to Celia Jensen," said Thatcher with equal bluntness. "Are you sure that . . ."

"It's not just that. When you get out here, I think you ought to talk to Riley. He isn't influenced by Cele."

"Riley? You mean the Department of Justice man?"

"That's right. He knows more about the front office at MM than they do themselves, and he's convinced that Jensen was murdered to keep him from talking."

Thatcher was dubious. "He may be riding his hobby-horse."

"Sure he may be. But did you know that Jensen was threatening to start a real hunt for whoever gave the feds the tip on the conspiracy?"

"Oh, so that's the way the wind blows." He frowned

into space as he recalled MM's general reluctance to speculate on the rapid promotions following Ray Jensen's downfall. "It makes sense," he admitted. "That murder was certainly convenient for someone."

"Exactly. And Glen Madsen is one of the few people up there who didn't stand to gain or lose a thing from the antitrust trial. That's what makes Riley think everything is too pat. Anybody could have dumped that gun in Madsen's file. He was the obvious fall guy."

It was also obvious that Berman was firmly enlisted in the pro-Madsen forces—a group not to be despised, if it included the Department of Justice.

"Doesn't Riley have any idea where that tip originated?"

"No. But he's putting his records through a sieve again. You really ought to come out."

"I have no choice," said Thatcher with acidity. "Waymark and Withers between them seem to cherish an ineradicable affection for Michigan Motors."

Berman's moroseness made itself felt across a thousand miles. "Well, the way things are going, MM will probably make a mint even if its whole management goes to the chair."

That really settled the whole thing. Promising to arrive some time the next day, Thatcher rang off and buzzed imperatively. When his secretary presented herself, he announced his forthcoming departure and his need for a plane seat. Silently she made a note.

"By the way, where in the world did you find Miss Whatsername?" He gestured toward the outer office.

"At the Acme Mail Service, which rents the fourteenth floor. Miss Tourene," the name was enunciated clearly, "is both helpful and conscientious." Miss Corsa was coldly reprimanding. Her voice suggested that these were qualities conspicuously lacking in some she could name.

Thatcher reconciled himself to the fact that Miss Tourene, eye shadow and all, was now numbered among the many objects Miss Corsa felt obliged to protect against the depredations of her employer.

"I am going to Detroit to visit Michigan Motors, a company of which you would approve," said Thatcher smoothly. "There they shoot objectionable executives."

Miss Corsa was not amused.

17 • Stop, Look, and Listen

ON WEDNESDAY Thatcher flew to Detroit. He was met at the airport by Arnold Berman, puffing his cigar with rare vigor. "You in a hurry to get out to MM?" he asked conspiratorially as he led Thatcher to the lot where a beaming Mack had illegally double-parked the waiting Sceptre.

"What alternatives can you suggest?" asked Thatcher. Berman was not, he knew, the man for idle sarcasm.

"Bloomfield Hills," Berman directed Mack. As they swung out of the airport, he expanded further. "We're having a conference, John. I'd like you to be there. Riley and I got to talking the other day. . . ."

A gathering of the forces believing in Glen Madsen's innocence was convened for three o'clock. Ironically it was to take place at Ray Jensen's home, the only site remote from curious eyes. Celia Jensen, hounded by the press since Madsen's arrest, had taken refuge in her own home. The civic authorities of Bloomfield Hills, while deprecating murder, reserved their strongest disciplinary action for those intruding journalistic vulgarities into the community.

"I see," said Thatcher. "Are you getting much support from Michigan Motors?"

Berman's lips twisted. "Like hell we are! They're all so relieved that the pressure's off, they could barely get out a company statement withholding judgment." He glared at his cigar. "And let me tell you, John, some of them make me sick! That poisonous Holsinger woman, for example. She's going around saying, isn't it too bad, but Madsen's been chasing Celia for years."

"Is her husband saying anything?" asked Thatcher.

"Not a damned thing," said Berman angrily. "He and Wahl and the whole bunch . . ."

"What about Frank Krebbel?"

Berman shook his head.

Thatcher frowned slightly. "You know, I was with Krebbel the day they found the gun, and I got the distinct impression that he couldn't believe Madsen was guilty. After all, planting the gun in his files wouldn't have been impossibly difficult. Krebbel isn't a fool, by a long shot. I should think he'd be a good man to have on your side."

Berman shook his head doubtfully as Mack turned off the expressway. As an index of rising income levels, trees began to appear at the roadside, their delicate greenery arching overhead. Thatcher would have known they were nearing Bloomfield Hills even if it had been midnight.

"You're right," Berman said. "But Krebbel isn't in a position to help us, no matter what he thinks privately. And he's really busy these days." This led to extended discussion during the remainder of the drive concerning the business aspects of Berman's sojourn in Detroit. He did not share Hugh Waymark's simple-minded enthusiasm, but he agreed with his superior that MM sales were going to yield a higher net than he, for one, had anticipated; spectacular performance by Holsinger's Buccaneers, together with expanded military contracts, accounted for the improvement. Despite everything, management had effected a respectable cost-cutting program. Financially speaking, Michigan Motors looked like a good bet.

"If anything does these days," said Thatcher. "What's that?"

For Mack had braked at a modified road block: a police cruiser, parked on the side street with a policeman leaning against its fender. He was carefully watching the passing traffic, occasionally—as witnessed by a car at the side of the road—flagging one to a halt.

"They're checking up on who goes near the Jensen place," reported Mack when the policeman gestured them to proceed. "They had a lot of trouble when Mr. Madsen was arrested—complaints about the damage the reporters did to the lawn. And one guy from a Chicago paper tried to break into the house—only he picked the wrong one. Then there were people just cruising around, looking. They kept throwing beer cans. . . ."

"Do they know you? Is that why they didn't stop us?" Thatcher asked.

"Mr. Thatcher! *You're in a Plantagenet!*" Mack turned, a little sharply, into the winding driveway of a long, low house characterized by the half-timbering and casement windows of pretentious mock-Tudor. It was all very reminiscent of Riverdale, New York, in the thirties, except that this house had been saved from banality by the absence of frizzled bushes and cluttered borders. Only a giant willow swayed gently in the breeze on the smooth green lawns stretching back to woodland. At a guess, Thatcher would have said that the late, unlamented Ray Jensen had decided upon the house and left the landscaping to his wife.

She greeted them at the door, thinner than Thatcher remembered. "Arnie! And Mr. Thatcher! It's wonderful of you to come. Do come in. . . ."

As they followed her across the hall to a sunken living room, they caught glimpses of shrouded furniture and dust-coated oak paneling. The house had been empty a long time, and whatever arrangements its owners had made for the upkeep of the grounds had not been extended to the interior. The general air of abandonment was further emphasized by the gritty small-paned windows grudgingly admitting the light of a clear spring afternoon and, in the process, transforming it into a pallid murk suggestive of the closing scenes of *Götterdämmerung*.

In the living room there were signs of effort. Chintz slip covers and masses of spring flowers fought a rearguard action against the all-enveloping gloom. And from the shadows under a small minstrels' gallery, Fabian Riley emerged, pencil in hand, an array of papers on the table beside him. "I'm glad you came. I've been hoping we could get together for some time," he said, shaking hands with Thatcher. Then he looked questioningly at Berman, who was settling himself on the sofa next to Celia. "I don't know if Mr. Berman has told you . . ."

"John is convinced that Glen Madsen is innocent," Berman said firmly.

"I am," Thatcher agreed, earning a warm smile from Celia. "But I'm not sure what you—or we—can do. The police are satisfied with their case—"

"All they care about is arresting somebody! It's so unfair," she burst out. "Dragging Glen through this, just because we want to get married. He's the last man on earth . . ."

John Thatcher cleared his throat. "Mrs. Jensen," he said, "as long as you have brought the matter up, would you mind explaining . . . that is, were you actually separated from your husband?"

Both Riley and Berman looked respectful.

Celia Jensen snorted. "It was impossible to be separated from Ray," she said. "I left him and was starting to think about divorce last summer. Then after he was indicted, he called me. Of course I had to stand by during the trial, and I couldn't very well divorce him while he was in jail. But I wrote to him and explained that this was all just a delay, that I hadn't changed my mind! Then . . ."

"Yes?"

"I should have known better. Ray paid absolutely no attention. He came out to Lansing and said I had to come back here. It would make things look better at the company. Then I knew Glen had been right—Ray would always find some reason why I had to come back temporarily . . . for six months . . . for a year . . . and it would go on and on, with Ray considering nothing but how a divorce would affect his position at Michigan Motors, while Glen and I got older and older. I had it out with him. I wasn't going to wait anymore. So you see, Glen didn't have any reason to kill him. We didn't care what Ray did, or what the company did, or what anybody thought. . . ."

"Now take it easy, Cele," said Berman, patting her hand. "No use getting excited. This is the situation, John. Celia here is convinced that Glen is innocent—no, don't interrupt, Cele—because she loves him. Riley and I, on the other hand, are concerned about the business side of the whole thing."

"You mean that the motive is in the company?" Thatcher said. He was delighted to leave the subject of Ray Jensen's personal life in favor of his professional activities; in view of Mrs. Jensen's comments, however, he could not believe the prosecuting attorney would feel the same.

"That's it," said Berman, puffing his cigar to a satisfactory kindle. "We thought that by pooling our resources—and our confidential information about MM—we might come up with something."

"Highly unethical," said Thatcher, amused. This caused both Riley and Mrs. Jensen to break into a spirited defense of the propriety—or the justifiable impropriety—of such behavior. "No, no," he said hastily. "Merely a pleasantry. What do you hope to gain?"

"What we hope to gain," Riley said precisely, "is the following: evidence which Georgeson and the police are not equipped to understand, that will lead to Madsen's release—"

"Oh, we must, we simply must," whispered Celia. Berman again squeezed her hand.

". . . or," Riley continued, "a really excellent defense

for Madsen. It's probably unlikely that we can get him released, but we can give his attorney—"

Eagerly Celia interrupted to say: "We've retained Leo Chastens. They say he's a brilliant criminal lawyer. . . ."

"But this kind of business detail isn't the sort of thing Chastens could dig up himself," Riley concluded. "When we've got our facts straight, we'll talk to him."

"I see," said Thatcher temperately. Had Mrs. Jensen not been present, he would have added that Glen Madsen's prospects were unpromising, to say the least.

Riley consulted a paper. "Now, Mr. Berman and I were discussing the conspiracy conviction. We agree that it must figure in the murder. We decided that the sensible thing to do is to review the Department of Justice information."

Celia Jensen, Thatcher could see at a glance, would connive at the fracture of virtually any law to free Glen Madsen. Love is a powerful force—as the Michigan State Police recognized. Arnold Berman was strong on family feeling. Skeptical by nature, indolent by inclination, he nevertheless exerted himself to help a lifelong friend of his wife.

But Fabian Riley? Thatcher, watching the thin young man rearrange papers, decided that the force moving him was probably a disinterested attachment to the cause of justice.

In many ways this was as heartening as the discovery of managerial competence at Michigan Motors.

". . . so we had been interested in the automotive industry for a long time. The question was how to prove conspiracy. Our investigators uncovered a lot of economic information about price fixing, but the courts demand hard evidence on collusion."

Arnold Berman, of Waymark-Sims, exchanged a look with John Putnam Thatcher, vice-president of the Sloan Guaranty Trust. Two men who knew more about pricing policies in American industry would be hard to find.

"Then, out of the blue, we got everything we wanted. On the morning of March twentieth, a brown manila envelope addressed to the Assistant Attorney General, Antitrust Division, Department of Justice—with a Detroit postmark of March eighteenth."

"Whoever addressed it knows who's in charge of antitrust activities," Berman pointed out.

Riley nodded. "Yes. Up at MM I know that they suspected the clerks, but the department has assumed that it was someone much more sophisticated. We don't know, of course . . ."

"What about tracing the typewriter?" Mrs. Jensen asked. "You said that the address was typed."

"Officially our story is that we had no reason to trace it." Riley swept on without a blush. He had already made his decisions about revealing inside information and could only hope that Julian Summers would approve. "But we established it was done on a coin-rental typewriter in the YMCA downtown. We went even further than that. One of our men traced the photostats—to a copying machine at the main branch of the library, again a coin-operated job."

Celia slumped back dejectedly. "He certainly wasn't taking any chances."

"Oh, our friend was careful, all right," said Riley. "Anyway, in the envelope were copies of your husband's handwritten notes of the March fifteenth meeting. It was an important meeting and lasted two days. You see, they knew they were going to have to correspond with each other, at least on a minimal basis. And nowadays one of the problems in a big company is keeping incriminating documents out of the files. You know all the classic stories —the sales manager who's instructed all his area supervisors to burn their correspondence with a competitor, so they burn the correspondence and file the manager's instructions. Or the files on a proposed merger that contains answers to questions in letters that have been destroyed. Or the memos with a big circulation list where the company's lawyers get hold of all but one copy. Well, the long and short of it is that Jensen and his pals decided to play it smart, and work out a code that made their letters look harmless. Then everything could go into the file, and they'd keep the code at home. Jensen's notes had that code and all the names. Once we had the code, it was easy enough to keep track of them and their meetings. And, of course, we had a field day when we subpoenaed their files."

As he spoke, Thatcher was examining the photostats; handwritten jottings, with names and numbers listed in neat columns. "Tcha," he said disapprovingly.

"Well, they had to keep some records," said Berman indulgently, reaching for the documents. "Tell me, Cele, what did Ray do when he came back from one of these meetings? What was the procedure?"

Mrs. Jensen shook her head helplessly. "Arnie, I never knew a thing about it. Ray didn't talk to me about business . . . and we haven't been close for the last few years. I thought these were just ordinary business trips."

Riley, a bit embarrassed, said, "We looked into it. What happened was that Jensen and Holsinger would go to one of these meetings. Then Jensen would bring back some short notes—he acted as secretary, really—and write up a memo and have it circulated—"

"But Orin Dunn?" Thatcher interjected, recalling that unhappy young man.

Riley explained that Dunn, as a subordinate, had not been part of the inner brain trust. He had no role in making policy; his job had been to police its execution. On occasion he had also acted as decoy; for instance, registering under Jensen's name in New York when a meeting was taking place in Chicago.

"It doesn't seem fair that he had to go to jail, too," said Celia. "Not that I ever liked him. Orin is a cold-blooded boy on the way up. . . ."

"He is," said Berman, "but not at MM anymore. He's quit, you know."

Celia Jensen was genuinely surprised. "I thought he lived and breathed Michigan Motors."

Once again Riley reflected the thoroughness of the Department of Justice. "It was resign or get fired," he said. "Jensen—I beg your pardon, Mrs. Jensen—was trying to get rid of him. And I gather that after the murder Dunn felt he had even less of a future at MM—" His words gave him food for thought; he broke off abruptly.

"Is Holsinger in the same position?" Berman asked after a pause.

Buck Holsinger was in no immediate danger, said Riley, rather abstractedly. He was a division manager—and a very successful one, at that. It made a difference. And he had a rich wife, a wife who was very active on his behalf.

"That's one way of putting it," said Thatcher, recalling his encounters with Mrs. Holsinger. "I interrupted you, though. What did Jensen do with these notes? After he brought them back, I mean."

Jensen had been in the habit of giving them to his secretary to be coded and transcribed. Invariably she was asked to do it at home so that no unauthorized personnel could catch sight of her work.

"Naturally," Fabian Xerxes Riley said stiffly, "we investigated Miss Price very thoroughly. We are convinced that she was totally innocent."

"Naturally," Thatcher said. He recalled the attractive Miss Price very well.

Riley became human. "And if Susan was the tipster, I'll eat my hat."

"Of course not. But couldn't she make a rather shrewd guess who was?"

"You don't understand." Bafflement settled on Riley's features. "To Susan they're little tin gods—Jensen, Wahl, the whole bunch of them. They can do no wrong. And as for the ones she genuinely likes, such as Madsen—" He drew a deep breath and ran a hand through his hair. "Take Krebbel, for instance."

As Riley recounted Miss Price's tribute to Krebbel's conduct in their contretemps, a decided vein of rancor entered the narrative. Like most men, he was not fond of having held up to him a beau ideal of which he must inevitably fall short.

Thatcher repressed a grin. He had no difficulty in identifying the younger man's emotions.

Riley ended abruptly. "Dunn's the only one she doesn't have a good word for."

"That seems to be beyond all of us."

Berman, rising to help Celia with a tray of drinks, said that he didn't understand how Ed Wahl, for example, or Frank Krebbel—or even Glen Madsen—could claim to be ignorant of the fact that Michigan Motors was up to its ears in price fixing.

Celia Jensen, hostess rather than distraught woman, answered him. The corporate world was just that—a world complete with rival factions, with top secrets, with divided interests. Executive A, expecting benefits from certain developments, might very well hide them from Executive B.

"Be specific," said Berman, handing Thatcher a Scotch and water.

"Take the current feud," Celia said. Her guests looked at her blankly. "Didn't you know? I ran into Audrey Wahl the other day. Apparently Ed and his whole division are at the throat of the Publicity Department."

"Lincoln Hauser," said Thatcher appreciatively.

"Everybody denies responsibility for driving the Super Plantagenet to the pool. . . ." She faltered and bit her lip.

The fate of both her late husband and the man she loved was intimately involved with that car. Before she could continue, Berman, moving swiftly for so big a man, went to her side and left Thatcher and Riley to make covering conversation.

"I take it Jensen was killed in the car," Thatcher said in an undertone.

Riley nodded.

"Killed at Plantagenet, transported to the pool—I can see why everyone's denying responsibility for moving the car. Particularly when one of Hauser's men is already involved as the passenger on that trip. I don't suppose anybody will ever voluntarily identify himself as the driver."

Riley looked sober. "I'm inclined to think it was the murderer," he said. "And I'd swear that it was the man who sent us the information."

"On the whole," said Thatcher, "I tend to agree with you."

It was five thirty before Thatcher and Berman started for the Telegraph Motel.

"Don't you think it's a little cruel to raise that woman's hopes? An acquittal is the most they can hope for," Thatcher remarked.

Berman shifted unhappily. "I know that things look bad for Madsen," he said. "But I'm sure . . ."

"A lot of good that does us!" Thatcher replied tartly.

Silence descended in the Plantagenet. Thatcher found himself thinking once again of the movements of the Crown Prince Bulbul's car.

". . . big farewell party for Dunn, tomorrow night," he woke to hear Berman saying. "You can imagine what that's going to be like! There's this fight between PR and Plantagenet, and between you and me, whatever is going on with Mrs. Holsinger and . . ."

Thatcher leaned back. "If we were younger and more foolhardy, we should attend it. Probably it will be awkward enough to turn into one of those situations where the truth must out."

A moment's pause, then, "Well, John, that's what I thought when I accepted for both of us."

18 • Flat Tire

JOHN THATCHER did not expect to enjoy the party for Orin Dunn. Going-away parties are apt to be strained, even when the severance is voluntary and the guest of honor romping off to greater glories. In cases of retirement they are too often pitiful. And when the employee has just been "let go," the resulting function can generate the exquisite embarrassment normally associated with adolescence.

Especially for the outsider, thought Thatcher savagely as Ed Wahl completed his anthem to the departing Orin Dunn. Wahl was displaying a talent for unctuous platitude which was surprising and, under the circumstances, well-nigh indecent.

"Of course, we'll all miss Orin," he said. "Particularly those of us at Plantagenet who've had the privilege of working closely with him. His contribution to our company will long be remembered, and I know you join with me in saying his departure is the automobile industry's loss and the aircraft industry's gain. In conclusion, Orin, I just want to say that we'll often be thinking of you, and we hope that somewhere in California you will be thinking of us."

A burst of applause signified either the audience's participation in the sentiments expressed so turgidly or its relief at their conclusion.

Dunn then rose and, with an unconvincing air of breeziness, thanked everybody for the festivity in general and for a heavy rawhide suitcase in particular. This was followed by more clapping and a surge toward the bar.

"Well, I'm glad that's over," remarked Buck Holsinger as he waited for the barman to provide him with two drinks. "I don't mind these parties once they liven up, but it's hell sitting around a table looking at a division manager behind a bunch of roses."

Thatcher agreed that most division managers looked better without garlands.

151

"Reminds me of Hawaii," said Holsinger inconsequently. "Did I ever tell you what happened to Eberhart when he landed there to open the new agency?"

Happily the arrival of Mrs. Dunn interrupted Holsinger's reminiscences.

"You've all been splendid, simply splendid," she burbled, affectionately clasping the arm of her husband's fellow jail inmate. "I can't deny this has been a difficult time for us, but Orin has always said that you and Di were simply marvelous."

"Oh, Orin's all right," said Buck without fervor.

Mrs. Dunn tightened her hold. "Now, I want you to take me to Diane so I can thank her personally. I wouldn't feel right if I didn't have a chance to talk to you both. Orin and I are setting forth on a new period. . . ."

Ignoring the appeal in Holsinger's eye, Thatcher excused himself and let his companion be swept off by Mrs. Dunn, who was displaying that easy flow of language so markedly lacking in the speakers of the evening.

He had not gone more than two steps before he was accosted by Arnold Berman.

"This is turning into a real celebration," he said, looking around the room with disfavor. "And if you ask me, what they're celebrating is Madsen's arrest."

"Not in my circle," Thatcher replied crisply. "We're celebrating setting forth on a new period of life, though we can't deny that things have been difficult."

Berman had no trouble identifying the source. "You've been listening to that Dunn woman," he said with simple certainty. "Never mind her, she's a crackpot. It's those others, especially Wahl. They're only too relieved. . . . Oh, hello there, Stu. How are things going?"

Stuart Eberhart came to rest beside them. "I'm glad you could make it, Thatcher." Although Eberhart was Michigan Motors' ex-president, he shook hands and surveyed the room with a proprietary air. "These occasions are always painful, I think."

Thatcher agreed heartily. It developed, however, that Eberhart was referring to something loftier than social discomfort.

"I've seen many men come and go at Michigan Motors," he pontificated, "but I never really get used to it. Of course there are those who don't make the grade. They haven't got what it takes. Some adjustment there is necessary," he conceded. "But these men who change for the sake of change, who can't wait for a division to open up . . . There was none of that when I was a young man. You may not know this, but I came to Michigan Motors in 1931. Of course the industry wasn't what it is today."

Thatcher could scarcely help knowing that Stuart Eberhart had come to Michigan Motors in 1931. Complete biographical details of his affiliation with the company (and with price fixing in the automobile industry) had appeared in the press during the conspiracy trial. Thanks to a cover story in *Time*, Thatcher also knew that Eberhart invariably drank hot chocolate rather than coffee at breakfast. For a moment he was tempted to remind Eberhart of the massive documentation available to anybody seriously interested in the subject. But no, if he was to act as the enemy within the gates—and that seemed to be Berman's intention—it behooved him to be tactful.

"Nothing is the same today," he agreed encouragingly. "Why, I remember at the Sloan, in the twenties . . ." There followed a long anecdote about employee stability in banking between the two wars.

Eberhart laughed politely. The automobile industry had become so overrun with young men that he was unaccustomed to having his stories about the thirties capped by those of the twenties.

"Ah, you're one of the lucky ones," he said maliciously. "You're still at your desk. It was a sad day for me when I had to hand in my resignation. Bad health, you know. But when we get to our age, it's only wise to look ahead."

"Three sets of tennis a day," said Thatcher coldly, "keep me in condition."

Hastily Berman said he anticipated no trouble at all with his retirement. His intentions were good, but since he was forty-three, his contribution was not well received.

"You'll find that many of the things you plan to do now are just too damn much trouble." Eberhart sounded plaintive. "Take deep-sea fishing, for instance. I've always gotten in a couple of weeks, but somehow I didn't manage it this year."

Berman could have pointed out that this was probably due to the exertions required to keep out of jail. Instead he changed the subject.

"Here's your guest of honor," he said. "I can't let him pass without saying good-bye."

Orin Dunn favored them impartially with a fixed smile. "Just going the rounds. I don't want to miss anybody."

"Orin, my boy. I hope we're not going to lose sight of you entirely." Eberhart clapped a paternal hand on the young man's shoulder. "Let us hear from you. It seems as if it were only yesterday you came to us."

"It wasn't very long ago," agreed Dunn. "And who would have thought that in a few short years we'd both be out of the company?"

"Now, now. This is no time for bitterness. Think of the future. You have your whole life ahead of you. And a great career, I'm sure."

It occurred to Thatcher that, barring a few differences in style, both Mrs. Dunn and Stuart Eberhart favored the transcendental approach to job relocation.

"Well, let's hope so, Stu. Anyway, aircraft's the business of the future. I've got to think in terms of the long haul, you know."

"You certainly haven't done much thinking about the short haul," said a tart voice.

Dunn started nervously.

"I'd like to see you for a few minutes, Orin," continued Diane Holsinger.

"Now look, Di, this is no place . . . Why don't . . ."

Mrs. Holsinger interrupted ruthlessly. "But then, it's so hard to find you in the right place. Your maid keeps telling me you're out."

"Well, I've been pretty busy lately. And—"

"I don't care how busy you've been. If you think you're slinking out of town without seeing me, you're insane! Now, are you going to come with me, or do I do my talking here?"

Mrs. Holsinger was not making the slightest attempt to moderate her voice. Everybody in the immediate vicinity was listening with rapt attention.

"For God's sake, Di, do you have to yell?" Dunn complained.

"I am using normal conversational tones," replied his adversary. "And what's more, I don't have anything to be ashamed of. I'd be only too delighted to settle this right here!"

"I don't know what there is to settle," exploded the unlucky Dunn. "So I'm leaving. I've got every right to leave. In fact, you ought to be able to see that I don't have any choice."

"I'm not talking about your leaving," Diane snapped. "I'm talking about this federal agent—this Riley, or whatever his name is—stirring everybody up, looking for a tipster. He's been out at the plant every day this week, Buck tells me. And I want to know what you've been up to!"

"Diane, you've got it all wrong," Dunn intervened hastily. "Come into another room, and I'll explain it all." Grabbing her elbow, he started to steer her to the nearest doorway.

"If this is just another rigmarole," she began on a warning note.

"No, no," he said soothingly. "Just come on. But don't say anything more here," he pleaded.

It was Berman who broke the silence occasioned by this interesting departure.

"A very forceful woman, Mrs. Holsinger," he offered.

Eberhart frowned in thought. "Yes, she is," he said abstractedly. "Tell me, did you get the impression that those two might know something about our . . . our informer to the Justice Department?"

"I don't see how one could avoid that impression," rejoined Thatcher.

Berman had reduced himself to an almost inhuman stillness as he willed Eberhart to prolong his confidences. Thatcher could feel his tension. Was it too much to hope that this might be a breakthrough?

Meanwhile Eberhart continued: "You know, I've often wondered about those two. You have to admit that it's queer."

"O-h-h-h?" Berman crooned invitingly.

"I have never agreed with the company decision to forget that we have a spy in our midst. That sort of thing," said Eberhart with heat, "should be Rooted Out."

"Absolutely."

"Do you gentlemen realize that it is almost certain the tip came from someone in the confidence of our senior management?" The ex-president of Michigan Motors lowered his voice to an appropriate level of horror.

"Unbelievable," said Berman.

"But in that event," interjected Thatcher, "you would expect it to be someone who gained something from the trial."

Eberhart was inclined to cavil. "Unless it went wrong. That's what I've always wondered, you know. What I mean is that somebody might have been behind the tipping who knew a lot but not quite enough."

"In fact, a company wife?"

"Or a wife in collusion with somebody else?"

"That's what I was thinking," said Eberhart.

"You'd think if Mrs. Holsinger wanted to collude with somebody, it would be with her husband," speculated Berman.

Eberhart shook his head. "No, Buck wouldn't touch this kind of thing with a ten-foot pole. But it's just the sort of thing she'd think of. She's ambitious for him, you know, very ambitious. But she'd need somebody to work with. Somebody with inside information. And Dunn was aching for Jensen's job."

"But surely if Dunn were in on it, then he would have worked things better."

"I think," said Thatcher, "that what Mr. Eberhart is driving at is this. Mrs. Holsinger can plan, but she doesn't have information. Dunn has information but can't plan. Between them they might have flubbed the whole thing."

"Exactly." Eberhart beamed at Thatcher's solution to the problem of communication. But then, as the implications of this extremely plain talk came home, his satisfaction faded. "This is all guesswork, you understand. Probably some other explanation entirely. You mustn't let this little imaginative effort of mine mislead you. No doubt Mrs. Holsinger and Dunn have many things to discuss. Ah, Miss Price, not leaving us so soon, are you?"

Susan Price, her arms laden with a large wooden box, halted in her progress toward the door. She smiled at them in slightly muzzy fashion. Everybody seemed to be doing a good deal of drinking.

"Good evening, Mr. Eberhart. No, I'm not leaving. Mr. Dunn brought this model of last year's Planty. He's cleaning house and it belongs to the company. I said I'd take it back. I'm just going to put it in the car."

Berman offered to carry it out for her. As he prepared to depart, Frank Krebbel bore down on the group. He was frowning slightly, though he welcomed Thatcher back to Detroit with his usual calm.

"I thought our sales figures might fetch you," he said as Berman, before leaving, explained Thatcher was interested in having a second look. "And I see that Dunn is trying to get you to run his errands, Miss Price. You should have told him to call a company messenger."

"That's all right, Mr. Krebbel," replied Susan, who was

radiating affection and indulgence for the world at large. "Oh, I forget to tell Mr. Berman which Drake to put it in." She laughed up at him. "I'll go after him, or else we'll have *you* doing Mr. Dunn's errands."

She skipped off in hasty pursuit, leaving Krebbel with a faintly puzzled expression. The sight would have warmed Fabian Riley's heart. Presidents do not remember chance encounters with secretaries quite so vividly as secretaries remember those with presidents.

"I think Lionel was looking for you a few minutes ago, Stu," Krebbel said briskly. "He's in the other room."

Thatcher began to suspect what was coming.

As soon as the coast was clear, Krebbel resumed.

"I heard Stu blowing off steam about Mrs. Holsinger and Dunn. There's nothing I can do to stop him, but you might as well know that he's got a bee in his bonnet about the Justice Department getting inside information."

"I can see how he might."

"The company policy is clear. We've weeded out our troublemakers, and I intend to run such a clean shop that there won't be any more material for tipsters. As for what happened in the past, I intend to forget it. And I'll see to it that everyone on the payroll does likewise."

Krebbel paused. Thatcher was far too experienced to contribute anything of his own until he was convinced that no further information was forthcoming. Then he spoke.

"You may not be able to persuade outsiders to write off MM's past so readily."

Krebbel nodded. "Oh, I know. Riley's been haunting the front office. He's another one who's obsessed. But the point is, that's his business. It isn't mine."

Thatcher regarded the new president reflectively. He decided to take a chance. "Tell me, Krebbel, you wouldn't care to give me your personal opinion as to whether Glen Madsen shot Ray Jensen, would you?"

"No, Thatcher, I would not."

And smiling gently, Frank Krebbel, who regarded himself—with a good deal of justification—as a vehicle of company policy rather than personal opinion, turned to join another group.

Ten minutes later Thatcher had been swept up by the Wahls and had endured an exuberant analysis by Ed Wahl of the anticipated earnings of Plantagenet for the next two quarters. It was during a lull in this monologue, caused by Audrey Wahl's insistence on another drink, that Thatcher heard the most illuminating conversation of the evening—although he did not realize it at the time.

"It isn't true what they're saying," proclaimed Mrs. Wahl largely. "Ed had the job sewed up, right from the minute Jensen went to jail. Jensen was just putting up a good bluff when he told people he was coming back. He was always a bluffer. Big on talk, you know," she waved vaguely, imperiling a table. "But he got taken care of, all right."

19 • High Octane Rating

It BECAME abundantly clear the next day that the indiscretions had not been limited to those of Stuart Eberhart and Audrey Wahl the previous evening. An early morning phone call from Fabian Riley, wanting the story on Diane Holsinger and Orin Dunn, proved that the fertile rumors of Michigan Motors were being channeled, presumably via Susan Price, directly into the Department of Justice.

And arrival at the MM presidential suite brought Thatcher and Berman face to face with a figure busily generating its own contribution to that channel.

"It's disgraceful. Absolutely disgraceful," spluttered Lincoln Hauser, his meager body rigid with indignation. He was standing in the anteroom to Krebbel's office and had seized on the two new arrivals as an audience for his grievances.

"What seems to be the matter, Hauser?" Thatcher asked benignly. It was such a relief to be spared the publicity director's relentless cheeriness that sympathy for his plight, whatever its nature, sprang forth unbidden.

"That man Wahl is a maniac! Do you know what he's done?"

Gravely Thatcher shook his head. The stoic calm with which Krebbel's secretary continued her typing told him that Wahl's latest atrocity was common gossip in the front office.

"He's distributed a memo to List C saying that all Plantagenets, whether production or design models, are the property of the division and are not to be moved without a clearance from him. To List C, mind you! Why, that's almost general distribution!"

The enormity of this behavior rendered Hauser momentarily speechless.

"Well, now, that's too bad," said Berman, dimly aware

that he was not measuring up to the magnitude of the event.

The inadequacy of his comment revived Hauser.

"Too bad! Why, he's accusing us of having taken that damned Super Plantagenet. I tell you, I'm not going to stand for it! If there's one thing a director of public relations has to do, it's stand up for his men. And nobody is going to use one of my boys as a scapegoat while I'm around. He thinks we don't know—"

"Is there something you want, Hauser?" Krebbel's ironic tones interrupted his impassioned subordinate in full flight. The president had emerged from the inner office and was viewing the gathering with a quizzical expression.

But the Hausers of this world, once their blood is up, are not so easily silenced.

"Yes, there is," he replied with dignity. "Have you seen this?"

He rattled the offending memorandum under his superior's nose.

"I suppose that's the one from Wahl," said Krebbel wearily. "Yes, I've seen it. But couldn't we go into it some other time? I have"—and he indicated the presence of Berman and Thatcher—"another appointment just now."

"No, it can't wait. I want a countermanding memo issued this morning. This ought to be settled right here and now."

"If it comes to that, I'd like to settle things too," said a new and ugly voice as Ed Wahl made his appearance.

"So you knew I'd be up here as soon as I saw this," accused Hauser with a martial gleam in his eye.

"I didn't know anything," said Wahl shortly, "but I could hear you down the hall."

Krebbel, resigning himself to the situation, suggested that perhaps they should all come into his office to avoid drawing even more participants to the scene of combat.

There was a brief exchange of glances between Berman and Thatcher. The invitation had been ambiguous enough to be distorted for their own purposes.

"Splendid," Thatcher said briskly, marching through the doorway. "We were getting a little noisy."

Whatever Krebbel may have thought of these tactics, his attention was instantly claimed by the demands of his division manager.

"I'm getting sick of this," announced Wahl. "I've got more important things to do than squabble about who drove that damned car around with Jensen's body. So PR made a mistake. All right. I can understand that. There was a lot of confusion with changing plans at the last minute and Hauser, here, wanting to make a circus of the thing. But I'm not going to sit still while he tries to weasel out of the whole mess and put the blame on my division."

"*We* made a mistake! I like that. You were sending the car down to the pool without even letting us know. In spite of the fact that the procedure manual is quite clear on our responsibility. If Winters hadn't seen your man driving the car away, we wouldn't even have known where to send the photographers."

Wahl laughed nastily.

"That's a good story," he jeered. "Even I didn't know anything about the Planty being moved until I saw it stolen. And I notice you've been careful enough to get Winters out of the way."

"Who the hell is Winters?" Krebbel demanded testily.

Wahl was quick to give him the information. "He's the PR man who was driven over to the pool in the Super Planty. Nobody else got a good look at the driver, and now Hauser has shipped Winters off to Canada or somewhere."

"What do you mean by that?" cried Hauser.

"I mean that you made goddamn sure we couldn't ask him who gave the order for that car to be moved."

Opening and shutting his mouth like a mechanical toy, Hauser made several false starts before he was able to give coherent expression to his sentiments. Under cover of the tides of passion swirling through the office, Berman whispered to Thatcher, "Didn't Riley say the police theory is that the murderer drove the car?"

"Yes, but I think that fact has eluded Hauser."

And indeed both Hauser and Wahl seemed completely incapable of comprehending anything outside the scope of their quarrel.

"Who the hell are you to cross-examine anybody in PR?" demanded Hauser, irrevocably sloughing the last veneer of professional cordiality. "We're *staff*, and we report to the front office! The police asked Winters all the questions they wanted before he left."

"They don't seem to have gotten much help from him."

"What was there for him to tell them? He's new here, and he didn't look at the driver closely. All he could describe was an ordinary-looking man in Plantagenet overalls and a visored cap. If you'd let him take a look at everybody in your division, no doubt we'd know who drove that car."

"Like hell we would! I let him look at every man we've got who's assigned to driving. If you think I'm going to close down a whole shift when we're already running behind, just so your fancy Dan can pretend to be trying to recognize somebody, you're crazy."

"Ah ha! First you say I got Winters out of the way so he wouldn't be able to recognize anybody. Now you say he's in on the whole thing."

Krebbel intervened. "That's right, you know," he said judiciously. "You can't have it both ways."

"Well, then, why did he send Winters off?" demanded Wahl sullenly.

"I didn't send him off specially," Hauser screeched. "The front office wanted someone to cover the Canadian parts procurement. He was the man who got sent."

Wahl was recovering from Krebbel's umpiring. He riposted smartly. "I suppose he just *happened* to be the man who got picked."

"For God's sake! We've had a murder in our front yard. My best men have more than enough on their hands right here."

"Very pat. And as slick a coverup as I've ever seen!"

"Coverup, is it! If you're looking for a coverup, don't look at us. You know damn well the police say that Jensen was stuck in that car because it was supposed to be trucked to New York. We were the ones who stopped that and arranged for the poolside display. And," said Hauser, his artistic instincts rising to the fore, "it was a magnificent idea."

"He must have gotten along great with Withers and Waymark," muttered Berman *sotto voce*. "Sticks with his ideas through thick and thin."

"Banking didn't have enough latitude for him," whispered Thatcher.

"If you're implying that it was someone at Plantagenet who was taken by surprise," Wahl began threateningly.

"I'm not implying, I'm saying it," said Hauser stoutly. "Which division was Jensen mixed up with? Who had the most to gain by getting him out of the way?"

Too late Krebbel tried to play peacemaker.

"Now, boys. Link, you're just talking off the top of your head. Ed, he doesn't mean what he's—"

"Why, you little pipsqueak!" roared Wahl. "Running

around with a popgun, trying to pretend we're selling tanks. You probably held a dress rehearsal in the garage and managed to gun down Jensen through sheer incompetence. It wouldn't surprise me if your whole gang isn't running around trying to whitewash a massacre. Ask yourself a few questions! Who knew you were going to stage a shooting act as the grand finale to your rodeo? Whose idea was it to take potshots into the back seat of that car?"

Under this barrage of accusations Hauser was turning an alarming crimson. Krebbel's injunctions to keep calm went totally unheeded. Berman's cigar hung from his hand unnoticed, while Thatcher found his head swinging first right, then left, as if he were in the gallery at Forest Hills.

So Michigan Motors' public posture was that Glen Madsen had murdered Ray Jensen, was it? On the contrary, wherever one or more of the senior management were gathered, you would find as many theories about the murderer. Whether any of this helped, Thatcher was doubtful. But certainly the injection of a few grains of irritation would bring to the surface all the subterranean suspicions running riot through the front office. He immediately began to prepare several useful irritants to apply wherever they would do the most good. In the immediate situation, however, he could see no necessity for outside assistance. The roiling was going along splendidly under its own steam.

"I'm not going to stand here and listen to this sort of thing," squeaked Hauser in a futile attempt to maintain his dignity. "What kind of fools do you think we are?"

"I'll tell you," Wahl offered with menacing sincerity.

"Oh, no you won't. I'll tell *you* something. Don't talk about accidents in the garage! Everybody knows Jensen was murdered with a stolen gun. Somebody planned the whole thing. Jensen said he was going to track down the tipster. You were scared stiff. You're the one who got Jensen's job. And even then, you couldn't have held on to it if you hadn't murdered him! Did you let Winters take a look at *you* when he was looking at the Plantagenet drivers? You drove that car yourself!"

Thatcher fully expected Krebbel to weigh in with a firm negative. If one thing in the whole episode seemed proven, it was that Wahl had distinguished himself by racing pathetically after the murder car as it set forth on its journey to the poolside.

But Krebbel favored a more expansive approach to the contentions of his employees. "Now, that's enough!" he said sharply. "We've got too much trouble to have you two hurling murder charges at each other. I let you in here so you could blow up in decent privacy." He looked doubtfully at Berman and Thatcher but continued without pause. "But I'm not going to have this sort of thing going on in public. I expect some disagreements among management personnel. There always have been, and there always will be. But we've gotten along for years without accusing each other of murder, and I don't see any reason to start now. Particularly now, when it's dangerous to throw this sort of thing around."

"If you think I'm going to let him get away with . . ." began Wahl.

"I don't think so. I know so." Krebbel could exert authority. "Not only are you going to let him get away with it, he's going to let you get away with it. My job is to see that we turn out cars at a profit, and we're going to do it, no matter how much you have to swallow. I'm not going to have this operation undermined because you, or anybody else, can't stand the pace."

Wahl began to bluster. "Now just a minute . . ."

"No, I've given all the minutes to this that I plan to give. This is it, Ed. I don't care— Yes, what is it?"

Krebbel's secretary looked doubtfully into the room, whose occupants were ranged in warlike postures. Hauser stood in the exact center of the rug, his legs angled apart and his Adam's apple bobbing up and down. Sputtering noises bubbled forth in an involuntary rhythm. Wahl hovered over Krebbel's desk, with jaw outthrust and weight suspended on one beefy hand.

"Yes, Miss Shaw?" said Krebbel impatiently.

"It's Mr. Wahl's secretary. She says he has an appointment, and are you coming?"

"Me?"

"It's the union negotiation," explained Susan Price over Miss Shaw's shoulder. "They're starting to . . . ker-choo!" She sneezed heroically. Her eyes were red and watery, and she clutched a handful of tissues.

"God bless you," said Wahl automatically without relaxing.

"Thank you, Mr. Wahl. Mr. Casimir and his staff have arrived. And you said that maybe Mr. Krebbel would come, in Mr. Madsen's place. As a gesture of management solidarity."

"Oh, for God's sake, I forgot," grumbled Wahl.

Krebbel smiled wanly.

The mention of the union had brought Hauser's head up alertly.

Miss Price sneezed again.

"Having a little union trouble?" asked Berman blandly.

"Certainly not," said Wahl, Krebbel, and Hauser as one.

Susan shook her head. Her eyes were now streaming.

"You'd better come, Frank," urged Wahl.

Krebbel was thoughtful. "Yes, you're right," he agreed. "And, Thatcher, why don't you and Berman come too? After this morning you really owe us a chance to show you a little . . . er . . . management solidarity, was it, Miss Price?" he said pleasantly.

"That's right." Wahl joined his persuasions to those of the president. "At least for the first session. I'll be tied up with them for the rest of the day. In fact, it might be a good idea if you went home, Miss Price. You've been under the weather all morning, and there won't be anything for you to do."

Susan produced a watery smile and admitted that she would like to nurse her fruity head cold at home.

And, with a very convincing demonstration of *esprit de corps,* the front office of Michigan Motors marched forth to meet Local 7777, UAW AFL-CIO.

In Union There Is Strength.

20 • Fringe Benefits

HOWEVER ADMIRABLE the unity it evoked, the battle was scarcely a scene of storm and strife. Cold-blooded calm was the order of the day, thought Thatcher a half-hour later as he sat listening to the mellifluous voice of Thaddeus Casimir.

The union leader, flanked by bespectacled men in conservative attire, was reading a prepared statement on the topic of "additions to the agreed list of full-pay holidays." Although presumably he felt strongly about this subject, he did not indulge in a public show of naked emotion. Thatcher approved.

Across the table, listening intently, was Management: Frank Krebbel, courteously expressionless as usual; Buck Holsinger, restively fiddling with pencil and paper; Ed Wahl, glowering across at Casimir. Behind the principals was the Michigan Motors staff—accountants and lawyers at the ready.

"You have to watch him," one of them had confided when he ushered Thatcher and Berman to the table. "He's a smooth operator!"

Listening to Casimir's persuasive tones, Thatcher agreed. He was extremely—almost offensively—reasonable. Without batting an eye he was arguing that the hourly staff at Michigan Motors insisted—to the point of being willing to strike about it—on five additions to the paid holidays guaranteed by the current contract. Fender assemblers, so Casimir claimed, felt very strongly about Citizenship Day, Yom Kippur, Veterans' Day, St. Patrick's Day, and Flag Day.

Thatcher, a veteran of many prolonged conferences, watched the brisk passing of notes on Management's side and the visible thought-gathering that culminated in statements (1) identifying Labor's demands as grossly inflationary, (2) protesting the unyielding and stubborn nature of Labor's negotiators, and (3) deploring Labor's refusal to

166

discuss the real issue of the current negotiations, name-ly, revision of the work rules to standardize coffee breaks on a company-wide basis.

Wage rates were to be negotiated later.

"I don't understand why we're here," said Thatcher in an undertone to his neighbor. Berman merely gave a shrug of fatalistic resignation comprehending the whole range of experiences undergone at the hands of Michigan Motors.

Thatcher himself was not in top form. The Sloan Guaranty Trust might make money from Michigan Motors, he thought as Frank Krebbel spoke at length; it would take a quite unusual profit to compensate for the discomfort to which John Putnam Thatcher, senior vice-president, had already been subjected.

Thaddeus Casimir, having listened to Krebbel's incisive explanation of why Michigan Motors was totally incapable of acceding to the union's irresponsible and preposterous demands, smiled and resumed speech. There was no likelihood of fireworks here, Thatcher saw. Krebbel's imperturbability was matched by Casimir's oiled determination. Both were all business—in marked contrast to their seconds. Impatience on Holsinger's face, mulishness around Ed Wahl's eyes, pursed lips among the assorted attorneys regardless of side—these indicated the second-string men. The principals had no feelings.

"Without assuring our men of a day off on Citizenship Day, Yom Kippur, Veterans' Day, St. Patrick's Day, and Flag Day," said Casimir, "I don't see how I could submit any contract to the membership for ratification."

"I could not go to our stockholders and report that, next year, September seventeenth, October eighth, November eleventh, March seventeenth, and June fourteenth, were being added to our already generous roster of holidays with pay," said Krebbel.

"Nice balance of interests there," Berman roused himself to comment during the lull while notes spread around the table. "Smart cooky, Krebbel. Doesn't mention the day, just the date."

Thatcher nodded agreement. He had come to the conclusion that he and Berman, representing Waymark-Sims, the Sloan—and the money markets of Wall Street—had not been pressed to attend this meeting through any juvenile pride in the success with which Hauser and Wahl could compose their differences. Krebbel was too subtle

168 • MURDER MAKES THE WHEELS GO 'ROUND

for that. Instead he was giving them a long-delayed opportunity to see the kind of managerial competence that
would guarantee profitable performance by Michigan Motors. And high time, thought Thatcher irritably, that Krebbel realized that involvement with alcoholic wives, intra-
mural battles, and convulsive emotional scenes was not
calculated to sway the financial man. At least not favorably.

Berman and he were being given a view of business as
usual. Thatcher had to admit that this prolonged duel with
Thaddeus Casimir showed more thought, preparation, and
general efficiency than he had believed available to Michigan Motors.

Glen Madsen, he recalled, had organized the staff work.
Was he preparing notes and briefing his superiors from
his cell?

Berman had not forgotten either. "Madsen did a lot of
the homework on this," he leaned over to say.

Unfortunately a good economist and a first-rate re-
searcher can still be a murderer. Moved by rage, by
love—by God knows what—Glen Madsen might have shot
Ray Jensen at some chance encounter in the division, during an inspection of the internal wonders of the Super
Plantagenet. Thatcher did not think it likely, but it was
certainly possible. More important, the state of Michigan
was convinced of it and was doing its best to assemble
proof to that effect. No wonder Berman was depressed.

To keep from asking himself if Michigan had the
death penalty, Thatcher turned his attention back to the
bargaining table. Frank Krebbel and Thaddeus Casimir,
like rival chieftains, had retired from the spotlight; two
juniors, armed with dissimilar and conflicting statistical
data, presented information on Michigan Motors' output
per man since 1936.

Neither pessimist nor statistician by nature, Thatcher
retreated again to his own thoughts and dispassionately
examined management. The union was presenting results
of a study proving that Michigan Motors' profits were
excessive—by no means the most favorable moment to
view Frank Krebbel, Buck Holsinger, and Ed Wahl. Thatcher narrowed his eyes slightly. Were they troubled by un-
answered questions? Did Buck Holsinger know what his
wife was saying? Did he realize that she and the enig-
matic Orin Dunn gave every evidence of being up to something? Holsinger was listening to the union statistician

intently. His good-natured, rather foolish expression had been replaced by one of exaggerated sobriety.

What did Frank Krebbel think of the scene he had just left? How did he feel about Ed Wahl? His confidences to Thatcher had been careful and calculated. What did he really think of his newest division manager?

Thatcher found his glance returning to Ed Wahl, now biting his lip with restrained aggressiveness. Wahl was enjoying his sudden elevation. And Mrs. Wahl made no bones about her open satisfaction. The Wahl income, the Wahl future—both had been improved by Ray Jensen's murder.

Wryly Thatcher realized that once again he was thinking about the economics of murder rather than the emotions of murder. Nevertheless, he regarded the management side of the table with the same cool speculation that he saw in Thaddeus Casimir's eye. What were these men capable of? What did they want? What would they do to get it?

In the last analysis this was what mattered to the man who represented organized labor at the bargaining table. It was also what the investment community wanted to know.

And for Glen Madsen and his supporters, it was vital. Unless Ray Jensen had been killed because Glen Madsen wanted his wife.

Thatcher did not believe it.

The statisticians, having clarified nothing, finished their presentations; the first team again took the field.

"In these exploratory conversations," said Frank Krebbel, consulting a note, "I'd like to suggest a step that may lead to some progress. The company would be willing to consider adding October eighth to next year's list of accredited paid holidays. Solely as a means of expediting these discussions and without prejudice to dates. . . ."

The real horse trading had begun. Michigan Motors, through Krebbel, was going to suggest that, with unparalleled generosity, it might consider absorbing one more paid holiday.

"Any discussion of increased holidays that gave us only Yom Kippur would be a waste of time," said Thaddeus Casimir affably. The union side of the table, apparently amused by a rare pleasantry, looked merry.

Extended silence.

"But," continued Casimir, thoughtfully examining his

manicured nails, "purely on an exploratory basis, we are willing to consider dropping Veterans' Day from our current list of holiday demands. I don't know what our men —men who fought in two world wars—are going to say. But I'll try to convince the membership. . . ."

His staff shook its head, admiring this selflessness.

In short, brass tacks.

Michigan Motors would yield one holiday. The union would insist on four. The statisticians would be recalled. After discussion Michigan Motors, on a purely exploratory basis, might consider two holidays. It would point out the fearful competitive position resulting from this largesse; it would speak strongly about cost-price squeezes. But it would consider, just barely, two holidays.

The union, sympathetic, aware of the difficulties, would reply that it understood Michigan Motors' position; unfortunately feeling among the membership ran so high that unless it could guarantee at least three holidays, why, it might not be able to control the men. They would probably . . . just walk out.

Thatcher let himself consider the gamesmanship of the situation as somebody introduced the ominous word "arbitration." (This was a newly hired lawyer who was severely reprimanded after the meeting by his superior from the Michigan Motors Law Department. "Our general position, Brewster, is against government intervention!") Apart from the strength of the relative bargaining positions, Thatcher felt there was something in the intrinsic content of the demands that predicated the outcome of these proceedings, namely, the nature of the holidays. Citizenship Day seemed doomed to him.

Chairs scraping woke him up. The meeting was adjourning for a short break.

"Let's say fifteen minutes," said Krebbel. There was an automatic synchronization of watches before Krebbel, gesturing to Holsinger, retired for a brief caucus, and Casimir, huddled with his staff, engaged in half-time pep talk.

Thatcher, rather bored, drew a small sheet of paper to him, a neat mimeographed list of the union's original demands. "St. Patrick's Day, March seventeenth," he said idly.

Arnold Berman, settling back with a new cigar, roused himself to speech. "You know, this gives you an insight into those long sessions they have at the bargaining table, doesn't it? I'm surprised that they ever get finished—Where are you going?"

For John Thatcher, not hearing a word that Berman said, had pushed back his chair and was striding from the room. "Telephone call," he said. "I didn't realize that St. Patrick's Day was March seventeenth."

Puzzled, Berman watched him push his way through the cluster of men at the door.

There had been a snap of urgency in Thatcher's voice.

"So," murmured Berman. "March seventeenth is St. Patrick's Day?" He considered this, then came to a conclusion. "We've been in Detroit too long."

21 • The Open Road

ONE-HALF HOUR LATER Arnie Berman sat alone in the deserted conference room. He was out of cigars. Celia Jensen and Glen Madsen waited for good news that did not come. Everybody at Michigan Motors had gone mad. Berman sighed.

John Thatcher, hurrying back into the room, stopped short at the sight of the solitary mournful figure. "I thought the meeting was going to resume," he said abruptly.

Berman looked up. "Yes. Well, it resumed for all of two minutes. Then the MM boys discovered urgent business elsewhere, so we're adjourned until tomorrow. And, to be honest, Casimir was none too pleased at the way Krebbel and Wahl and Holsinger stamped out of here—"

Unceremoniously Thatcher interrupted. "You didn't mention that business about St. Patrick's Day, did you?"

He sounded deadly serious. Briefly Berman wondered how to explain things to the Sloan Guaranty Trust. "As a matter of fact I did," he said, automatically searching his breast pocket for a cigar. "They noticed you weren't here, and I did say that you were busy calling Brad Withers to tell him that St. Patrick's Day is on March seventeenth—"

"Good God!" said Thatcher, turning on his heel.

For a moment Arnie sat considering things. Then he got up and hurried after Thatcher. He was hard put to match the older man's stride. "John," he said breathlessly, "would you please explain in words of one syllable—"

Thatcher ignored him. He turned the corner and pounded down the rarely used stairway, taking some steps two at a time. Arnie, trotting behind, could see his face only at the turns. He looked forbidding.

"Just tell me what the hell we're doing!" Berman called after him.

Thatcher scarcely heard him. He strode into the lobby, where a flurry of secretaries returning from a coffee break scattered like agitated pigeons before him. Their flight revealed the thin figure of Fabian Riley, studiously consulting a notebook.

"Just the man I want," Thatcher muttered without breaking pace. "Riley! We're going to need your help."

Fabian Riley looked up.

Thatcher, with a humorless smile, said, "We've all been inexcusably slow, my friend. Has it occurred to you that St. Patrick's Day is March seventeenth?"

"St. Patrick's Day is March seventeenth?" Riley echoed, looking as blank as Arnie Berman felt. Then, with an expression of shocked consternation, he dropped his notebook and hurried after Thatcher, who was already outside the building looking around for Mack and the Sceptre.

"That damned car has been hounding us every minute we've been here," he murmured irritably, "but when you want it . . . oh, there he is. Mack! Mack!"

From the far side of the Mighty Michigan Motors Pool, Mack hastily disassociated himself from a friendly game of five card stud and hurried to his vehicle.

"What are you doing?" Riley demanded. "Where are you going?"

"Miss Price has already left," Thatcher said impassively. "She's probably home by now. And I think she's in danger. . . ."

"You mean—"

"I do."

"I'm coming with you," said Riley with determination.

"What's going on here?" Arnie asked patiently. His companions ignored him.

"You are going nowhere, Riley," Thatcher ruled. "You are going to stay here and use the authority of your office to rouse the police. We'll try to head him off."

"There won't be time. . . ." Riley protested mutinously.

Thatcher was already hastening into the front seat of the Plantagenet now at the curb. "You are wasting time as it is. And endangering Miss Price's life, I might add." He turned to exchange a few words with Mack, then leaving him in severe shock, he turned back to say, "He's driving a 1966 Viscount, black with white sidewalls."

Obedient to Thatcher's command, the great limousine was already moving down the driveway (and Fabian Riley was pelting back toward the lobby) when Arnie Berman emerged from his trance and scrambled into the back seat of the car.

". . . and hurry," Thatcher said from the front seat. "It's literally a matter life and death."

Arnie brushed himself off, groped for a cigar, and the scenery on Michigan Motors Road began to go by faster, faster, and faster.

"Goddammit!" bellowed Fabian Riley into the telephone on the reception desk. "I don't care what Georgeson's doing! Put me through to him."

Riley picked up a memo pad and deliberately crushed it between long, nervous fingers. The receptionist cowered in her chair.

"Georgeson? Thank God! Now, listen to me. We've discovered who killed Ray Jensen. . . . What? No, it was not Glen Madsen, you damned fool. I don't care. . . . Listen, it doesn't matter what you think. . . ."

Meanwhile the driver of the 1966 Viscount, black with white sidewalls, drove carefully, just five miles over the legal speed limit. He was heading for the Willow Run Expressway and downtown Detroit, and it wouldn't do to get picked up the police. It wouldn't do at all. Automatically he checked the rearview mirror; the normal flow of traffic heading for the access ramp. No avenging fates, no nemesis. . . .

"Now's the time to keep calm," he said calmly and aloud. "Nobody really has any notion of what you're doing. It was pure coincidence, that's all. You'll have to protect yourself against having anything come of it, but at the moment you're perfectly safe—if you keep calm. . . ."

But instinctively he pushed the accelerator nearer the floorboard.

"I thought you said this car had power," said John Thatcher scornfully as the Plantagenet screamed onto the access road.

"But Mr. Thatcher! There's a stop sign—"

"Mack, this is no time for a lot of nonsense about stop signs," replied Thatcher impressively. "Is this the best way to town?"

Perspiration glistened on Mack's forehead despite the air conditioning. "Well, if we cut off onto old Route five, we might save a few miles—"

"Do it!" Thatcher ordered.

In the back seat Arnie Berman, bracing himself against another wild careen, had a sudden vision of heaven, an extended MGM array of lovely young women bearing large trays of Havanas. "John," he said wearily, "will you please tell me . . ."

The question was never completed; the super-powered road-tested Magna-Grip brakes of the Plantagenet Sceptre clamped several tons of steel, glass, rubber to a shivering halt.

DO NOT ENTER
ROAD UNDER CONSTRUCTION

John Thatcher began to swear, softly but fluently. Mack, visibly trembling, took a deep breath. It was a mistake.

"Back it out," Thatcher broke off to demand. "Back onto the expressway."

The reverse speed of the Crown Jewel of Motoring lived up to its advertising.

". . . dammit, you fool," Riley said savagely, primitively, into the telephone, while the receptionist began to feel faint. "You're going to have the blood of a woman on your fat stupid hands if you don't do something. . . . What do you mean 'What'? Put up road blocks, call the Detroit police! . . . What do you mean, you'll look like a fool. . . . Listen, Georgeson, if you don't get moving, I'm coming over to take you apart. . . ."

The 1966 Viscount ("Elegance in Driving") pulled into the left lane to pass a produce truck. Ridiculous to feel nervous with everything under control and only one detail left. But there was a sultry oppressiveness in the air—that was it. The weather. Unpleasantly hot. The car pulled sedately into the right lane.

Suddenly the scream of a siren made the driver start compulsively. A squad car, howling hideously, streaked past. Past. The driver took an unsteady breath. That just showed what an uneasy conscience could do. The police —why, they weren't a menace. Must be an accident up ahead.

Suddenly, with the cold, calculating intelligence that had stood him in good stead before, the driver realized that if there was a serious accident, there might be a delay.

There might even be officials noticing, taking license numbers. . . . No use to risk observation. He pulled the Viscount off the expressway at the next exit. Grand Island Tollway was several miles longer. But it was safer.

The driver of the 1966 Viscount was a man who valued safety.

"Thank God!" Riley murmured weakly, sagging against the desk. Georgeson, dim, distant, aggrieved, and distorted, had finally yielded to his appeals. The phone emitted an interrogative squawk. "What? License number? Oh Lord . . . wait, I'll get it . . . I'll get it. . . . I'll call you back. . . . Please God!" said Riley, racing toward the far hallway. "Let us be in time!"

The Plantagenet Sceptre was capable of doing 147 miles an hour. John Thatcher was in a hurry. These facts, neatly as they meshed, were extrinisic to the situation; the Plantagenet's speed and John Thatcher's desires were imbedded in one of the great verities of modern America—the traffic jam. The Willow Run Expressway was one attenuated monster parking lot. From horizon to horizon an unending line of cars, motionless, steaming, panting, remained bumper to bumper.

Mack returned from an exploratory expedition.

"Accident up ahead," he reported unhappily. "Couple of Volkswagens ran into each other. Then a lot of these cars backed up here are getting vapor locks. You know . . ."

"Vapor lock," said Thatcher bitterly.

"We're going to be quite a while," Mack persisted, bravely putting his cards on the table.

"That's where you're wrong," said Thatcher, opening the door.

Arnie Berman, upon whom the morning's events were beginning to act hypnotically, mopped a streaming brow. "Planning to walk to Detroit?" he called.

Thatcher, however, was not heading straight ahead down the highway; instead, with a display of the superiority of shank's mare to eight thousand dollars' worth of automotive know-how, he was striding brisky off a restricted access highway. Motorists, imprisoned behind their wheels, stared hostilely.

Momentarily Arnie was tempted to let Thatcher go his eccentric way. Then mindful of his responsibility to Waymark-Sims, he hitched himself forward and set off to follow.

Mack, a broken man, buried his head in his hands.

"What do you mean you don't know the license number of that car?" Fabian Riley said ferociously.

Lincoln Hauser, already much tried, attempted sweet reason. "We keep a whole rank of cars out there for executive use, for those of our visitors who want to drive themselves, old man. I can give you a list of the numbers of all of them—"

With a snarl Riley snatched the paper from his hand, then, without asking permission, reached across Hauser to the phone.

"Oh, now see here!"

"Shut up!" Riley said between clenched teeth. "Georgeson? Here are the tag numbers. . . . Yes, I said numbers. . . ."

The 1966 Viscount had pulled onto a spur road that paralleled Canal Road by a distance of two fields and a string of hamburger stands and seedy motels. While he drove, the driver could keep an eye on traffic through an occasional gap in the depressing façade. As he had expected, there was no police activity on Canal Road. The Grand Island Tollway, while time-consuming, was going to be worth the detour.

The driver smiled grimly. If anybody ever asked, he had been someplace far, far away during the next hour. He had to think about where it would be—but he had already successfully done this once before. And quite ingeniously. There was no reason to suppose he couldn't do it again. With a thrill of pure pleasure at the lively response of the motor, he accelerated slightly.

"We are at the Texaco Gas Station at the corner of Elwood Street and Sebago Road," said Thatcher to the phone. "Have you managed to get in touch with Miss Price? Oh, it's just as well, if she's not home. . . . And the police? Thank God! Yes, yes, I know it's a question of time. . . . Just come along and don't take the expressway. It's snarled up. . . . Yes. . . ."

Hanging up, he took an impatient turn around the station office while Arnie Berman, collar open, tie askew, and coat jacket off, looked at him with mute inquiry.

"Riley will be here in a few minutes," Thatcher finally said.

"Good," said Arnie.

"If anything happens to that girl, it will be because we were incredibly obtuse," Thatcher continued somberly.

"Obtuse, schmobtuse," said Arnie to himself. "What the hell is going on?"

The driver of the 1966 Viscount threw twenty-five cents into the hamper and sped ahead onto the Grand Island Tollway, exactly two minutes before the reluctant police contacted the attendant.

"There are a lot of Viscounts on the road," the toll-booth keeper said disagreeably when asked if he had seen it. "How would I know?"

"Well, keep an eye out for it now, will you?" was the exasperated reply. "Killers."

"Aahh," said the tollbooth keeper.

Meanwhile the 1966 Viscount, carefully remaining even with the flow of traffic, was in the clear. Its driver breathed a sigh of relief, a sigh that showed how much pressure he had been under. In the clear. Tomorrow, business as usual. . . .

"Did the state police call the Detroit police?" Thatcher asked immediately as he got into the car which Riley had ruthlessly commandeered from the Michigan Motors complement.

Berman's spirit was broken. He merely climbed into the back seat.

"Georgeson was getting in touch with them," said Riley, goaded by a recollection of that lethargic official. He started with a shriek of tires. "But Susan isn't home . . . and it's a question of time. For all we know, he may be there already."

"Take it easy," Thatcher counseled. "He may be stuck in traffic."

"If anything happens to Susan, I'll tear Georgeson apart," said Riley, his frailty turned to pure power by rage. "I only hope . . . now, what the hell!"

For, as they drove up to the tollbooth of the Grand Island Tollway, the gate came down.

The attendant, barricaded in terrified isolation, refused to venture out of his booth to answer the demands of the killers in the car (although the one in the back seat

looked apathetic enough). The cars piling up behind
began the tuneless melody of automotive clamor.

"What's the matter?" demanded Fabian Riley, throwing open the car door and striding toward the keeper.

The man cringed away from him. "License plate . . .
police . . ." he whined in terror.

"License plate . . . oh, Lord! Look, I know that we've
got one of the license numbers," Riley shouted, "but we're
not a black Viscount with whitewall tires, you idiot!
We're a blue Majestic!"

At this moment a squad car raced up, coming to a
dramatic halt as the doors were flung open and two officers
emerged with guns drawn.

"Do you hear me?" Riley shouted at them, looking for
all the world like a mad killer. "We're a blue Majestic!
Not a black Viscount!"

Some minds do not readily assimilate new ideas; there
was a dangerous moment (during which the tollgate keeper ducked, and the woman in the car behind the commo-
tion told one of her four children to stop teasing Donny,
ignoring entirely the looming possibility of gunfire) when
Arnie Berman wondered if he were going to witness an as-
sault by the Sloan Guaranty Trust abetted by the U. S.
Department of Justice upon the armed might of the state
of Michigan.

"Say, Al," one of the officers said. "That's right. It is a
black Viscount we want!"

Riley, ignoring their guns, hurried back to the car. "Get
that damned thing up," he ordered the gatekeeper.

"Twenty-five cents," that worthy quavered, recovering
courage.

Riley started the motor and shot forward.

The squad car, outdistancing him easily, sped ahead.

Arnie Berman tried to achieve a decent frame of mind
in which to leave the world. A cigar would have helped.

The 1966 Viscount was pulling onto Grand Island
Bridge, which would lead into downtown Detroit. The
thoughts of the driver, not a man who liked violence, were
on the regrettably distasteful, yet necessary chores that
lay before him.

Suddenly the twinkle of red showed in his rearview
mirror. Behind him a squad car was shortening the gap
between them with surprising speed.

The Viscount was at the crown of the bridge, with an

unimpeded view of the road ahead. Nothing. Nobody speeding, no accident. No cars in the breakdown lane. . . .

Suddenly the driver knew whom the police were pursuing. A pang of pure fright—the first he had ever experienced—shot through him. It suddenly blurred the road with a red mist; it convulsively tightened his sweating hands. . . .

It sent the 1966 Viscount into a turn that propelled it powerfully through the restraining wires, into an arch rising from the bridge . . . then, with the speed of death, crashing into gas-fed flames on the railroad tracks below.

Fabian Riley, shaken like every driver who had seen the terrible plunge, brought his Majestic to a halt. For a moment he and John Thatcher and Arnie Berman sat there. Then with the air of a man doing his duty, Riley got out and walked ahead to where the police were standing on the bank leading down to the railroad tracks, helplessly watching the blazing wreck.

"Not a hope," one of them said. "The fire truck's on the way. But the poor bastard didn't have a chance."

Thatcher and Berman, who had pushed their way through the gathering crowd to join Riley, heard this epitaph.

"Poor man," said a voice from behind them. "What a terrible way to go."

"Worse than the gas chamber?" Thatcher mused aloud. "I wonder." He looked at Arnie. "Oh, yes, Frank Krebbel was the murderer, all right."

22 • Pedestrians Only

"FRANK KREBBEL! I still can't believe it," protested Glen Madsen two days later. But he was sitting on the sofa next to Celia Jensen, and they were unashamedly holding hands.

Thatcher puffed cautiously. In a rare moment of indulgence he had allowed Arnie Berman to foist off on him a commemorative Havana. "Is it that hard to believe?" he asked thoughtfully. "After all, he was really the most logical suspect all along."

"And I thought he was so nice," said Susan Price ruefully.

Arnie Berman emerged from the depths of his armchair, where he was contentedly examining the ceiling. "Not nice. Just smart."

"Almost smart enough to get away with it," Thatcher agreed. "If it hadn't been for Mr. Riley here." He indicated the young federal investigator with a wave of the hand.

Fabian Riley sneezed gratefully.

Thatcher beamed at him paternally. During the past forty-eight hours, in the course of which Berman, Thatcher, Riley, and Susan had maintained an unrelenting attack on state police headquarters, Riley had displayed inexhaustible patience educating a reluctant Captain Georgeson in the intricacies of antitrust investigation. Susan Price had recounted her memorable Saint Patrick's Day again and again. But it was not until Thatcher began to speak of the movements of a certain red Drake that Georgeson finally abandoned his resistance.

"Because Mr. Riley was the one who insisted over and over again that Raymond Jensen was murdered by the original informant. And Mr. Riley has been living in the front office of Michigan Motors for a year. He knows much more than any of the rest of us possibly could about the atmosphere generated there by Jensen's return. What he said deserved respect. But it led to certain inescapable conclusions. The murderer had done two things.

He had sent the original tip, no doubt for excellent reasons, to the Department of Justice, and he had killed Jensen. And, if the state police were right, he had done another thing. He had driven the Super Plantagenet from the division to the pool. Add those three, and you have Frank Krebbel."

"I still don't see it," said Madsen. "To be honest, I always thought Ed Wahl must have been the tipster."

"We all thought that at one time or another. Probably because we made the mistake of thinking of Raymond Jensen in his present job rather than his future job. We discounted the fact that he was the acknowledged heir to Stuart Eberhart. But look instead at what the tipping actually accomplished. Eberhart was forced to resign. His two obvious successors, Jensen and Holsinger, went to jail. And the board of directors refused to consider anybody associated with production or marketing as a presidential candidate. Under the circumstances they were almost forced to go to their controller, and Frank Krebbel became president of Michigan Motors. In other words, he got exactly what he wanted. Whereas if you assume that Jensen or Dunn or Holsinger had anything to do with the tipping, you have to assume that they made an incredible botch of the job."

Riley shook his head. He was still feeling faintly aggrieved that the informer had been unmasked by someone else. "I dismissed him from the beginning," he confessed. "Of course, I could see how much he had gained, but it seemed impossible that he could ever have acquired the information. He was so remote from the entire conspiracy."

The tender glance that Riley directed toward Susan was just barely reproachful.

"But, Fabian," she defended herself, "how could I know? I never connected it with St. Patrick's Day."

"I've never understood what St. Patrick's Day has to do with all this," Celia complained, rousing herself from a daze of happiness to offer more coffee to her guests.

"It's all in the timing," explained Thatcher. "On March fifteenth the price fixers had their famous meeting. It lasted two days. On the morning of March seventeenth Jensen was back in the office giving his notes, as usual, to Miss Price for her to take home and transcribe. But that evening, things did not go as usual. Miss Price took her belongings—which included a small envelope with the

notes and twenty cupcakes decorated with shamrocks—
out to her car and then had to dash back into the building
for something. When she re-emerged she discovered that
she had mistaken another Drake for her own. And its
owner had driven off with her belongings. The next morning Frank Krebbel returned the envelope and gave her an
enormous decorated cake. By that afternoon a photostat
of those notes was on its way to the Department of Justice."

Glen Madsen was incredulous. "But didn't Ray ever find
out?"

"No." Susan shook her head. "You don't understand.
The trial wasn't until October. Of course we had suspicions before that. Mr. Jensen started to get worried last
summer. But he had been to lots of meetings in the
meantime, and he just asked me if anybody could have gotten at the notes of any meeting. Naturally I said No. I
never associated the meetings with St. Patrick's Day."

"It's surprising Krebbel gave you that cake," mused
Berman. "You'd think he'd be afraid to stamp the occasion on your mind."

But Thatcher did not agree. "On the contrary," he said.
"I think Krebbel was very clever. After all, Miss Price was
almost certain to tell the story. By presenting her with
that outlandishly inscribed cake he riveted her attention
on the exchange of pastry." Thatcher smiled reassuringly
at Susan. "Nobody is going to spoil a good story about cupcakes by introducing an irrelevant envelope. That's human nature."

Susan, suffering from a rare attack of chagrin, looked
relieved. It was mortifying, to say the least, to have her
arguments with Fabian Riley come to this conclusion.
She glanced at him doubtfully. What she saw reassured
her.

"Ray," said Celia, who could now speak of her late husband in a way satisfactory to all her guests, "was set to
move heaven and earth finding out what happened."

"Precisely. That, of course, is why he was killed." Thatcher stirred cream into his coffee contemplatively. "Ideal-
ly Krebbel would have liked to cut all links between Jensen and Michigan Motors before the jail sentence was
over. But his appointment was very recent, and he
couldn't consolidate his position quickly enough. So there
he was, with Jensen threatening to unveil the tipster unless
he was re-employed. Krebbel couldn't afford to have

Jensen around the front office in any capacity. And he couldn't afford to have Jensen dedicating himself to a ruthless investigation. Because by then Jensen knew enough to concentrate on the March fifteenth meeting. So Krebbel decided to kill him."

"They had that long conference the week Ray was killed," Madsen reminded them. "I wonder what went on."

"We'll never know. But look at what happened. They had their talk on Monday. On Tuesday the gun was stolen. I think Krebbel told Jensen he'd be taken back. That was to keep him quiet. Then Krebbel took the gun and waited for a favorable opportunity. It came on Wednesday. You remember we had looked at the Super Plantagenet and been unable to find Jensen, who was somewhere in the building. Then Krebbel left us before the plant tour because he had other errands to do in the building. We were all under the impression that the car was being trucked to New York on the following morning. It seems inescapable that Krebbel met Jensen somewhere near that car. The garage, you recall, was deserted. Somehow he induced him to enter the car, probably to look at something or for a private talk. There he shot him, made sure there were no fingerprints, rearranged the body on the floor so that it was hidden from view, and walked off, confidently expecting that no one would enter the car except for hastily loading it on a truck, until New York. By that time a good deal of confusion would have entered the picture."

"Not to mention a couple of hundred Arabs," grunted Arnie disapprovingly. "Including a reigning monarch on an official state visit."

Celia was shaken. "It seems incredible," she said.

Madsen squeezed her hand encouragingly. He was anxious to divert Thatcher from further description of the murder itself.

"What makes you so sure of what Krebbel said to Ray?"

"Wahl's reactions," said Thatcher promptly. "At the same time he promised Plantagenet to Jensen, Krebbel promised it to Wahl. After the murder Krebbel always maintained that there had never been any question of taking Jensen back. But before, he temporized with Wahl, telling him that a public announcement would have to be delayed because of trouble with Lionel French. This left Wahl—in fact, both the Wahls—explaining Jensen's assertive confidence as a monumental bluff. This sounded very thin, and Wahl knew it. People suspected that Wahl was doing the bluffing. The result was that he blustered in public and suspected a double cross in private. He realized what we should have realized. Frank Krebbel was a very decisive man. He was perfectly capable of making it clear to Jensen beyond the shadow of a doubt that his connection with Michigan Motors was terminated. I had the privilege of watching him handle two subordinates the other day. He was not the man to shilly-shally, waiting for French to approve an official memo."

There was no dissent as his audience brought to mind the vision of Frank Krebbel in his more authoritarian moments.

Susan Price looked up from some calculations of her own. "Then it wasn't until Thursday morning that Mr. Krebbel found out that the car was being presented here in Detroit?"

"And what a blow it must have been to him! He had calculated that the body would not be discovered before New York. With luck the car might even be loaded into the hold of some ship bound for the Suez Canal. Instead of which he comes to work the next morning and finds Hauser in the midst of elaborate preparations for a grand presentation right outside the front office. You know," said Thatcher, turning aside to speak to Berman, "I've often wondered why our early entertainment here was so badly handled . . . why Krebbel didn't give us a more solid business view of Michigan Motors and less insight into its social feuds. Now we know."

"The man had too much on his mind," Berman agreed.

Madsen, fresh from jail, was not overly sympathetic with the rigors endured by his two champions. "Yes, but what about the car? Who drove it over to the pool?"

"Krebbel did. We now have proof of that."

It was this proof which had caused Captain Georgeson's final capitulation. Milton Winters, summoned from Canada, had been escorted to the morgue, where he had viewed the body of Frank Krebbel, shorn of its distinctive rimless glasses. A visored cap firmly pressed down over the high forehead hid the receding hairline. "That's him," Winters had cried. "That's the driver!"

"Krebbel was in a frenzy when he heard about the Super Plantagenet. It was essential for him to delay discovery of the body long enough to obscure the time and place of the murder. Remember," cautioned Thatcher,

186 • MURDER MAKES THE WHEELS GO 'ROUND

"he had no idea where the rest of us had been during the critical period. It was just Madsen's bad luck that he wandered off. What if everybody had a cast-iron alibi? He had to introduce as much confusion as possible. And certainly he had to prevent any busybody going over the car for a last-minute brushing or cleaning. So he acted on the spur of the moment. He rushed over to Plantagenet, appeared publicly as Frank Krebbel, then retired to don overalls and cap. All he had to do was wait until nobody was near the car. He just got in and prepared to drive off. When young Winters hopped into the other side, he couldn't do anything about it. Nothing but pray that Winters wouldn't look into the back."

"Why didn't Winters recognize him?" asked Susan.

Celia replied with the assurance of a company wife. "A junior staff member would never suspect a man in overalls of being the company president. And I must say, Frank left rapidly enough when Ed Wahl raced into the garage." She remembered those fleeting taillights as the Super Plantagenet had sped off with an inflamed division manager in its wake.

"As a matter of fact, it turns out that Winters had never seen Krebbel except at public functions. And of course it was Krebbel who initiated the idea that Winters be sent up to Canada." Thatcher smiled as he visualized Lincoln Hauser's reaction to learning that Public Relations had served a killer's ends.

"You mean," demanded Madsen, refusing to be diverted by side issues, "that Frank Krebbel just parked the car by the pool, sauntered off in a pair of overalls, and called it a day?"

"I suspect that Frank Krebbel disappeared with the speed of light, whipped off his overalls in the nearest secluded spot—incidentally leaving Winters asking us if we'd seen the driver—stuffed them into his briefcase, and then reappeared in the lobby to tell Berman and me he would see us at the chamber of commerce dinner before stepping into his limousine." Thatcher shook his head. "That limousine was the key to the whole thing."

Fabian Riley, whose expertise on Krebbel's activities was bounded by the scope of the Clayton Act, did not understand. "Limousine?" he asked.

"Well, cars anyway," conceded Thatcher. He pointed accusingly at Celia Jensen. "You saw Krebbel drive up to Plantagenet in his Drake on Thursday. We saw him shortly thereafter in the front office, preparing to be chauffeured about in a limousine until he returned to Plantagenet the next morning. Then he arrived at the grand presentation to Crown Prince Bulbul in his red Drake."

"Well, what's wrong with that?" demanded Riley.

"How did he get from the plant to the front office on Thursday, if he had left his Drake at the plant over a mile away, and did not pick it up until Friday morning? That was the question that finally roused Georgeson. I will say for these Michigan police, they may be confused about the antitrust laws—and who isn't?—but they are alert to everything about cars. It was simple for them to check up and discover no company car was used, and nobody admits giving Krebbel a lift. That's what stirred Georgeson into sending for Winters and seriously considering the possibility that Krebbel had moved the Super Plantagenet."

"All these people are nutty on the subject of cars," said Arnie disparagingly. He was still shaken from his experiences in the great Krebbel chase. Traveling to work on the IRT had protected him from exposure to the commuter experience.

"But we had another clue also," Thatcher rebuked him. "Celia told us that when Wahl chased the Super Plantagenet, nobody but she dared to laugh. But Krebbel told me the same story, including a vigorous and rather funny description of how Wahl looked. Quite apart from the fact that Krebbel has a booming, boisterous laugh that Celia wouldn't have overlooked, I am quite sure that if the president of the company had been roaring his head off, the staff would have had no hesitation in following his lead. But the president was in the driver's seat, hiding behind a pair of overalls, watching the whole thing in the rearview mirror. And I daresay he didn't find it so amusing at the time."

The silence of repletion enfolded the little group, their appetite for information temporarily sated. Celia had closed her eyes and allowed her head to slip down against the backrest. The shadows were still under her eyes, but the tired lines had vanished, and she was at peace. Arnie Berman smiled at her. Susan Price and Fabian Riley had reached the self-conscious stage; they both rather ostentatiously avoided looking at each other. It was Glen Madsen, rumpling his hair and stretching out his legs, who spoke.

"And I suppose it was Krebbel who planted the gun in my file."

"I would expect so. You were the obvious scapegoat. Particularly with Riley egging everybody on to look for a connection with the conspiracy case. Krebbel wanted a good personal motive to take the spotlight off MM. It was simple for him to plant the gun in the file cabinet, then demand a report under circumstances which would insure a public disinterment. With you arrested he felt perfectly safe until he discovered I had been making cryptic remarks about St. Patrick's Day falling on March seventeenth. Then he knew that Miss Price was a danger to him, and with his customary decisiveness, he rushed off to do something about her."

Susan shivered slightly, and Fabian Riley moved to sit on the arm of her chair.

"What beats me," said Madsen, "is how calm he was throughout. God knows he was busy—but he never turned a hair."

"He was not the man to show his emotions," said Thatcher in a masterful understatement. He remembered the exchange between Krebbel and Casimir at the union negotiation. If he knew anything about Casimir, the fate of St. Patrick's Day as a working day at Michigan Motors was now foreclosed. At the next negotiation that redoubtable unionist would no doubt maintain that the memories of March seventeenth were too painful for his men to dedicate themselves to work with their customary zeal.

"And what in God's name were Dunn and Diane Holsinger up to anyway?" Madsen added to his list of complaints.

But Thatcher had no help for him there. "I have no idea," he admitted. "Certainly they were doing their best to look as guilty as possible."

Unexpectedly Celia spoke up. "I know. Buck called to wish me well." And then she blushed and suddenly looked years younger. "Anyway," she continued hurriedly, "he said that Diane had told him all about it. When she heard Ray talk about putting pressure on the company to take him back, she thought that Orin Dunn and she could play the same trick. What she was going to do was get together enough information to start another antitrust investigation. Then she was going to tell French that he had to take back Buck and Orin—or else! But Orin got cold feet, enough so that Diane was afraid he might be dealing with Mr. Riley behind her back. And of course when Buck heard about it, he clamped down hard."

Riley had stirred suggestively at this enticing piece of information. But Susan laid a restraining hand on his arm. Surely he must see that now was no time to . . .

"And does anybody know what's going to happen to Mr. Holsinger?" she asked swiftly.

Nobody did. Berman, who had been maintaining his contacts with a shattered front office, told them that Lionel French had temporarily assumed the presidency while he reviewed his depleted forces. Holsinger was almost certain to get his division back, just on the basis of manpower shortage. There was even talk of elevating him to be chief executive.

"They considered you, too," Arnie told Madsen, "but they had to discard the idea. French said he might just possibly get away with a jailbird like Holsinger, considering the circumstances. But he couldn't seriously recommend to the stockholders any executive who managed to go to jail for something he didn't do!"

Madsen laughed. "Just as well. While French is looking for people, he can get himself another tame economist. I've had enough of Michigan Motors. Celia already knows my mind's made up. It's back to research for me."

As if exulting in some new freedom, he rose to his feet and stretched luxuriously. Then he grinned down at them. "To hell with the money!"

As Thatcher heard these heretical sentiments he looked up at the relaxed, confident figure. He remembered the reckless refusal to stay away from Celia Jensen.

Then he leaned forward.

"That attitude, Madsen, confirms me in my opinion," said Thatcher gently. "You were not cut out to be a Michigan Motors man!"

Keep Up With The BESTSELLERS!

_____ 80432 CONVERSATIONS WITH KENNEDY, Benjamin Bradlee $1.95

_____ 80176 THE TOTAL WOMAN, Marabel Morgan $1.95

_____ 80270 TOTAL FITNESS, Laurence E. Morehouse, Ph.D. and Leonard Gross $1.95

_____ 80600 est: 4 DAYS TO MAKE YOUR LIFE WORK, William Greene $1.95

_____ 80446 NICE GUYS FINISH LAST, Leo Durocher with Ed Linn $1.95

_____ 80468 TOILET TRAINING IN LESS THAN A DAY, Nathan Azrin, Ph.D. and Richard M. Foxx, Ph.D. $1.95

_____ 80979 RUNNING FOR PRESIDENT, Martin Schram $1.95

Available at bookstores everywhere, or order direct from the publisher.

POCKET BOOKS
Department NFB-2
1 West 39th Street
New York, N.Y. 10018

Please send me the books I have checked above. I am enclosing $_____(please add 35¢ to cover postage and handling). Send check or money order—no cash or C.O.D.'s please.

NAME_____

ADDRESS_____

CITY_____STATE/ZIP_____

POCKET BOOKS

NFB-2

Keep Up With The BESTSELLERS!

_____ 80409 LOOKING FOR MR. GOODBAR, Judith Rossner $1.95

_____ 80720 CURTAIN, Agatha Christie $1.95

_____ 80676 TALES OF POWER, Carlos Castaneda $1.95

_____ 80588 FOREVER, Judy Blume $1.75

_____ 80675 THE MASTERS AFFAIR, Burt Hirschfeld $1.95

_____ 80445 SECRETS, Burt Hirschfeld $1.95

_____ 78835 THE PIRATE, Harold Robbins $1.95

_____ 80763 WEEP IN THE SUN, Jeanne Wilson $1.95

_____ 80762 THE PRESIDENT'S MISTRESS, Patrick Anderson $1.95

_____ 80751 JULIA, Peter Straub $1.95

_____ 80723 SEVEN MEN OF GASCONY, R. F. Delderfield $1.95

Available at bookstores everywhere, or order direct from the publisher.

POCKET BOOKS
Department FB-2
1 West 39th Street
New York, N.Y. 10018

Please send me the books I have checked above. I am
enclosing $_____ (please add 35¢ to cover postage and
handling). Send check or money order—no cash or C.O.D.'s
please.

NAME_____

ADDRESS_____

CITY_____STATE/ZIP_____

POCKET BOOKS

FB-2

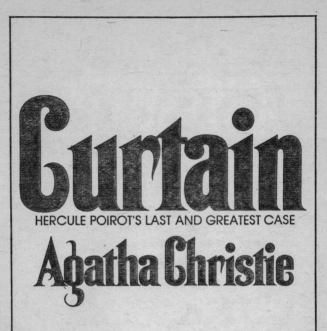

Curtain

HERCULE POIROT'S LAST AND GREATEST CASE

Agatha Christie

_____80720 CURTAIN $1.95

Available at bookstores everywhere, or order direct from the publisher.

POCKET BOOKS
Department CU
1 West 39th Street
New York, N.Y. 10018

Please send me the books I have checked above. I am
enclosing $_____ (please add 35¢ to cover postage and
handling). Send check or money order—no cash or C.O.D.'s
please.

NAME_____

ADDRESS_____

CITY_____STATE/ZIP_____

CU

POCKET BOOKS